Don't Be Gentle with Lord Tristan

BARBARA RUSSELL

trigger warnings

Trigger warnings: self-harm (non-cutting), addiction, fighting/boxing, a child is badly injured, stitches, grief/loss, depression, panic attack.

Being called Euphemia Calpurnia and being the thirteenth child of the Earl of Winchester did mean bad luck.

For an hour, Effie had searched for a quiet place to read her book and found none. If she couldn't find a nice spot for herself in a house with more than twenty bedrooms, then she should move to Grandmama's dower house and forget London.

Her elder brothers and sisters were either bickering or playing loud games while she wanted to finish the chapter on the muscles of a horse's back before going to bed.

Her governess thought studying veterinary medicine was a waste of time for an earl's daughter, but Effie found it fascinating. Women could become physicians and surgeons. It was only a matter of time before they would be veterinary doctors as well. No wasted time at all.

Carrying her precious book, she entered the piano room, but Mary was playing a fast-paced piece of music while James and Lena danced and jumped around. The big library was taken over by Colin and his rowdy college friends—as if there weren't enough people in the house already—the small library was occupied by Papa, who was working. And the sitting room on the ground floor was too close to the street; the noises from the carriages and people passing by thundered.

Now she understood why Mama hated London. Their house in Bedfordshire had more than two hundred rooms, and the birds chirping was the only sound she would hear in her bedroom. She could go an entire day without seeing any of her siblings.

But in London, everything was cramped together, and the house didn't have enough space for her noisy brothers and sisters and their friends.

Thank goodness she would soon return to Bedfordshire to her horses and dogs.

She had to be content with a small nook next to the window overlooking the garden, in the middle of the corridor. The glass was frosted, and not much light filtered in from the streetlamps. But the glow coming from the hallway was enough to allow her to read.

She barely finished a paragraph when footsteps came from the other side of the hallway. Voices followed. She lowered the book, resigned to being interrupted. Could she have a moment of peace to read?

The butler rushed to knock on the door of the small library.

She kept reading until Papa came out and a new pair of footsteps distracted her. The butler looked flustered. Papa frowned. She put aside the book. The universe had decided she couldn't study now.

A young man her age walked out of the servants' door. His chin was up, but the fear on his tense face belied his confidence. His dark suit had seen better days if the threadbare fabric at the hems was any indication. Stopping in front of Papa, the young man removed his worn hat, letting a mop of blond hair fall to his jaw.

She remained still in her corner, lest Papa tell her to leave. The young man couldn't be one of Colin's friends.

There was a quick exchange between the butler and Papa, but

she didn't catch any words while the young man nodded several times.

Papa eyed him with concern. "So you are the son of the Marquess of Montcrest."

"I am, my lord. I'm Lord Tristan." He gave another nod.

That surprised her.

Lord Tristan didn't exactly look like a poor man but not like the son of a marquess either, and not just because of his clothes. His face was gaunt, and his hands were bony. Even from her spot, she could see his protruding knuckles.

Living in Bedfordshire for most of the year, she wasn't informed of everything that happened in London, but she'd heard about the Montcrest family's fall from grace.

Papa and Lord Tristan spoke in a low tone with the butler who was seemingly shocked by whatever Lord Tristan was saying.

Papa shook his head. "I'm sorry for your situation, but I'm afraid we can't give you any food."

Lord Tristan didn't protest or beg, but the way his shoulders stooped showed his defeat. He didn't even ask for a reason why Papa had refused to offer help.

Lord Tristan swallowed hard. "My lord."

He seemed about to say something, but then he headed for the servants' door and was gone in the darkness of the stairs.

She remained still, in shock. They couldn't give any food to a young man who was obviously starving? They had plenty of food. Her family was big, and the pantry was always well supplied.

She waited for the butler to leave before knocking on Papa's door.

"Come in." He sounded annoyed.

She entered the warm room that smelled of old wood and freshly brewed tea.

He smiled. "Darling. Let me guess. The house is too noisy for you." He laughed. "Heaven knows you're just like your mother."

"Yes, the house is noisy, but I'm not here for that reason." She stepped deeper into the room. "Don't be angry, but I happened to have heard the conversation between you and Lord Tristan."

He leant back in his chair, sighing. "I'm sorry that you heard that. Nasty business."

"He asked for food. Surely, we can give him some."

He rubbed the bridge of his nose. "It's not that simple, and I understand the scene looked concerning, but Montcrest is in a terrible situation."

"Of course, he is if his son begs for food."

He drummed his fingers on the table. "Lord Tristan's grandfather was a suspected traitor to the crown. He also squandered the family's fortune due to some bad investments, and now his father, the current Marquess of Montcrest, is involved in who knows what scheme to regain his family's money."

Lord Tristan's dejected face haunted her. Who cared about schemes?

"But they're starving."

He held up a hand. "The point is, I don't want to get involved in whatever they're doing."

She walked closer. Arguing openly with Papa was never a good strategy. Finesse was required. "Why did Lord Tristan come here? Why did he choose you to ask for help?"

He straightened a few documents on the desk. "I was with his father at Eton, and we used to be friends before the tragedy struck the Montcrests. First, their financial disaster. Then the supposed high treason. Montcrest and I fell out when he was at the centre of a huge scandal. I guess Montcrest exhausted the list of people to ask for favours."

"But Lord Tristan has nothing to do with his grandfather's and father's problems. He's a young man who needs food. Please. Help him."

He scowled. "I won't be dragged into a scandal. I won't help a family accused of high treason."

"Almost accused, and it was Lord Tristan's grandfather."

"Effie, darling. These are delicate things you shouldn't be troubled with."

"I won't let someone, who asked for our help, starve when we have the means to help them. I know you have a good heart. You taught me we must be compassionate and help others whenever we can. Were you lying?"

"No, of course not. But this is different."

She folded her arms over her chest. When diplomacy failed, then a little threat was advised. "I will never take a walk in the woods with you again if you don't send help to the marquess, and if you refuse to help them, I'll do it. And if you try to stop me, I'll tell Mama and Grandmama."

He stopped tidying his desk. "You wouldn't dare."

"I would. I'll send Grandmama a wire if I have to."

He waved her away. "Please, darling, leave this matter to me."

She drew in a sharp breath. "Papa, I'm serious. We'll be as discreet as you want, but we will help them. Because I trust you to do what's good and right, as you taught me. As you taught all of us. If you don't do something, I will have trouble trusting you again."

When he rested his forehead on his hand, she smelled victory.

two

Tristan added another piece of wood into the meagre fire in the drawing room. The room had once been crammed with silk sofas, chintz armchairs, and people in fancy dresses. Now it was dark, damp, and bare, like a shipwreck abandoned on the shore.

He and his father had chopped up the less precious furniture they couldn't sell to fuel the fire, and the smell of burning paint made him queasy. Not that his stomach had any food to throw up.

Considering that Grandfather bankrupted the family and had been almost thrown into the Tower of London before dying of a seizure, it was a miracle they still held the title. A title that was more a curse than a blessing because it carried responsibilities and commitments they couldn't take care of. Tenants had lost their incomes because of his family's financial disaster.

Their butler, Harris, was the only servant who had decided to starve with them out of a loyalty Tristan didn't understand anymore.

"Where have you been?" Father carried a pile of old blankets he must have found somewhere in the house.

Tristan shrugged. "Around, searching for a job."

If Father knew he'd been begging for food in Lord Winchester's house, he wouldn't be pleased. He was fighting tooth and nail to find the funds to rebuild the family, but Tristan didn't have much hope.

"Tea, my lord." Harris brought them a steaming pot on an old tray. Although more than tea, it was a dubious potion made with old tea leaves and other herbs Harris found in the garden.

"Thank you, Harris." Father smiled at the butler, but Tristan couldn't bring himself to say anything.

Harris should run away from them and find employment in a house where he would be paid.

"Lord Tristan." Harris poured him a cup.

The smell wasn't terrible—a combination of mint, nettle, and black tea—but the taste had nothing to do with the rich, strong tea they'd been used to drinking.

Father winced when he opened his hands; they were covered in cuts since he spent hours chopping wood and furniture and meeting solicitors and old friends, asking for help.

"Things will get better," Father said. "Mark me. I will fight for us until my last breath. My friend George has a good plan to help us."

"I have no doubts, my lord," Harris said.

Tristan didn't doubt his father's determination either. He doubted the result. They'd exhausted their list of friends and associates to ask for help. There wasn't anything they hadn't tried. For the first time, he was glad Mother had died of typhoid fever years ago. She'd been spared the humiliation and suffering of the family's downfall.

The doorbell ringing caused the three of them to still. For a moment, Tristan thought one of Father's friends had come for dinner. But that type of life was gone.

Harris put the tray down. "I'll see to it."

Tristan stood up and wiped the ash from his hands. "No, I'll go."

If it was another one of their creditors, he would beg to give them more time, no matter how much Father was against begging, and he didn't want Harris to witness the scene.

Only a couple of candles lit the wide corridor, and their glows cast tremulous shadows on the faded wallpaper.

When he pulled the door open, the surprise tied his tongue. A young lady with large hazel eyes stared at him from under the cover of a hood. Her fine lines and expensive clothes made him sorely aware of the poor state of his clothes and pale skin.

She tilted her head. "Lord Tristan?"

He could only nod. He was so stunned he didn't ask her how she knew his name or what she wanted.

"I'm Lady Effie, the daughter of the Earl of Winchester." She cleared her throat. "I'm aware you visited my father this afternoon."

He was puzzled. Why the earl would send his daughter to his house was beyond him. "I did, but I won't disturb you again, my lady."

"Oh, no. It's not that." She stepped closer, and the scent of cinnamon wafted from her, reminding him of lazy winter after-noons spent reading in front of a blazing fire and eating cinnamon cakes. "My father has a small present for you. If you open the servants' entrance, the footmen will deliver it."

He craned his neck to see past her. A footman stood next to the carriage, waiting.

"Of course." He didn't move.

She pointed to the other side of the street. "Then I'll tell them to walk around the house."

"Yes." He still didn't move.

She smiled, and he didn't care anymore about his poor looks. "I hope it helps. Good night, Lord Tristan." She bowed her head and walked to the carriage.

"Good night."

In a daze, he closed the door and crossed the hallway.

Father came out of the drawing room. "Who was it?"

He hesitated before speaking. Hunger had played tricks on him in the past weeks. Maybe what had just happened wasn't real. "Lady Effie, the daughter of the Earl of Winchester, asked me to open the servants' entrance so her footmen could deliver something for us."

Harris didn't need to hear more. He made a dash for the rear door.

Tristan was about to run down the stairs as well when Father took his arm.

"Why? Did you see Winchester?" Father narrowed his eyes to slits.

"I met him by chance when I was walking home." He was glad the semidarkness hid his face, or Father would understand he was lying. "He asked me how we were faring."

"Did he now?"

"Let me go, Father." He slid out of Father's grip and rushed downstairs.

When he stepped into the anteroom to the kitchen, the two footmen were already there next to an astonished Harris. They didn't speak, and he was grateful for that because the shock had taken control of his ability to talk.

The small gift consisted of crates of potatoes, apples, salted meat, and potted vegetables. The footmen carried everything quickly and efficiently in the anteroom and left, bowing, as no one had bowed to him in a while. Harris closed the door, muttering something.

Tristan stood in front of a rich feast.

Emotion thickened his throat, and his stomach groaned.

Father came down as well. He stared at the crates, walking around them. Hopefully, he wouldn't decide to send the gift back to the earl. Tristan wouldn't starve because his father was too proud to accept help.

"Blimey." Father scratched his beard.

"The earl was generous." He waited, ready to argue in case Father complained.

They stared at each other across the room, both tense and determined.

Harris cleared his throat. "I shall store everything in the pantry and the larder, my lord, before the food gets spoilt."

Father slouched his posture. "Let's start then. We don't want to waste anything."

Tristan exhaled in relief.

His first thought when he opened the parcel with salted meat was that he hadn't thanked Lady Effie.

three

London, 1897

Tristan was a simple gentleman—he wanted something; he got it.

And right now, he wanted to have a chat with the bloody Earl of Winchester.

He hitched Zeus to the fence around Archer Hall, the earl's white townhouse in the middle of Belgravia, and marched to the front door. Zeus shook his head, and his black mane flapped around his strong neck. For a moment, Tristan thought he'd heard an odd noise from the horse, but he had more pressing matters to pursue.

Drops of mud fell from his dirty riding boots to the pristine paved path cutting through the front garden, and he couldn't care less.

He'd been riding in Hyde Park when his footman had found him to deliver a message from his secretary: Lord Winchester had rejected his offer again.

Tristan hesitated to knock only for a moment, remembering that night, many years ago, when he'd used the servants' entrance to beg for food in this very house. That sad time was long past gone.

He wasn't that beggar anymore, and while he was still grateful to the earl for his help, he had a business to run and responsibilities to care about.

He and his father had thanked the earl for his generosity years ago. The food supply hadn't simply kept them alive, but it had also renewed their hopes.

But the past was the past. The end. No one could accuse him of sentimentalism.

He knocked on the front door, gripping the riding crop hard. An earl couldn't be the reason for his failure to expand the London and West Marches Railway. He'd worked too damn hard for that. Hell, his father had died from working too hard. Now he was the Marquess of Montcrest, and it was his duty to complete the job.

The butler opened the door.

"Montcrest to see Lord Winchester." Tristan walked inside.

The butler gazed around, still holding the door open. "My lord, His Lordship isn't available."

Tristan wasn't surprised. Winchester must have ordered his butler not to let him in.

"Is he hiding in his study?" He climbed the marble stairs two steps at a time.

"My lord!" The butler closed the door and moved towards the stairs.

An itch started at the base of his neck, that nervous nagging demanding attention, but he closed his fists and focused on his imminent confrontation. Once he finished with the earl, he would have plenty of time for a long boxing session at The Octagon to silence '*the twitch.*'

"I must see the earl." He strode to the study and pushed the door open.

Three voices cried out at the same time—two were human, one wasn't.

"My lord, I beg you," the butler said, catching up with Tristan.

At the same time a woman said, "What is it?"

And a dog barked.

Tristan surveyed the study. The room was drowning in brown wood and ancient bookshelves, as if it were out of the Bodleian Library. The woman standing behind the desk stared at him with annoyance. An English setter peeked at him from behind a chair, his large brown eyes on him.

"My lady." The butler entered the study as well. "Lord Montcrest was looking for your father."

"My father isn't here," the lady said, brushing a lock of chestnut hair from her cheek.

She was familiar, but he couldn't remember where and when he'd seen her.

"I can write down any messages you want to leave him." She nodded at the butler. "Thank you, Doyle. You may go."

"My lady?" The butler sounded shocked.

Tristan ignored the increasing intensity of the twitch in his neck and reluctantly bowed his head. "When will your father return, my lady?"

The dog whimpered. He had a lame leg he dragged behind as he hid behind his mistress.

"You're scaring Pepper with your tone. Would you terribly mind being quieter?"

He glanced at the setter again. "He's a gundog. He should be used to loud noises."

That wasn't what he meant to say. He blamed the lady's attitude; it distracted him.

"He isn't." She scratched the dog's head. "He was born with a bad leg. The breeder wanted to put him down because of it, so I took him home with me. Pepper has never been on a hunting trip and thank goodness for that. I personally think it's barbaric in this day and age. Don't you agree? Or are you one of those red jackets hunting a scared animal?"

What the hell was happening?

"As a matter of fact, I do not hunt. It's a waste of time, and I do find it cruel." He gripped his riding crop harder. Again, she'd distracted him. "My lady," he gritted out, "when is your father going to be here?" He forced his tone down, lest she start with another piece of Pepper's story.

Not at all bothered by his scowl, she walked around the desk. "Let me see." She slowly flipped through the pages of a personal appointment calendar, as someone with all the time in the world. "I'm afraid you're out of luck. Papa will return late this evening. He'll probably dine at the Criterion with his friends."

"I must talk to him immediately. Where can I find him?"

She drew her fine eyebrows together. Even Pepper frowned.

Her large hazel eyes seemed to ignite like brandy, and her autumn red gown enhanced them. "If you tell me the reason for your unexpected visit, I'm sure I can help."

Fair enough. It would be quicker to tell her everything. "Your father again refused my very reasonable offer to buy his land in Easthollow for the extension of my London and West Marches Railway. I would like to know the reason why he rejected my offer."

She twitched her mouth. "I can't help. I have no idea what you're talking about."

"Great." He pressed his lips hard. "Now, would you please tell me where your father is?"

"I doubt he wants to be disturbed."

"I don't care about what your father wants."

A hiss came from a corner. A large black cat was perched on the top of a shelf; its yellow eyes narrowed to slits.

"And now you've upset Kettle as well, poor boy." She balled a fist on her hip.

Without taking his eyes off Tristan, Kettle jumped silently on the desk and settled himself into a sphinx-like pose.

She caressed Kettle's head. "Black cats are awfully mistreated. Too many people think they bring bad luck and refuse to adopt them, but my Kettle—"

"Honestly!" Tristan strode to the desk and grabbed the appointment calendar. At least he would know where Winchester was.

If meeting this woman was a test in patience, he was gloriously failing it.

"What are you doing?" She put a hand on the calendar, blocking him. "It's called a *personal* calendar not because it's a pretty name."

"Tell me where your father is, and I'll leave."

She pulled the calendar towards her. "You're welcome to come back tomorrow after arranging a proper appointment."

He pulled the calendar towards him. "I don't have time for games."

"Neither have I. I have plenty to do with my animals."

Tristan gave a yank to the calendar, but she didn't admit defeat and pulled it back. He couldn't believe he was having a childish tug-of-war with the daughter of an earl while under the scrutiny of a frightened dog and an upset cat.

"My lady." He controlled his voice. "Time is money, and you're wasting both."

"That tone again."

In the blink of an eye, there was a black blur. Kettle unsheathed his claws and aimed at him with the speed of a swordsman. Tristan withdrew his hand but not quickly enough and couldn't avoid being slashed by the sharp nails.

"Bloody hell!" He closed his hand as blood trickled down his wrist.

Getting punched in a ring for the pleasure of feeling pain was one thing. But being slashed by an angry cat was another matter.

"Kettle!" She picked the cat up and laid him on a chair. "Mind your cattitude!"

He wrapped his handkerchief around the cut; actually, there were three thin slashes.

She kissed the head of the panther. "I'm truly sorry. Kettle has a problem controlling his anger."

"He isn't the only one."

"But fear not. I have the perfect remedy for those scratches." She opened a drawer and took out a small glass jar.

"I'll live. Would you just tell me where I can find your father?"

"This balm will—" She rose on her tiptoes to look out of the window. "Is that wonderful Andalusian yours?"

"What?" Words failed him.

In the span of a few minutes, she'd jumped from one topic to another without completing any of them.

She set the jar on the desk. "You let him drink in the park, didn't you? I bet your horse gulped down gallons." Her alarmed tone caught his attention.

"Yes, why?"

Her frown matched Kettle's. She stared at him as if he were an imbecile. "Never allow your horse to drink large quantities of cold water. I think he's suffering from colic."

He forgot about the bloody cut and looked out at Zeus on the pavement. "How can you tell from here?"

"He keeps biting his flank and looking at his side. Quickly. We don't have much time." She rang the bell and the butler arrived. "Doyle, I need my coat."

"But what—"

"Your horse might die. We must stop the colic from getting worse." She beckoned him to follow her. "Our stable is just around the corner. Quick now, or you won't lose just a business deal."

four

After Winchester's chatty daughter declared Zeus was in danger, Tristan hesitated for a moment before following her out of the study.

From the moment his family had regained their fortune, people often tried to trick him, using the most outlandish claims, from telling him his roof was about to collapse to diagnosing him with an incurable disease, only to steal money from him. Hence his lack of trust towards people. But she sounded genuinely concerned for Zeus.

"Are you sure Zeus is sick?" he asked.

"Very." She went down the corridor.

The butler handed her a coat. "Will you be gone for long, my lady?"

"It depends on the horse."

"Will you need the carriage, my lady?"

"No. I'll be at the stables for a while." She rushed outside with Tristan following her.

Zeus was pawing the ground, his muscles tense and his eyes wide.

"Mate." Tristan ran a hand down Zeus's neck, feeling the tension under the horse's coat.

"Quickly. He's starting to feel pain." She untied the reins and beckoned at him to follow her again. "He's growing nervous."

It was true. Tristan had been so enraged when he'd ridden to Archer Hall that he might have overlooked Zeus's state.

He sped up, caressing the horse's side. A sickening lump was growing in his throat at the thought of Zeus dying. It would be his fault. In the park, his mind had kept drifting to business matters, and he hadn't paid attention to what Zeus had been doing.

"I'll take care of you, mate."

"I'm Lady Effie, by the way." She cast him a glance as if expecting him to say something.

But he didn't understand what—the memory hit him when the sunlight played in her shining hazel eyes.

"Lady Effie. I believe I met you before." For a handful of moments nearly sixteen years ago. But he never forgot that night when she'd knocked on his door or the gratitude he'd felt. He'd met her father occasionally, but not her.

"We did. Briefly." She waved a dismissive hand. "Let's think about Zeus first."

She led him under a stone arch and into a secluded, cobbled alleyway lined with stables. "This is the second time we see each other, but on both occasions, we weren't introduced formally. Not that I mind."

He said nothing. She always caught him off guard, and it wasn't exactly pleasant. From the little he remembered, she didn't seem to have changed much. Her spectacular hazel eyes struck him as extraordinary, the same as they had done years ago.

"I'll be right back." She disappeared behind a door.

Tristan stroked Zeus's muzzle again. "I'm sorry," he whispered to him only. "I'm an ass."

The horse made a noise between a snort and a squeal.

"Here we are." Lady Effie returned with a bucket of water. "I dissolved some chloride of lime in the lukewarm water. The stomach isn't too distended. This trick should work to solve the problem. I also added some apple juice. It does wonders to encourage a horse to drink."

He was taken aback again. "Chloride of lime corrodes metal."

"But in very small doses, it helps with intestinal gas. Trust me. It's a sure remedy and a safe cure. I tried it several times with great success. The dose makes the poison."

He watched Zeus closely as he drank small sips from the bucket.

Lady Effie leant against the wooden stall. "Please be careful next time. No cold water, especially in the morning. After he finishes that bucket, I'll give you some asafoetida. It's perfect for curing stomach problems. Then light food and light exercise until we're sure he's safe."

"How do you know so much about horses?" He caressed Zeus's neck and abdomen gently; it was bloated, but not too much.

"Mama hates London. She never wants to spend time here. So I grew up on an estate in Bedfordshire with my siblings. Papa divided his time between Bedfordshire and London, but he's staying here longer as of late. He does feel lonely, so I decided to keep him company. I'm his thirteenth child. My brothers and sisters are scattered all around the kingdom and the Continent." She waved a hand. "For business or because their spouses are from another country."

"Thirteenth?" He kept caressing Zeus, more to calm himself than the horse.

"I also grew up surrounded by horses and animals, and Mama has never stood on ceremony when we were out of London. Papa is the opposite. He prefers the city to the country."

Zeus finished the water and licked his lips.

She took the reins. "We'd better let him walk for a while." She led Zeus along the stable alley.

The clip-clop of Zeus's hooves echoed off the walls of the stables. The chatter of the stable hands and grooms came from every corner.

"Do you have siblings?" she asked.

"No." He exhaled. "I mean, yes. A brother."

Almost. Rowan was the son of Father's second wife, who had eloped with a Scotsman, leaving her son behind. Such a lady.

"Do you get along? I love all of my siblings. They're my best friends."

"Rowan is a boy."

"And? Is age an impediment to brotherly friendship and love? You love Zeus, and he isn't even human."

So his test in patience wasn't finished yet.

"Lady Effie, I'm grateful for your help, but I'd rather talk about your father. I really need to see him."

Her hazel eyes flashed with a quick glint. "Papa is visiting Colin, my eldest brother, who lives in Greenford. So he'll be back late this evening and have dinner at the Criterion."

"Greenford, West London. I bet he paid a ticket to my railway company."

She let out a nervous chuckle. "I don't know. That would be ironic, wouldn't it?"

They reached the end of the alleyway and turned around. Zeus's moves were less stiff and his muscles more relaxed.

"Why is it so important to see him?" she asked.

"I told you. He rejected my more than reasonable offer."

"Well, maybe your offer wasn't so reasonable." She laughed. He didn't.

"I offered him thrice the value of a piece of land he owns in Easthollow."

"Easthollow? Isn't it that strip of uninhabited rocky land where not even grass grows?"

"Precisely, yet he refused my offer."

Out of spite. Winchester was convinced Father had robbed

him of a great business deal, which was ridiculous. Father hadn't robbed anyone; he'd simply been a clever businessman.

She checked Zeus's belly. "Papa must have his reasons." She smiled, and he had to admit her smile was disarming. "And he helped you once," she added in a whisper.

"We both know you were behind the earl's generosity." Otherwise, she wouldn't have come to his house.

Her cheeks flushed. "He needed to be persuaded, but he made the final decision. Anyway, I'm glad you overcame your troubles."

"I did." It'd taken nearly two decades, but his family wasn't starving anymore. Quite the opposite.

They reached the other end, so she turned Zeus around to walk back again.

"Why did Papa refuse your offer?"

He cleared his throat, pondering what to say. "You should ask him that next time you see him."

"I will."

They walked in silence among the noises from the other horses in the stables and the chatter of the stable hands.

She touched Zeus's belly again. "Much better."

He checked him as well. The muscles weren't tight anymore, and Zeus's eyes were less wide.

"We should take him home. Where's your stable?" she asked.

"Close to my house at the end of the street."

"Don't mount Zeus. It would be better if you walked him. I'll be right back." She handed him the reins and entered the stable.

Tristan scratched the spot in Zeus's neck the horse loved, making him sigh. He kissed Zeus's muzzle, scolding himself again for letting his temper neglect his stallion.

"I'm sorry," he whispered.

"He's better, isn't he? He should be all right now." Lady Effie ran a hand along Zeus's neck. "Such a gorgeous stallion."

"He's my favourite."

"That's for you." She handed him a pot with a tight lid.

"Asafoetida for Zeus to drink. Pick a measure of powder as big as an egg and dilute it in lukewarm water. It does wonders."

He took the pot. "Will do."

"Don't make him run until tomorrow. He needs rest."

"Of course."

"Well, I'll see you soon, then. If something happens, send for me."

He loitered another moment, wondering why leaving right then didn't seem right. "Lady Effie, thank you for your help. I mean it. You've been wonderful."

"You're welcome." Her smile could melt a glacier. "Have that cut disinfected." She pointed at his hand. "Who knows where Kettle sank his nails into?"

"I don't want to know." He bowed his head.

Zeus nudged Lady Effie with his muzzle before pressing his muzzle against his master.

"Goodbye." She waved at them.

He waved back. "I'll try again to meet your father. Perhaps tomorrow."

"Excellent."

He walked away with Zeus. That wasn't how he'd supposed his day would have gone.

five

It took Effie hours to finish tidying Papa's study, sorting through the correspondence and arranging the books on the shelves.

The secretary had volunteered to do the job, but she loved putting things in order and keeping herself useful, and Papa was always happy to have her help.

He was messy, but her slow work wasn't due to his lack of organisation. The encounter with Lord Montcrest had given her a lot to think about.

First, he'd barged into the room unannounced and uninvited, scaring poor Pepper and Kettle, and then his beautiful horse had risked dying.

He loved his horse, but he also had a temper; a hot temper that was a contrast with the coldness in his blue eyes. They were the only thing about him that hadn't changed. She'd hardly recognised him as the scrawny young man who had stared at her speechless when she'd offered him a few crates of food.

What bothered her wasn't his temper or his stiff manners, but something else. Something she couldn't quite explain. He'd been restless and nervous, closing and opening his hands repeatedly and scrubbing the back of his neck. His facial muscles had smoothed only when Zeus's health had improved.

That had been the moment when he'd completely changed in her eyes. He'd looked genuinely horrified at having neglected his horse. She didn't trust people who mistreated animals and those who couldn't defend themselves.

At least he wasn't completely heartless, although his annoyance at Papa for a business deal had seemed exaggerated. On the other hand, he claimed he didn't hunt. She liked that about him.

Once the study was tidy, she went to the library. The scent of walnut wood and leather was a cure-all, and the light of the sunset tinted the room in warm red. She ran a hand over her worn copy of the latest edition of *A Compendium of the Veterinary Art*. She knew the book backwards. Every sketch, description, and procedure. It was funny how her dream lay in those six hundred pages.

More than a dream, it was an impossible goal.

Women could study medicine, could even be registered as physicians. But they weren't allowed anywhere near veterinary medicine. Yet she was as knowledgeable as any graduated man from the Royal Veterinary College. She even had experience in dealing with cattle and sheep in the remote, muddy farms in the countryside. Her pleas to be admitted to the college had fallen on deaf ears. The college hadn't even bothered to reply to her.

But anyway, she held the book against her chest. She wasn't searching for glory, nor did she care about revolutionising society. She only wanted to be recognised as a veterinary doctor. Although she could help sick animals with or without formal recognition.

A loud purr distracted her from her musing. Kettle bumped his head against her leg and coiled his tail around her skirt.

"You didn't like Lord Montcrest at all, did you?"

He raised his yellow eyes with an air of innocence.

"You shouldn't have scratched him."

His reply was another deep purr.

Thank goodness Lord Montcrest wasn't one of those people

who became violent towards cats. She'd seen her share of people raising a fist at a hissing feline.

Now that she thought about it, Lord Montcrest had a few redeeming qualities, but she would reserve her final judgement on his nervous character once she saw how he took care of Zeus in the next few days.

Kettle made a soft trill, a sign he wanted to retire and sleep, and demanded she follow suit.

"You're right." She opened her arms, and he jumped in her arms. "You had a stressful day."

Dinner was a quiet affair with Pepper and Kettle for company. Papa had felt lonely in London after her elder siblings had flown the nest and started travelling, and she'd moved there to spend some time with him, but he was often out until late.

After going upstairs, she sipped a tisane in her bedroom, reading in front of the blazing fire. Pepper was asleep on her bed, and Kettle was keeping a watchful eye on London from the window, having changed his mind about a nap.

When Papa's carriage stopped at the front door, she hoped he would come upstairs before going to bed.

"Effie?" He knocked on the door.

"Come in."

"Darling." He showed a bright smile, carrying with him the cold air from outside.

She rose from the chair and hugged him.

He held her back. "Still up?"

"I was waiting for you."

"Thank you for tidying my study." Papa stroked Pepper's head and stretched out an arm towards Kettle tentatively. After Kettle tilted his head and made a soft sound, Papa caressed his head gently.

"I like being useful."

"Is something the matter?" he said in a low voice because Kettle didn't like harsh sounds.

"Lord Montcrest came here this morning."

He stopped touching Kettle. "What?"

"Didn't Doyle tell you?" she asked. "Montcrest was distressed and demanded to see you."

"Did he upset you?"

"Not at all." A little, but not in the way Papa imagined. "He was worried about a deal he had with you."

"He shouldn't have bothered you. Like his late father, he doesn't care about rules of behaviour." He started towards the door. "I'll write him a message immediately."

"Wait." She went after him. "He'll probably come back tomorrow."

"Will he now? I don't have any intention of seeing him. He can talk to my solicitor if he needs to communicate with me, but certainly, he shouldn't come here uninvited."

"Why did you refuse to sell him the land in Easthollow? You've always said that land was as useful as a rock."

He patted her cheek. "Don't worry about that. It's nothing."

"But his proposition sounded reasonable."

"I really have to go." Papa walked out of the room without waiting for her to finish.

She scowled at the closed door. Papa had never involved her in the management of the estate. Why would he? She didn't have any training or knowledge about farming or stock market. But his abrupt departure was out of character as if she'd struck a nerve.

Lord Montcrest wasn't a destitute man anymore. He didn't need her help. But she would be lying if she said she didn't want to help him both because he was intriguing and because Papa's reaction had been exaggerated. And, like Kettle, she was curious.

six

The next day, Effie pondered whether to go to Lord Montcrest or not for about two minutes. He hadn't sent a message, asking to see her father, and she was worried. Knowing how Zeus was faring was more important than any dispute he and her father might have had. Curiosity about him had a role in her decision, too.

After breakfast, she hurried along the already busy pavement with her friend Jane, Viscountess Vaughan.

The end of winter was being generous to Londoners. The sunny days drew everyone out but made the smell of horse dung stronger. Not that she minded it, but it covered the scent of the evergreen trees coming from the park.

"Did you see those parasols? So pretty." She pointed at a couple of ladies twirling their light blue parasols.

Jane glanced at them. "I agreed to come with you, but we shouldn't call on a gentleman without having an appointment. Gossip spreads quickly, especially when Montcrest is involved."

Effie chuckled. "You don't like Lord Montcrest, I gather."

Jane patted her dark hair styled in a complicated French braid with curls and rolls. Her lady's maid had a gift when it came to hairstyles. "From what I heard about him, he seems a rather ruthless person. Inviting him to next week's ball was my husband's idea."

She perked up. "Is he coming? I didn't know."

"He hasn't confirmed his presence yet. I agreed to send him an invitation, only because not inviting him would have started rumours. Montcrest's father was..." Jane shook her head. "I shouldn't speak ill of the dead."

"Why not? They won't gossip."

"Very funny."

"I want to know your opinion." She paused before turning the corner towards Montcrest House. "Did something happen between my father and Lord Montcrest's father?"

"I would say between the late marquess and everyone in London. My father-in-law told me the late marquess was a ruthless businessman. He tricked more than one gentleman with his greed, and I fear the apple didn't fall far from the tree."

"Did Lord Montcrest's father damage Papa as well?"

Jane leant closer. "I don't know the details. I heard the late marquess didn't behave like a gentleman in a business deal. The rumours about his second wife are rather muddled, though. Apparently, she moved to the country to visit a relative and died of fever or something similar."

Effie understood little of Papa's business; animals were more interesting than numbers, but she could easily believe Lord Montcrest was a determined businessman.

Well, for now, she cared only about Zeus. And Lord Montcrest had nothing to do with a quarrel that had happened years ago between Papa and Lord Montcrest's father.

Montcrest House towered over a cul-de-sac in its dark glory. Despite the fact its whitewashed walls sparkled, the glossy black front door, black-framed windows, and heavy-looking black fence gave the house a gloomy atmosphere. The cypress trees did nothing to cheer up the look, and the dark amphorae on the porch resembled two guardians ready to kick out intruders.

Jane hesitated before knocking. "It looks like a cemetery."

She agreed. "Anyone living here would have a temper."

A tall, imposing butler opened the door, staring at them as if they were thieves.

Effie forced a smile. "Good morning."

"Lady Vaughan." Jane handed her calling card gracefully. "Lady Euphemia and we would like to see the marquess. if he's accepting calls. If not, we'll leave immediately. Good day." She half-turned around.

"Or…" Effie stopped her. "If Lord Montcrest isn't home, I may pay a visit to his stallion, Zeus, and see how he's faring, if you would be so kind as to tell me where he is."

The butler arched one of his bushy black eyebrows, the tails of which were completely white, so the eyebrows resembled two small skunks. "Please come in, my ladies. I'll inform His Lordship you're here."

Effie and Jane entered the cavernous hallway. Only a small console table and a painting decorated the entry hall. Lord Montcrest didn't waste space on frills, although the table was an expensive Sheraton piece and the painting looked like a Jacques-Louis David. Her footfall echoed in the domed ceiling.

Jane whispered, "The butler looks like a mortician and is just as cheerful."

"You're being influenced by the stern house."

The butler showed them to the drawing room and bowed his way out with a quick, "Please wait here, my ladies."

Effie took a stroll around the room, trying to learn more about Lord Montcrest. But the serious room didn't reveal any secret passion for animals, sports, or music. The expensive furniture had been likely chosen by someone who had heard about cheerfulness as a passing comment. The brocade drapes were so heavy they could be used as theatre curtains, and no recent family portraits or still nature hung on the wall.

The only touch of colour was a wooden toy horse on a shelf.

"Lady Vaughan. Lady Euphemia?" Lord Montcrest's deep voice rose in question as he said her name, but still...it could be interpreted as frightening or accusatory, depending on one's mood.

His dark suit matched the house and drew attention to his limpid blue eyes. They were such a contrast to the rest of his grim persona that they attracted her attention.

"Good morning, my lord." She smiled.

Jane gave a nod of her head but kept her gaze on him.

"I didn't expect your visit." With his bright golden hair and clear blue eyes, one would expect him to have an angelic look; it couldn't be further from the truth.

He was anything but angelic. His lines made him handsome, but they were rough, and his stern expression broke the illusion of a celestial appearance.

"I'm here to see Zeus. How is he faring?" she said.

He nearly smiled, but he must have changed his mind because the smile never had the chance to fully develop. "He's recovered, thanks to your prompt intervention."

"May I see him?"

Jane slanted her an alarmed look, perhaps because Effie had taken the initiative and not waited for him to offer.

He took his time. His face gave nothing away. "Of course. The stables aren't far." He rang the bell.

"Are you enjoying the sunshine?" She waved towards the window.

"Not really. I'm working." He showed again a fleeting smile.

Jane became suddenly fascinated with a ribbon on her sleeve.

"My lord." The butler appeared a moment later.

"Harris, I'll be showing the ladies to the stable. I will be back shortly."

Harris glanced at her. "Yes, my lord."

She and Jane followed the marquess out of the house and around it towards the stables in the rear. The stables were essentially part of the house; one of the advantages of being a marquess and having a very large backyard, she guessed.

Jane grimaced as she sidestepped the puddles of mud and dung. "Effie, dear, you know I'm not fond of mud."

"We'll be quick."

"My lord." A stable hand bowed at his passage as he swept the stable alley.

"My lord." The groom removed his flat hat to bow.

He acknowledged them both with a few shy nods. Inside the stalls, he turned to Effie. "There's Zeus."

At hearing his voice, Zeus lifted his head from the manger and whinnied, relaxing his ears. The change in Lord Montcrest's face was immediate. A full smile stretched his lips; dimples appeared on his cheeks, and a certain softness appeased the hard lines of his face. If he looked like that all the time, she would swoon.

"He's in excellent shape." She caressed Zeus's muzzle.

"The asafoetida works." Even his voice sweetened and sounded more excited. "He's more lively than last night."

"Good morning," a young voice said from behind them.

Effie turned around. A boy in riding breeches took off his hat and bowed.

The resemblance with Lord Montcrest was striking, the same blue eyes and blond hair, but his expression lacked Lord Montcrest's confidence or harshness.

"Good morning," she said.

Lord Montcrest stiffened a little. "Lady Euphemia, Lady Vaughan, this is my brother, Lord Rowan."

The boy showed a bright smile. "Tristan told me how you saved Zeus, my lady. Thank you. I don't ride him because he's too big for me, but he's my friend."

"We both love Zeus." He stared at his brother and for a second there was a fond understanding between them.

"It was my pleasure, Lord Rowan," she said.

Rowan took a step closer. "May I ask you something?"

"Please go on."

Rowan hesitated, twisting the hem of his jacket with nervous fingers.

"Perhaps you could tell me how you became so knowledgeable. I wish to study veterinary medicine, but I don't know where to start."

Lord Montcrest's soft expression changed to surprise.

"Lord Rowan, I'll be delighted to share my knowledge with you."

When Rowan beamed, his resemblance with his brother increased. "Thank you, my lady."

Jane cleared her throat discreetly. "We should return home."

Effie stroked Zeus again. "I'll be back again if you don't mind, Montcrest, to see Lord Rowan and Zeus."

He shifted his weight and took a breath before saying, "I don't mind at all. Allow me to escort you to the high street."

"I'm looking forward to seeing you again, Lady Effie." Rowan showed his brilliant smile again, and two dimples appeared on his cheeks, like those of his brother.

The marquess walked them back to the high street in silence, and Effie paused before heading home.

"Are you honestly happy about Lord Rowan learning veterinary medicine?" she asked. "You didn't seem to approve."

"I do approve." He clasped his hands behind his back. "Rowan is young and enthusiastic. I hope you meant it when you said you wanted to give him your time."

"I did. I wouldn't have said so otherwise."

"I'm grateful. Ladies." He gave a quick nod and waited for them as they stepped out into the street, then he turned and left.

She was confused. "I don't understand. Did he think I was lying?"

Jane clicked her tongue. "The horse is a better gentleman than he is."

seven

Anticipation for a boxing session burnt in Tristan's veins as he walked to The Octagon. A chilly breeze blew from the north, and the humidity blurred the glow from the streetlamps. After the scare about Zeus and his anger at Winchester, he needed a good boxing session, or the twitch would become unmanageable.

Meeting Lady Effie again had set him on edge. For whatever reason, her simple and spontaneous behaviour kept intruding into his thoughts. Not to mention she'd saved Zeus.

His life was a back and forth between the damn urge to feel pain and thoughts of her kindness, smiles, and beautiful eyes.

When nervous energy consumed him as it did now, a fast walk to the edge of Chelsea was the best way to warm up his muscles and lower his anxiety.

His heart pounded, and tension rode him hard. He walked down seedy alleyways filled with drunken men and bored constables. The smell of urine singed his nostrils.

The Octagon was situated under a busy brothel, and he made his way through a queue of clients eager for another type of relief.

By the time he went down the stairs to the illegal bare-knuckle fighting ring, sweat damped his shirt and his body screamed for some pain.

One night years ago, when he'd finished working late at the factory where his first locomotive had been built, a group of anarchists had attacked him. They had been upset about him being a rich and powerful lord. No matter that he'd worked as hard as anyone to rebuild his family's business after the financial disaster his grandfather had caused. A disaster that had nearly finished the Montcrests.

There had been five angry men against one that night, and he'd been barely alive when they'd left him bleeding in an alleyway. He'd spent months in a deep sleep, only to wake up confused and weak.

Since then, something had changed within him, and not just his sense of safety, or lack thereof, when he walked alone at night. Between a punch and a kick, something other than his ribs had cracked deep inside him, and darkness had poured out of that crack.

He'd started boxing seriously, become more guarded, and learnt how to fend for himself. Though his body had learnt that lesson quickly, his mind had learnt something else.

He craved the pain and the excitement of a fight, as an opium addict craved his drug. He needed to calm the twitch that nagged him, the urge to feel pain. If he ignored the urge, those five men would invade his mind, and then fear would grip him until he threw up and collapsed.

Inside the underground boxing club, the smell of sweat and blood brought immediate relief to his ache.

The fights in The Octagon didn't follow many rules. The place didn't rely on money or bets either. If someone wanted to wager a bet, that was their business, but The Octagon wasn't for gambling. It was a place where those who wanted to fight could do it without too many worries. No gloves. Bare-knuckled. Violent.

He walked along the border of the fighting pitch, searching for a free partner. Just watching the others throwing punches and hearing the grunts of pain charged him with violence. The need for pain grew in intensity to the point that his vision became dark at the edges.

Dark pillars surrounded the octagonal space where people fought. The hall was as big as a cricket pitch with light coming from gas lamps and a few braziers, reminding him of an illustration of the Elysian Fields he'd seen in a book. But he was no hero.

Humid, heavy air pressed against his chest, teasing his need for a release further.

He found a man leaning against the wall. "Are you free?"

The man sized him up. "I am."

Tristan beckoned him to follow, eager to find a free spot. His fingertips itched, and blood pumped in his muscles.

They chose an unoccupied spot and raised their fists. The man grinned, showing a row of yellowed teeth.

"One rule," he said. "Don't punch my face."

"Why?"

"I like to stay pretty."

The man shrugged. "Let's start."

AFTER A GOOD, bloody fight, there was nothing better than some peace and quiet. Tristan sprawled on his favourite armchair next to the fire in the sitting room, a glass of brandy in his hand. One might find the room bare, with only the essential furniture and no frills. But to him, the room was airy and spacious without burdens.

For no reason, he thought of Lady Effie's eyes, how they brightened or darkened according to her feelings. She was a free spirit, the opposite of who he was. He was trapped by his unhealthy urges, his unbreakable duty to his family's honour, and his burning desire for redemption because the Montcrests deserved to be remembered as a powerful family, not as traitors.

He lifted his glass to take a sip and winced. His body burnt and ached. The opponent he'd faced in The Octagon had been no amateur. Strong punches, quick footwork, and clever strategy had assured the man's absolute victory.

Not that Tristan cared. He didn't go to the ring to win a boxing match; he went there for the pain, and he'd got plenty, especially since one of the fighters had slashed his abdomen with a shard of glass. The cut was long but not deep, and it burnt. Weapons weren't allowed in The Octagon, and the man had been kicked out, but not before leaving a memento for Tristan.

Finally, the twitch that had bothered him for days was quiet. His mind was free, and his thoughts were clear. He would sleep peacefully that night.

There was a soft knock on the door, and Harris entered. "My lord, Mr. Fleet wishes to see you."

"At this time?"

"He came twice while you were away." Harris gave him a long, appraising look. "Again. My lord, I must speak—"

"Show Mr. Fleet in. Thank you, Harris."

Harris pressed his lips. "Very well, my lord."

Tristan waved his hand in approval. He was too relaxed to be bothered by his business partner's late visit or his butler's worried tone.

George stepped into the room and eyed the glass of brandy and Tristan's pose.

"Not again." He poured himself a glass from the sideboard. "One day, you're going to get seriously hurt or lose a limb for your foolish addiction."

Tristan shrugged. He didn't care about anything after a good session at the ring. Not even about the truth. "What did you want to tell me?"

George winced as he sipped the brandy. "This brandy is awful."

"You came here late at night to inform me of the quality of my liquor?"

George sat in front of him, giving him a paternal look that made him feel guilty. But what was he supposed to do? Take opium? He would be dead in a matter of months.

"I knew it." George tried the brandy again before putting the glass on the low table. "I feared you were out to get yourself punched. You, your father, and I made many sacrifices to rebuild your family's business, and getting yourself almost killed—"

"Don't."

"—it's a poor way to repay our work."

He polished off his glass with one sip. Yes, maybe the brandy didn't taste good. "If you've come to serve me with a sermon, you can leave."

"Because I can only discuss business with you and nothing else?"

He didn't answer. There was some truth in George's words. Since Father's death, George had grown closer to him, but he had kept him at arm's length. He didn't need George's help to sort out his personal, intimate problems. They worked together, and it was better not to mix feelings with business.

"No, I came here to know if you talked with Winchester yesterday." George went to the sideboard again. "We must start working in Easthollow and finish the new line before autumn begins."

"The ass was visiting his son outside of London."

"Rubbish." George paused pouring himself a glass of Scotch. "I saw him in London."

He sat bolt upright. "Where?"

"Close to the warehouse of Lord Carnegie after my meeting with him to discuss the steel supply. I was about to hail a cab when Winchester came out of the Russian anarchists' centre, shaking hands with them."

Anger flared up again, but it was of a different type; it wasn't the dark anger burning him when the twitch bothered him. It was a less destructive one.

"Since when did Winchester befriend the anarchists?"

George tasted his scotch and gave a nod of approval. "Who knows what business he has with them? Nothing good, mark my words. The point is, he was in London."

Tristan drummed his fingers on the armrest but stopped when the simple movement shot pain up his arm. "The fact he avoids me is nothing new. But is he hiding his association with the anarchists? Those people keep placing bombs everywhere and killing innocents."

Only two years before, the anarchists had bombed the Royal Observatory in Greenwich, and the Fenians placed bombs all over the kingdom as well.

"I don't know what Winchester is doing. He'll soon realise that dealing with the anarchists only leads to destruction. What I care about is that he sells us that bloody piece of land first." George curled up his upper lip in annoyance. "That barren strip of rocks is worthless. No tenants live there. And he's acting as if we asked him to sell us his home estate."

Another thing bothered Tristan. Effie might have lied to him about her father's whereabouts. Or maybe her father had lied to her. Why he cared about that insignificant detail, he couldn't tell. Perhaps because he hadn't thought she was capable of deceit. But then again, he couldn't expect her to show him loyalty.

George exhaled. "Winchester will be at Lord Vaughan's ball next week. You must go."

"Must?" He gritted out. "Are you giving me orders now?"

George's dark eyes flashed. "The day you show some common sense and stop letting strangers use you as a punching bag, I'll stop telling you what to do. Right now, I don't trust your judgement."

"Get the hell out. That's my judgement."

George didn't flinch. "Your father would be ashamed of you."

"Father would be happy to see the progress we made to rebuild our fortune."

"He cared more about you." George's tone was too serious to answer back, and he spoke the truth.

"What I do in my free time is none of your business, especially since it doesn't have consequences on my work."

"It does." George exhaled. "I'm disappointed. All those expensive tutors, schools, and books, and you haven't learnt the most important lesson about business and life."

"Which is? Enlighten me."

George stood up and finished his scotch. "Five hundred soldiers can't win against five thousand, but five hundred friends can. It's from the *Hagakure*, the samurai's handbook. Good night, Tristan. I hope your personal bloodbath was worth it."

Tristan rubbed his face when George left. Damn George and his books. And his truth.

Father wasn't there; he couldn't ask him what he did or didn't want. And his twitch was starting again.

eight

Effie's head spun after her third dance in a row. The last galop had tested her endurance and her slippers, but she couldn't stop smiling.

Lord Vaughan's ballroom wasn't as wide as the one in her home in Bedfordshire; the dancers had less space to jump around, but the music sounded louder, thanks to the low ceiling, and she loved it. The large windows offered a nice view of the garden, which was better than a busy London street.

She took a glass of lemonade from a passing footman and watched the dancing couples performing a quick mazurka. The ladies next to her clapped their hands in rhythm with the music, and she couldn't resist. She tapped her foot as well, following the dance.

Papa walked over to her, elegant in a dark suit. "Are you enjoying yourself, darling?"

"Very much. My card is full."

He beamed. "Anyone you fancy?"

She chuckled at the eagerness in his voice. "I met a few interesting gentlemen."

"Anyone I know?"

"You know everyone. Isn't a father supposed to be reluctant to marry off his daughter?"

"I just want to see my youngest daughter settled. You're the last one. We've been so blessed. Thirteen healthy children, and twelve of them are married. I couldn't be happier."

She hooked her arm through his. "You didn't seem so happy last Christmas when you were surrounded by your fifteen grandchildren."

He feigned being outraged. "I had to pretend to drink invisible tea and eat wooden cakes with three little girls and their dolls for an entire afternoon. Then Margaret's doll got sick, and we pretended to cure her. Such a long affair. I'm glad the doll survived, or there would have been a service as well."

She laughed. "You adored every minute of it."

He gave a shy nod, but his smile faltered when he gazed towards the set of double doors on the other side of the ballroom.

"Can't I have a moment of peace?" he muttered in a harsh tone in stark contrast to the playful one from before.

"What is it?" She searched the room.

Lord Montcrest stood at the entrance, drawing gazes and murmurs from every corner. In his shiny dark evening dress and with his golden hair, he was easy to spot. But above all, his dark aura drew in everyone's interest. His confident posture and glacial stare added to his persona.

"Didn't you know he would come?" she asked.

Papa worked his jaw in a nervous gesture she'd rarely seen. "He usually doesn't attend balls. I bet he's here only to see me."

"Why don't you simply talk to him?"

"Because he doesn't deserve my time."

"You agreed to help him when he was in need," she whispered behind her fan.

"Yes, and he and his father showed no gratitude afterwards."

"But you didn't help him only in the hope he would remember the gesture, did you?"

He said nothing.

The dancing couples slowed their paces but started again when Jane prompted them to keep going with a charming laugh, dancing with her partner.

When Lord Montcrest crossed the ballroom, heading for their corner, Papa straightened, and Effie sighed.

"Good evening." Lord Montcrest shot a glare at Papa. "Winchester, Lady Effie."

"Montcrest, what a surprise," Papa said in a sharp tone.

He ignored him, fixing his intense stare on her. "Lady Effie, I would like to dance with you." The words formed a request, but the tone sounded like an order.

"What..." She cleared her throat to take the time to recover from the shock. "I would be delighted, but my card is full."

"Who's next?"

"Montcrest, my daughter was clear," Papa said.

"So was I." He radiated coldness. Those blue eyes seemed chipped out of a glacier.

Just not to let her father argue with the marquess, she said, "Lord Henry."

He gazed around before marching towards an oblivious Lord Henry who was chatting with a friend next to the window.

"What is he doing?" she asked.

"What he does best." Papa scoffed.

Lord Henry stood at attention as Lord Montcrest interrupted the conversation. She couldn't hear what they said, but Lord Henry flushed red and bowed and dabbed his forehead with a handkerchief too many times in her opinion. Then both gentlemen walked towards her.

She fiddled with her fan, not sure what a lady was supposed to do in a situation like that.

"Lady Effie." Lord Henry's mouth twitched in a nervous smile. His thin moustache seemed drawn with a pencil, and when he moved his mouth like that, it went up and down, making her want to laugh. "I agreed to exchange my spot on your card with Lord Montcrest."

She shifted her gaze from Lord Henry's embarrassed face to Lord Montcrest's stony one. '*Agreed*' didn't sound peaceful at all.

"I must protest," Papa said.

"Protest away, Winchester, but it's the lady who decides." Lord Montcrest offered her his hand. "Lady Effie."

That was why she preferred dealing with animals. They weren't bossy. Well, Kettle was bossy, but he also was cute and adorable.

If she refused, an argument would ensue between Papa and Lord Montcrest, and while Papa should solve whatever problem he had with the marquess, she didn't think a ball was the right place to do so. Lord Montcrest had already attracted too much attention. Several heads were turned their way, and she didn't want Papa to have yet another reason to dislike Lord Montcrest. Lord Henry seemed about to melt on the spot.

So she slid her hand into Lord Montcrest's.

"Do not worry, Papa." She gave him a pointed look, hoping he would understand she didn't want him to make a scene.

He pressed his lips in a hard line but didn't say anything.

A corner of Lord Montcrest's mouth quirked up. "We'll talk later, Winchester. Do not fear."

Effie forced a smile as he led her to the centre of the ballroom. "There was no need to frighten Lord Henry."

"I didn't. What makes you think I frightened him?" He took her waist and pulled her closer in a possessive gesture she found shocking.

No warm, fluttery feeling started in her belly. Absolutely not.

"He looked upset." She placed her hand on his shoulder, feeling his steel-like muscles underneath the smooth fabric of his jacket.

"Of course he was upset. He lost the opportunity to dance with a beautiful lady."

"Flattery won't lead you anywhere."

He cocked an eyebrow. "Why, do you know where I'm going?"

She was about to answer but then closed her mouth. Actually, she had no idea what game he was playing.

The music of a slow contradanse started, saving her from giving an answer she didn't have.

He was a great dancing partner—she ought to give him that. He moved with grace and elegance, never stepping on the hem of her skirt or hitting her slippers with the tips of his shoes, as her former dancing partners had done.

He held her gently but firmly and was protective of her, making sure she could easily follow his wide strides. She was enjoying herself. A great dancing partner was the best way to savour a dance.

The tension left her shoulders, and as he made her twirl quickly without letting her trip, she couldn't hold back a laugh.

He smiled back, a charming, warm smile she had no idea he could produce. Still, she wasn't so easily fooled by good looks and dancing skills. He'd invited her to dance only to upset Papa, and she couldn't overlook that.

"You stopped smiling," he said, sounding genuinely concerned. "What is it?"

"I would be grateful if you would leave me out of your business quarrel with my father," she said as they turned around.

"I don't have any quarrel with your father. It's him who does with me."

"Is it possible to have a normal conversation with you?"

"Yes, by being honest." He drew her closer, and his clean citrus scent engulfed her.

Another inch and she would be flush against him, and Papa would intervene.

She wasn't sure how she felt about that. "I don't know what you mean. I've never lied to you."

"Did you know your father wasn't visiting your brother the other day when I came calling on him?"

"What are you talking about?" She had to break eye contact with him to turn around under his arm. "Papa was in Greenford, as I told you."

"No, he was in London."

She narrowed her gaze. "Maybe he changed his plans at the last moment. Maybe he missed the train. I don't know. What I know is that he told me he would be there. Is this why you asked me to dance? To interrogate me?"

"No." He led her through a series of quick steps flawlessly. She was gliding over the polished floor; it was like flying.

Jane gave her a shocked stare as she danced past them.

Effie waited for him to say more, ignoring her friend. Of course, he didn't say anything else. The more time she spent with him, the more similarities she found between him and cats.

"Then why did you ask me to dance?" she asked.

"Because I wanted to."

"No, you wanted to annoy my father."

He leant scandalously closer to whisper, "If I'd wanted to annoy your father, trust me, I would have found something more effective."

Talking about honesty, she was more annoyed with herself for the little shiver his closeness and deep voice caused than with him. Nevertheless, she wouldn't be used like a pawn between Papa and a grumpy marquess.

"I'm never sure if you mean what you say or if you only want to provoke me." She huffed and came to an abrupt halt in the middle of a turn.

The quick stop broke his momentum and, since he was still holding her waist, he slid forwards. She tottered on her feet as well. Her elbow hit his abdomen, causing him to bend over in a deep bow. The impact did almost nothing to her balance, but he grimaced in pain and clutched a hand over the spot she'd hit.

He gritted his teeth, his cheeks paling. "Damn."

"I'm so sorry." Although she didn't understand how a simple poke in the ribs could have hurt so much and brought him to swear. She'd barely touched him.

He straightened. The tendons of his neck stood out over the rim of his collar.

"It's nothing." His voice sounded strained as well.

"It can't be nothing. You look in pain."

As he removed his hand from his abdomen to take his handkerchief, she caught a glimpse of a blossoming red stain.

nine

Standing in the middle of the ballroom, Effie drew in a breath as she stared at the growing red stain on Lord Montcrest's waistcoat. "That's blood."

"It's nothing."

"The stain is growing larger."

"I have to go." He walked towards the edge of the dance floor, hiding the stain with his hand.

She followed him at a close distance. He did his best to remain straight, but he kept hunching. She must have hit a freshly stitched wound or something similar.

Pressing the handkerchief against his side, he walked out of the ballroom with her at his heels.

"Montcrest." She chased him along the corridor. "Let me see. I feel responsible for hurting you."

"It's not your fault. It's nothing." He sounded as if he were choking.

"I can help." She caught up with him. "Trust me." Even though the scene would be scandalous.

He came to a halt and studied her for a long minute. Pain drew deep lines around his mouth. "You shouldn't worry about me. You shouldn't waste your time on me." The laboured and haughty tone was replaced with a vulnerable one.

Shock caught her at his resignation as if his statement were definitive. What had happened to him to make him so certain about his unworthiness? Guilt for having judged him gnawed at her.

She touched his arm as the instinct to pull him into a comforting hug rose. "Let's discuss that after I've taken a look at that bleeding cut."

"You take care of animals."

"You would be surprised to know how many things we have in common with them." She opened the nearest door and beckoned him inside a sitting room.

He didn't move. In the semidarkness of the corridor, he looked pale and hurt, guarded like a wild animal.

"Trust me," she said again.

He closed his eyes briefly before following her.

The moment she closed the door behind them, darkness fell in the room, and a certain stirring of uneasiness flickered within her. She was alone with a man she barely knew, in the middle of the night.

Her hand trembled when she locked them in. It was better to make sure no one entered, but being locked in with him meant she couldn't get out easily.

The thick door muffled the music from the ballroom, and his uneven breathing sounded louder.

She lit a few lamps. Their yellow glow spread over a couple of armchairs, bookshelves, and a large Chesterfield sofa. The fear he might take advantage of her vanished when he gritted his teeth and hung his head. He was in pain and needed her help, and she wouldn't refuse it.

"Over there." She pointed at the sofa.

He didn't move, his hand still on his stained shirt. "We're alone."

"Well spotted."

"You know what I mean."

"I do, but you're bleeding. The handkerchief is all red. If you cooperate, we'll be quicker and leave this room faster."

Exhaling, he sat on the sofa, not without wincing.

She sat in front of him. "Let me see."

He removed the bloody handkerchief and unbuttoned his waistcoat and shirt. She shifted on the seat. If Papa saw her now, she would have a difficult time explaining what she was doing. Lord Montcrest was a gentleman Papa wouldn't be happy to consider among her suitors. And if they were caught alone together, Papa wouldn't appreciate the gossip. She wouldn't appreciate it.

"You hit an existing cut. That's all." He showed her a thin but long slash across his abdominal muscles.

The edges were puffy and raw, and judging by the lack of a proper crust, the cut had kept bleeding often.

"Heavens. How did you get that? And why didn't your physician stitch it?"

He ignored both questions. "Now that you have seen it, you may return to the ballroom."

"Absolutely not." She rose. "The cut needs to be cleaned and stitched. I always carry with me the necessary equipment for an emergency. One can never know when something happens. Wait here."

One of his golden eyebrows shot up. "You want to use animal medicine on me?"

"Medicine is a science that works whether your flesh is human or not."

"You gave my horse chlorine of lime." There was an amused tone in his voice.

"Yes, and it worked, didn't it?" She waved a dismissive hand. "Medicine is complicated. I won't give you anything lethal. Besides, this is a cut, and cuts are cuts."

"What does that mean?"

"It means that you have to wait for me." She exited the room and darted to the cloakroom where she'd left her capelet, hat, and emergency bag.

"My lady?" A startled footman straightened when she stopped him.

"I need my bag, the big leather one."

"Of course." He left and returned with her bag in a moment.

"Thank you."

When she pushed the sitting room door open, she half expected not to find him. Instead, he was sitting where she'd left him, shoulders hunched and a sad expression on his face. At that moment, he looked nothing like the cold man who had entered the ballroom earlier, but like someone fragile and in pain.

"You're still here," she said, her voice quivering a little.

"Well spotted."

She locked the door again but with less anxiety. "So how did you get that cut?"

"I fell on a piece of glass."

She gave him a sceptical look. "I remember you saying something about honesty."

The ghost of a smile graced his lips. "Are you going to give me stitches?"

"I'll clean the cut first." She selected clean gauze and diluted iodine from her bag.

He pulled up his shirt to allow her to work. She wiped the blood, but since he was sitting and arching, the cut kept gushing blood.

"I need you to lie down." She gave him a little push, putting a hand on his shoulder, but he didn't move an inch.

After he gave her one of his *'Are you joking?'* looks, he did as told. Once he was stretched on his back, she touched the wound and the swollen sides.

"There's the beginning of an infection. What did your physician tell you?"

He shrugged. "I didn't see him."

"That's irresponsible. You need stitches."

"I'm sure I'll live."

He wasn't going to see a doctor.

"I can stitch it now." Her offer was a challenge to prompt him to see a physician although she could attend to his wound.

He propped himself up on his elbows. "Are you serious?"

"I stitched dozens of cuts on dogs, cattle, and bulls. It's not that different." It was. Animals' skin was thicker than humans', but the technique was the same. She closed her bag. "But if you prefer seeing your physician, as you should, I understand."

"No." He tilted his head back, exposing his strong neck and bobbing Adam's apple. "He would ask a thousand questions. Yes, do it."

"You're welcome. I love it when someone I'm trying to help gives me orders."

He lifted his head just enough to stare at her. "Thank you. I didn't mean to order you around."

"Honestly." She prepared everything she needed to stitch the cut. "I would appreciate a bit of respect and good manners."

"Fair is fair. Apologies." He swallowed. "Did you study at a college?"

"Women aren't allowed to study veterinary medicine. We can study medicine in many universities and can become surgeons, but heaven forbid if we touch a cow."

"That sounds unfair. Like many other things in life." He sounded genuinely sorry.

"Thank you for understanding. People don't usually react like you did when I tell them about my aspiration."

He flushed and mumbled, "You're welcome."

Had she embarrassed him? "You aren't used to praise."

He gazed around. "Not exactly. Let's say people don't praise my understanding."

His abdominal muscles tensed when she took out the needle and the thread.

"Is it going to hurt?" he asked.

"No. I'll apply cocaine to your skin to numb it. You won't feel anything." She worked quickly, applying the cocaine first, then stitching the wound with the thinnest curved needle she had. "The scar shouldn't be very visible, but you'll have one."

"Why are you so kind to me?" His tone of voice was the same as the one he'd used for Zeus—sweet, calm, and patient. He stared at her as if she were his guardian angel.

"Because I feel sorry for you." And she wasn't referring to the cut.

"Pity then."

"Compassion. It's different." She finished the last tiny stitches. "You're always so defensive. Why? Not everyone is your enemy. I certainly am not."

He lay down again and blew out a breath as if he were exhausted. When he met her gaze, the tense lines on his face smoothed. "I'm going through a rather difficult moment."

"May I ask what exactly?" She wiped the cut again.

"You know the story of my family." The guarded tone was back.

"I know you lost everything and rebuilt your fortune. I grew up in the country. I came to London twice a year. I don't know much about what happened here." She wiped the excess of disinfectant with a clean cloth. "Tell me. Everything I know about your family comes from other people."

He released a long breath through his teeth. Maybe the attitude was reluctance, but she suspected it was more about shame.

"My grandfather made a few bad investments, then some more bad investments in the attempt to repair the damage. He was a good man but with no sense of business or understanding of the market. He bled so much money he bankrupted my family. One of those investments dealt with an enemy of the crown, so he was almost accused of high treason on top of everything else. His title and life were at risk, and his coffers were empty. The shame and the pain were too much. He died of a seizure."

She stopped wiping his skin. "I'm sorry."

He wasn't looking at her as he spoke but at the ceiling. Perhaps he felt more comfortable talking about himself that way.

"You were the first person who helped us. I never forgot your kindness. My father and I started to rebuild our family's status and money. It was long and relentless work, made of late nights, begging people who hated us for favours, and humiliations. We worked side by side with clerks and builders, broke our backs to keep our land, and succeeded. People believed the relationship with my father was strained because I'd worked with him since I was a boy, thus they thought he'd forced me or been unfair to me. But it couldn't be further from the truth. But I'm still fighting. I fear the fight will never end, as if I lived in a loop that gets tighter..." He swallowed hard, his gaze fixed on the ceiling. "People assume that, because I'm a lord, I don't know what it means to be starving, be cold, or work so hard your body aches. I don't take my fortune for granted. I wasn't always surrounded by servants and wealth. I'm not complaining, but I'm not whom people think."

Emotion tightened her throat at his suffering. She put her hand on his, and he snatched it back like a scared animal.

"Sorry," she said. "I didn't mean to startle you."

A deep frown appeared between his eyebrows. He sat upright and buttoned his shirt. "I don't know why I talked so much." He tugged at his shirt and waistcoat hard enough to rip the fabric. "Bloody hell."

"I'm afraid I can't stitch that." Her attempt to lighten the mood didn't end well.

"I don't usually bother people with my family's history."

"You didn't bother me."

He stood up, changing into the stony Marquess of Montcrest in the span of a moment. "Thank you for your assistance. I should leave now."

"I should bandage the cut."

He raked a hand through his hair, messing it. "No. It doesn't matter. My lady." He bowed formally and left the room in a hurry as if she told him she meant to neuter him.

She sighed and packed her tools.

Lord Montcrest's problem wasn't a cut on his abdomen.

ten

For the second time in a row, Tristan had failed to talk with Winchester. For the second time in a row, he'd been distracted by Effie's radiance and spectacular eyes.

After the ball, he had trouble focusing on anything that wasn't sitting and staring at the fire. Alone in his warm study, he wondered what the hell had happened that night. He'd blabbered about his family for no reason, but seeing her sweet, kind eyes, he'd known she wouldn't judge him or dismiss him. Still, he'd talked too much.

It was the first time he'd lacked the focus and determination to complete a task. The first mistake had been dancing with her. It'd been a decision made on the spur of the moment, not to annoy Winchester. He didn't care about petty teases. He wasn't that cold-hearted.

Effie had looked so beautiful in her dark red gown and flushed cheeks that he'd ceded to the temptation of holding her for a moment. And he loved how she stood up to him.

And then there was her kindness—the most dangerous and attractive of her qualities.

He put a hand on his stained shirt over his sore flesh. She'd given him stitches. He chuckled, feeling them pulling at his flesh. A beautiful, excellent veterinary doctor had attended to his cut.

He could have easily told her not to bother and sent for his physician although Dr. O'Neil would have asked too many questions. But the truth was he'd wanted her to do it. His skin tingled with the memory of her gentle fingers and fast chatter.

His family had made quite a few enemies in the past years. Between Grandfather's mistakes and Father's aggressive economic expansion, the other peers didn't exactly sing the Montcrests' praise. He didn't care about that either. He didn't give a damn about what the others thought of him. He only cared about his family's finances and the tenants depending on it.

But Effie had made him realise how much he was used to being treated with coldness at best and disdain at worst.

She'd revealed a side of him he didn't like. A part of him craved simple social relationships. It would be good to chat with his friends at the club and enjoy a ball without ulterior motives, like a normal person would.

He exhaled when someone knocked on his door. Not George again. "Come in."

The door was pushed inwards, and Rowan peeped inside. "May I? Uncle George is here as well."

"Of course." He buttoned his jacket to cover the blood.

Explaining the injury to Dr. O'Neil would be difficult but explaining it to Rowan would be impossible.

George followed Rowan inside, his gaze immediately falling on Tristan's abdomen as if he knew. "Was the ball productive?"

"We'll talk about that tomorrow." He was too tired to discuss business strategy. "Why are you still up?" he asked Rowan.

"I couldn't sleep, and I played Ludo with Uncle George."

George's facial muscles relaxed as he ruffled Rowan's hair. "He won. Three games in a row."

"The secret is how I throw the dice." Rowan mimicked the gesture of tossing the dice.

They laughed together as old companions. A pang of loneliness struck him. He was happy Rowan had a good relationship with George, but he'd spent hours working side by side with George and had never developed anything but a strained friendship. Business had always got between them. Different views, decisions, and the business strategies of two stubborn men weren't the best premises for a smooth friendship.

"It's late. I'd better leave." George hugged Rowan fondly. "And you need to talk to your brother."

"Thank you, Uncle George." Rowan squeezed him tightly, and suddenly Tristan felt like a stranger invited to a family dinner.

After they exchanged a few laughs and private jokes, George opened the door and started to leave. "We'll talk soon, Tristan."

"I'm sure we will."

George closed the door behind him, and the atmosphere in the room became heavy as if a pea soup fog had descended.

"Is something the matter?" he asked.

Rowan shuffled forwards in his dressing gown. "I wanted to ask you something."

"Ask away."

Rowan chewed his bottom lip and twisted the belt of the dressing gown.

Tristan rubbed his temples. "If you're waiting for me to read your thoughts, we can stay here forever."

Rowan nodded and cleared his throat. No words came out of his mouth.

"Why are you so frightened of me?" He wished his tone sounded less intimidating, but hell, Rowan needed to become more determined.

At his age, Tristan had already been working with Father, travelling with him across the country and doing the combined chores of a farmer, secretary, and manservant while George had put his business expertise at their disposal.

Rowan flinched. "It can wait." He turned around and started towards the door.

"Rowan."

The boy stopped and faced him.

"I don't mean to frighten you. What is it?" He forced his tone down.

"I want to ask Lady Effie to come tomorrow," Rowan whispered.

A little shot of energy went through him, which annoyed him. He might not see her tomorrow, even if she agreed to see Rowan.

"And?" he asked.

"Is it all right?" Rowan regarded him from underneath the curtain of his golden curls.

"Yes, why wouldn't it be?"

Rowan fiddled with his hands. Tristan waited for an answer, but aside from shivering and tormenting his hands, Rowan didn't say anything else.

"I'm glad you like her and that you're making friends," he went on to encourage him. "I didn't know you wanted to become a veterinarian." That had surprised him, but he hadn't wanted to show his shock in front of everyone.

His half-brother remained silent.

"Rowan—"

"May I go now?" Rowan stared at the carpet.

"Yes, you may." He threw a hand up.

Rowan ran out of the study before Tristan could say more. His half-brother was terrified to death of him, and he had no idea what to do to change that.

～

Effie tried to hide behind her cup of tea as she was having breakfast with her father. Her dancing with Tristan had caused quite a stir, and Papa had given her a hard time with his questions.

"Did Montcrest say something about me?" he asked.

She buttered her slice of bread. "The answer isn't going to change after you ask me the same question for the fifth time. No, he didn't."

"But you must have talked about something." He folded and unfolded his copy of *The Times*.

"I told you. It was a normal chit-chat." Aside from Tristan's heartbreaking story about his family and his obvious loneliness. "Nothing to do with you."

"I don't understand why you don't want to tell me the truth."

Pepper stopped chewing his rubber ball to stare at him.

She put the knife down. "Honestly, am I at Scotland Yard now?"

"He rushed out of the room, seemingly in distress, and you went after him. I noticed that." He tapped the table nervously. "There. I didn't want to mention that, not to embarrass you. But you gave me no choice."

She tried to remain deadpan. "He didn't feel too well all of a sudden and left. I simply followed him to make sure he was all right. That's all."

"His health shouldn't concern you."

Oddly enough, that was what Tristan had said.

"Can't I be worried about someone feeling sick?" she asked.

"Yes, but...why him?"

"Because I can make my own decisions, as you've always encouraged me to do."

Finally, silence filled the room.

She scowled when he opened his mouth, likely for another round of questions, but the butler coming in saved her from an argument.

"My lady, this is for you."

"Thank you, Doyle." She opened the small envelope, and a little flutter started in her chest when she saw the emboldened golden M at the top of the paper.

> *Dear Lady Effie,*
> *I hope you will see me today to go to the stables with me.*
> *I'm eager to become a veterinarian like you.*
> *Lord Rowan.*

She smiled at the simple request. Rowan's enthusiasm and curiosity were touching, and she would encourage him gladly.

"What is it?" Papa used his interrogation tone again.

She rose to go to the small table to pick up a pen. "I'm going out today."

"For what reason?"

She wrote her reply on the back of the letter. "Doyle, would you please make sure this is delivered soon?"

He bowed his head and left.

"What is it?" Papa closed a fist around his knife. "Is it *him*?"

Rebellious traits had never been in her character. Her eldest sister was the rebel of the family after she'd secretly studied nursing science and paved the way for her younger sisters to do what they wanted. Yet Papa's tone and commanding attitude—a novelty— urged her to get closer to Tristan, instead of obeying him.

"Papa, please. No, it's not a message from Lord Montcrest, but from his brother, Lord Rowan."

"I hope you aren't seeing him?"

The more he ordered her to keep her distance from Tristan, the more she wanted to see him.

She stood. "Lord Rowan is a thirteen-year-old boy, Papa. He is very sweet and well mannered. I certainly want to see him."

"Effie, don't challenge me on this."

"I'll follow your warning and not get involved in your business, but I want to see the boy. I won't be rude to him only because you have a quarrel with his brother."

He dropped the napkin on the table. "I don't understand your attitude. You've always been so reasonable."

"Funny, but I was about to say the same thing." She left the dining room before he could order her to stay.

eleven

Morning tea and arguments were an awful combination to start the day, especially since Tristan had spent a troubled night and awakened late, not refreshed at all. He'd barely got dressed before George had ambushed him in the dining room.

"I didn't want to bother you last night, especially not in front of Rowan, but you still haven't talked to Winchester." George was sitting in front of him at the table, ignoring his cup of tea and buttery scone.

Harris shifted his gaze between the two of them.

"You were supposed to talk to him last night. Did you read the newspaper?" George pointed at *The Times,* where Tristan's name had made an appearance on the scandal sheet.

Nothing new. The only novelty was that, for once, they didn't gossip about his ruthless attitude in business, but about a slow dance with a stunning lady.

His presence had drawn more attention than he'd predicted thanks to his dance with Effie.

"The anarchists planted a bomb in a train station in Birmingham," Tristan said. "And another one at Liverpool Road Station in Manchester. They're targeting train stations."

George leant back. "I read about that. Awful business. But can we talk about Lord Vaughan's ball? Why didn't you talk to Winchester?"

He finished his tea and folded the ironed newspaper on the table. "An unforeseen difficulty happened."

A sweet, very charming unforeseen difficulty that had shown him compassion, understanding—he sniffled, catching a whiff of a pungent smell coming from his abdomen—and iodine. Lots of iodine.

George ran a hand through his greying hair. It might be Tristan's imagination, but since they'd started to expand their railway company, George's grey hairs had multiplied.

"Did you go to the ring last night?" George asked in an annoyed tone.

Harris seemed about to say something but remained silent.

The last thing Tristan needed was a double sermon. He rose from the table. "As we ascertained the other night, that's none of your business."

George stepped in front of him. He was as tall as Tristan, and his keen gaze saw too much. "I'm worried, and not because your fighting habit compromises your judgement in our business. That filthy place isn't only illegal but also dangerous. A passing thug could stab you, kill you, and dispose of your body without anyone being the wiser. The moment one of those crooks realises you're a marquess, you're as good as dead."

"That's ridiculous. The Octagon is a place for boxing. That's all. It's safer than a gambling den because there's no money involved." Although he'd been stabbed the other night, but George didn't need to know that.

"What if you get seriously injured? What if they break your spine or neck?"

He leant closer. "That's part of the thrill." He sidestepped

George to leave the dining room, and the footman opened the door.

"Tristan!" George's voice sounded sharp.

"What?" He didn't turn around.

There was an exhale. "Be careful. I mean it."

Not often did George use that kind, fatherly tone with him, and Tristan never dismissed it.

He turned around to face his father's best friend. "I will."

He was always bloody careful, but renouncing the ring wasn't an option.

He walked out of the room, wishing George would understand. Focusing on his work was easy after a good boxing session, and boxing in a boring, safe gentlemen's club, where the opponents followed the Marquess of Queensberry Rules, didn't do anything to silence his twitch. The rowdy, dangerous men at The Octagon were the best cure.

The cut Effie had stitched was still a bit stiff and itched, but every time a pang bothered him, he was reminded of her. He rushed down the corridor but came to a quick stop in the hallway where footsteps sounded.

Effie and her maid gazed up at him. The surprise froze him although Rowan had told him he was going to invite her. Effie's smile in the morning light was exactly what his life was missing. She was stunning in a rich-maroon gown with burgundy velvet ribbons and a matching hat. Autumn had always been his favourite season.

Why his mind had conjured up that thought was beyond him.

"Lord Montcrest," she said. "Good morning. I trust you are well."

He put a hand on the stitched cut. "I am."

Quick footsteps came from behind him. "Lady Effie, I'm here." Rowan slowed down as he walked past Tristan. "Thank you for coming."

"Lord Rowan, I'm glad to see you again," she said before

turning to Tristan. "I would like to see Zeus and talk to Rowan about veterinary medicine books." She tapped the large bag she was carrying. "Are you going to join us? It would be lovely."

Rowan shot a glance at her. Tristan could bet his brother had in mind another word instead of lovely.

He didn't have any urgent appointments that morning. Well, not very urgent.

While Rowan's scared face and the maid's hostile expression urged him to say no, Effie's bright eyes made him feel welcome. Someone genuinely wanted to spend time with him, as absurd as it sounded. And not because she had a business deal to discuss with him or worse, a marriage proposal.

His brain told him to say no and head to the factory in Pimlico to supervise the production. But his heart believed the factory could wait an hour or two.

"Gladly," he said.

George walked to the hallway as well. "Good morning."

Tristan stretched out an arm. "Lady Effie, this is my business partner and friend, Mr. Fleet."

Effie gave a graceful nod of her head. "Mr. Fleet."

George bowed. "My lady, you're Lady Euphemia, Lord Winchester's daughter, I believe."

"I am she."

"Interesting." George turned towards Tristan who lifted his chin, challenging him to say more.

He had to keep Effie out of the quarrel with Winchester.

"Lady Effie is going to teach me about becoming a veterinary doctor," Rowan said with a smile that Tristan didn't remember having ever seen.

George's face brightened. "Excellent. You'll be great with your love of animals. Only good things come out of a great passion."

Rowan blushed. "Thank you, Uncle."

"Backgammon tonight?" George asked.

Rowan nodded. "Yes! I'll tell you everything about today. We're all going to the stables. Even Tristan."

"Aren't you going to Pimlico?" George asked as the footman helped him don his coat.

He waved a dismissive hand. "Later. I would like to see Zeus as well."

"The more, the merrier," Effie said, but no one seemed to share her enthusiasm.

George shifted his gaze from Effie to Tristan, like a confused dog who didn't know which squirrel he should chase. "Yes, I often associate the word '*merry*' with Lord Montcrest."

Rowan started to chuckle but hid it with a cough.

"Excellent." Effie seemed oblivious to the awkward atmosphere. "Shall we go?"

"Peter, my coat," Tristan said to the footman.

George hugged Rowan and nodded to Effie. "It was a pleasure to meet you, my lady." He angled towards Tristan. "I'll see you later."

They walked together to the stables in an uncomfortable silence—though not uncomfortable for Effie. She hummed a tune and smiled at the warm sunlight. She pointed out this or that flowering plant or a cloud with a funny shape.

The maid was so serious and stiff she could be a statue, and Rowan walked close to Effie as if not wanting to stay close to his brother.

He regretted his decision to go with them—a decision that had come from nowhere. His relationship with Rowan had always been strained, not because Rowan's mother was a young, ruthless woman who didn't care about anyone but herself, as Father had said after she'd taken off with a lover. But because Rowan grew up during those years Tristan had spent with his father working relentlessly, he hadn't been present in Rowan's life much. He shouldn't be surprised that his half-brother considered him a stranger. George had spent more time with Rowan than he had.

Stable hands and grooms bowed and greeted them with low voices. Effie had been there only once, but she received warm smiles and devout bows from everyone.

She returned the greetings in kind. "Good morning, everyone. And here is mighty Zeus."

Upon hearing her voice, Zeus whinnied. His jaw relaxed, and his tail swung. He bumped his head against her palm when she caressed his head.

"How are you?" she said in a special, sweet voice.

Zeus replied with equally soft noises, forgetting about his master.

Tristan smiled. Even his favourite horse liked her, and he felt proud of that for some reason he didn't understand. But then again, where Effie was involved, many things didn't make sense.

The maid shifted her position, likely trying to find a clean spot. She would have a hard time. The stable hands did their best to keep it clean, but mud and dung were always present.

"Zeus recovered quickly, didn't he?" Rowan asked.

"Very quickly. He's young and strong. It's important to intervene as soon as possible when the symptoms of colic are spotted." She gave Zeus an apple she took out of her pocket. "Some horses are prone to digestive problems. That's why it's helpful to allow them to drink small portions of water at a time, instead of large buckets."

Rowan nodded solemnly.

"I once helped a horse with a twisted intestine," she said, "by using a stomach tube."

"That sounds incredible!" Rowan's enthusiasm struck Tristan.

His half-brother was truly keen to care for animals and study veterinary medicine.

Rowan focused on brushing Zeus's coat while Effie talked about the importance of removing the twigs, tiny pebbles, or parasites from a horse's coat.

"The bites of a horsefly get easily infected." She fished out a book from her bag and flipped through the pages. "See? This is a sketch of an infected wound."

"Nasty." Rowan brushed Zeus more gently, checking every inch of the coat.

As Tristan stroked Zeus's muzzle, he watched them talking like old friends, and a fit of longing bothered him. Although he wasn't sure what he longed for. Maybe for happy, carefree days he'd never had with his father. Not that he blamed Father. Those years had been all about survival, and Father had always been next to him through dark moments. But he'd never been simply happy, enjoying a moment of freedom with his friends, and even George had been obsessed with making money.

The sun beating on the back of his neck reminded him it was time to go. Oddly enough, he found it hard to leave the stable. Effie's chatter on how to spot and remove ticks wasn't just interesting but also relaxing.

He straightened, happy to see Rowan enjoying himself. "I have to go. Lady Effie, thank you for your time."

"You're welcome." She flashed another bright smile as if he were a normal person. If she only knew.

Rowan swallowed a couple of times. "Thank you for letting me be here today."

Every gaze was set on Tristan. He could bet they were holding their breaths, waiting for his reply.

He patted Rowan's shoulder. "You're going to be an expert in animals soon."

"I hope so." Rowan flushed. Effie's enthusiasm was contagious.

"My lady." He gave her a quick nod and walked to the end of the stable alley.

A smile tugged at his lips as he headed towards the high street. She gave him reasons to smile, and he wouldn't think too much about why.

He had barely turned the corner when Effie called out to him.

"Tristan." She ran towards him, her skirt lifting and exposing her ankles clad in leather boots. Nice, slender ankles, that is. And he loved the sound of his name on her lips.

Her bright eyes never failed to hold him captive. They weren't simply hazel but showed a riot of colours from golden specks to green hues. They changed according to the light.

"How is the cut?" she whispered when she stopped in front of him.

"Very well."

"No infection?"

"I wouldn't know."

She frowned. "Your cut was neglected before I stitched it. It's important to make sure the stitches don't get infected."

"I'll order them not to." He cringed inwardly. His attempt at making a joke was pathetic, to say the least.

She laughed, which made him chuckle, too. "If only it were that simple. I would like to take a look at it when you are available."

He stopped smiling. "Excuse me?"

"You're my patient."

"I'm sure you don't need to check on the cut."

She became serious. "I stitched your cut. It's my responsibility to make sure the wound doesn't get infected. Do you have an idea of how many animals and people die from infections every year? If you prefer seeing your physician, I understand, but someone must check on it."

If he had to choose between Dr. O'Neil and Effie, he had no hesitation in whom he preferred.

"I'll be home in my study in the afternoon."

"Excellent. Send for me when you're home." She gifted him with another smile. "I'll see you later."

He watched her running back to the stables, enthralled by the light radiating from her. She was like a bright star, and he wasn't despicable enough to keep her in his darkness.

twelve

Once again, Tristan had trouble focusing on his work. Being alone in his study with a nice cup of tea and the sunlight coming from the window didn't help.

The survey of the factory in Pimlico he had with his manager had been sheer torture. He'd asked the manager to repeat simple concepts a few times because he'd got distracted.

He'd gone through the meeting wishing for time to speed up so he could go home and wait for Effie. The situation was ridiculous, or worse, worrying.

She intruded into his thoughts with an ease that surprised him, almost as if she belonged with him.

The only saving grace of the day was that George hadn't joined him at the factory. He didn't have the patience to endure a new sermon from him or questions about his relationship with Effie. Besides, he wasn't sure what the relationship entailed, aside from pulse racing and sudden bouts of good mood that shocked him.

So here he was, sitting at his desk, unable to focus yet again as he waited for Effie. He'd sent her a message hours ago. No, actually, the clock on the mantelpiece informed him that only half an hour had passed.

He looked out of the window at the carriages driving by, and the people hurrying along the pavement. The smell of burnt coal sneaked inside the room.

He glanced at the mantelpiece again. Only five minutes had passed since the last time he'd checked the bloody clock. Ridiculous.

He'd burnt the midnight oil with his father for many hours in those earlier years, doing accounting or replying to urgent letters, and he hadn't had trouble staying concentrated. Nor had he cared about time slowing to a crawl.

He tried to start reading again, a document from his solicitor. Intruding thoughts were a challenge he was quickly losing. Then Harris opened the door.

"My lord, Lady Effie," Harris said. "And Lady Vaughan."

Effie entered, carrying her leather bag. Lady Vaughan wore a polite smile, holding a chestnut Pomeranian dog in her arms.

"Hello again, Lord Montcrest." Effie put her bag down.

"Lady Effie, Lady Vaughan."

"Montcrest, I hope you don't mind that I came." Lady Vaughan kissed the dog. "Effie was kind enough to take a look at my sweet Turi. He got something stuck in his teeth, and I couldn't get it out." She laughed.

"I don't mind at all. Shall I lie down?" he asked.

"Lie down?" Lady Vaughan stopped stroking Turi. "Is your dog going to jump on you, Montcrest, while Effie visits him?"

"Nothing of the sort." He wasn't amused.

"I'm not here to visit Lord Montcrest's dog." Effie opened her bag. "I need to check his stitches."

"Stitches?" Lady Vaughan paled, holding Turi more tightly.

"A nasty cut. Here." She ran a finger over her abdomen to mimic the wound. "It wasn't clean either."

"Isn't that a job for a physician?" Lady Vaughan raked a hard gaze over him.

"I trust Lady Effie to perform a good job." He returned the

hard glare. He was a champion in returning hard glares, and it worked because Lady Vaughan averted her gaze.

"It shouldn't take us long." Effie rummaged through the bag, muttering under her breath.

Lady Vaughan half-turned towards the door. "But Effie dear, you know how I feel about blood, sharp scalpels, and stitches. Montcrest should be attended by a physician. I thought you were here to see an animal."

She glanced at him then at Lady Vaughan. "Perhaps Jane you should wait for me somewhere?"

He didn't care one way or another. But spending some time alone with Effie wasn't a bad prospect. "I'm sure my butler will be happy to serve you tea."

"But—" Lady Vaughan fell silent when he lifted his waistcoat and shirt enough to uncover a couple of stitches. She swallowed hard. "Very well." She spun on her heels and left quickly.

"Lady Vaughan is a little sensitive," Effie said. "Even the smell of carbolic acid causes her to faint."

He waited a moment before reclining on the sofa, his skin tingling and pulling at the stitches as he moved. He undid the buttons of his waistcoat and shirt, careful not to reveal too much, just as he'd done the night of the ball. Bruises at various degrees of discolouring marred the rest of his skin, and how he'd got them was a conversation he didn't want to have with her.

As a veterinarian, she probably had no idea what sort of maladies a human mind could be afflicted with. He wouldn't be the one who shocked her into the world of pain and darkness that lived in his head.

"You didn't give me time to bandage the wound properly." She wiped her hands with a clear liquid, and a pungent smell reached his senses. But the disinfectant didn't cover her sweet scent of cinnamon.

A little line appeared between her delicate eyebrows, and he was, once again, charmed by her beauty and light. She didn't need to say anything to enthral him.

"I apologise again for having offended you the other day." She touched the wound lightly.

"Offended me?"

"You left in a hurry. I must have said something that upset you."

Yes, something had upset him, but she hadn't offended him. Her kindness had reminded him how unkind he was, and it hadn't been a pretty reminder.

"You didn't offend me. I was caught off guard by your compassion." The words tumbled out of his mouth without his explicit permission.

He blamed the power of her intense eyes. They made him tell the truth.

She dabbed the cut with a cloth. "You must have met some not-so-nice people."

He smiled ruefully. "Your heart is so good. It's unsurprising that you assume I met unkind people. I might be the unkind one, who was repaid in kind, if you allow me the play on words."

"If you admit you were unkind, then you can't be completely unkind, can you? An unkind person wouldn't confess to being one."

He gritted his teeth when she pressed her fingers to the sides of a particularly sensitive stitch. "One ought to show accountability."

"True." She wiped her hands. "The stitches are clean, and I don't see signs of infection. But I'll apply some more iodine anyway."

He watched her work with great attention, which was ironic. Until a moment ago, he'd had trouble focusing on reading a simple document, but now he could easily dedicate his full mind to her.

Her long eyelashes were chestnut at the base and golden at the tips. Her pert nose twitched when she focused on her work. And her skin had a warm hue as if she spent a lot of time outdoors without a parasol.

She was the first earl's daughter he'd ever met who knew both about farming and being a lady. The combination was extremely alluring and felt intimately close to who he was. Like her, he'd worked hard with his hands before being able to settle into the life of a lord.

"Done." She tilted her head to the side, studying her handiwork. "But this time I need to bandage the cut, or the fabric of your shirt might get tangled with the stitches and rip them."

"My valet wasn't thrilled when he saw my shirt stained with blood and iodine."

She signalled for him to sit up. "May I ask you something?"

"Yes, of course."

"Why is it so important to buy that land from Father?" She selected a wide roll of bandage from her bag.

Curious. She hadn't asked her father about the deal. Or more likely she'd asked, and Winchester had refused to answer.

"And please, don't say you don't want me to get involved. I really want to know," she added.

"I'm expanding my London and West Marches Railway towards the southwest. I want the railway to reach a small town, Fletton. It's in the middle of nowhere, but there's an old glass factory that will die unless the town gets modernised."

"With the railway," she said.

"Yes. The factory is losing relevance due to its isolation. A few hundred people live in Fletton, and almost half of them work at the factory. In order for them to have a hospital and a school, they need a train station. The railway will connect Fletton to Bristol and London, increasing job opportunities for everyone and making the transport of glass more efficient."

"It sounds like an important project."

He touched the stitches and groaned inwardly when his fingertips got stained with iodine.

"Why doesn't Papa want to sell? I don't believe he has any plans for Easthollow."

As much as he didn't like Winchester, he wouldn't speak ill of him in front of his daughter. "I think he should clarify that."

"Oh, I see." She stretched the bandage, becoming serious. "He doesn't approve of you."

He didn't deny or confirm, but his silence was likely more eloquent than his words.

She frowned. "I don't understand Papa's prejudice. I'm sure he would change his mind if he took the time to get to know you."

He heaved a breath as he felt strangely defenceless in front of her, fragile but not in a shameful way. She hadn't said anything too deep, but her trust filled him with warmth and confidence, like the hug of a loved one. It was the best feeling in the world.

"You don't know me," he whispered. "I might deserve the scorn."

"No, I don't believe that." Her eyes held too much honesty. "No one who loves animals as you do can be so terrible."

"You give me too much credit."

"You give yourself too little." She unravelled a large portion of the roll. "Stay still, please. You probably should remove your shirt."

Tension returned to his body.

"No. I'll help you wrap the bandage, but the shirt stays on."

Or she would see the devastation on his skin. His back was covered in bruises and shallow cuts. In fact, it was a matter of chance that his abdomen didn't have bruises. Usually, all his body, except his face, showed many contusions at different stages of healing.

"I understand. I didn't mean to make you uncomfortable." She practically hugged him while wrapping the bandage around him. "What did Papa tell you when he refused your offer?"

He swallowed hard, helping her to shift the roll. "First, he refused to give us a simple concession to let the railway go through his land. I offered to buy it. He refused. I tripled the price. He again refused."

She gazed up at him, and he forgot why he was angry. "That sounds unreasonable of him. Maybe he has some valid reason not to sell it, well aside from his personal dislike of you. I'll ask him if you want. I don't want to interfere in your business because, quite frankly, I don't know much about business deals, but I can talk to him."

"Do you really want to help me?"

She lifted a shoulder. "If I can, why not?" Her candour was out of a fairy tale, but he wasn't Prince Charming.

"You're too kind to me."

"You've met too many unkind people."

She brushed his skin and his hands as they both worked to wrap his abdomen. Shivers slithered down his back. For the first time, the twitch was completely silenced, stunned by her brightness. A sense of peace washed over him, leaving a trail of tenderness behind. Why was he so vulnerable with her? Sensations overwhelmed him, and he couldn't control himself.

He took her chin and stared at her mesmerising eyes. "What is it about you?"

She blinked. "I don't understand the question."

Neither did he. He stroked her chin with his thumb, wondering if he really wanted to find out why she caused so much turmoil inside him, or if he should simply accept it and succumb to it.

He brushed her plush lower lip with the pad of his thumb. How would it feel to suck it into his mouth until she moaned? Her scent was intoxicating. His pulse raced, for once not because he needed the relief that only pain could give him.

He released her chin and angled his head, giving her the opportunity to say no. When she inched closer, he brushed his lips against hers as lightly as he could, and a shot of pure, undiluted pleasure coursed through him. The lightness of the touch was inversely proportional to the emotion it triggered.

She drew in a breath and parted her lips, but when he edged closer to kiss her deeper, she moved back from him.

"Tristan." She stared at him as if begging him not to hurt her.

Hell. His name told in her sweet voice slapped him back to the present. The sense of peace was replaced by shame.

He buttoned his shirt quickly. He ought to apologise, but at that moment, controlling his voice was a chore; it would sound husky and heavy with desire, and he'd already made a fool out of himself.

She silently put the bottles and gauze back in the bag, her cheeks red.

He swallowed again, standing up. He was an idiot. "I didn't mean to make you uncomfortable."

She didn't look at him.

He was about to ask her to say something when a knock came.

"Effie?" Lady Vaughan asked from the corridor.

Turi barked.

He opened the door just to put some distance between him and her, and Lady Vaughan entered.

"Is it done?" she asked.

"Yes." Effie's voice sounded high-pitched.

Lady Vaughan frowned at Effie's flushed face. She turned towards him then to Effie again. "Is something the matter? Was there a lot of blood?"

Turi sniffled the air.

"No. All is good." Effie held the bag against her chest. "Lord Montcrest, have a pleasant afternoon."

He seriously doubted his afternoon would be pleasant.

thirteen

Effie ran the tip of her tongue over her bottom lip that kept tingling after Tristan had touched and kissed it. She didn't know what to think of his behaviour, her behaviour, and the whole world. But whatever had happened between them had been intense and shocking.

In the carriage with her friend, she was still shivering from the kiss. He'd stared at her with passion and hunger, as no man had ever done before. She hadn't had any choice but to stop him before the kiss went too far.

Actually, she didn't have a proper reason for having stopped him aside from the moment of panic that had caught her. If he'd kissed her properly, he would have found her lacking in technique. She'd kissed a few boys when she'd lived in the country, but the Marquess of Montcrest didn't seem like a man who would be satisfied by a simple country-style kiss. And kissing him would have been inappropriate.

She was a coward. She was a liar as well, because she had no idea why she hadn't kissed him back.

The rocking of the carriage caused the bag to slip from the seat, and she was so focused on thinking of Tristan's eyes she let it drop.

"Did something untoward happen with Montcrest?" Jane asked, picking the bag up while Turi stuck his head out of the window and enjoyed the breeze.

"No."

"I beg your pardon, but you were and still are flushed, and there was an awkward silence in the room. I shouldn't have left you alone with him. There are rumours about him being a rake, and rumours are usually true."

She tried again. "Nothing happened." And she was debating if she was disappointed or not. "You listen to rumours too often, and they're usually wrong."

"They can make or destroy your reputation. What's more important?"

"Honesty. Lord Montcrest is very honest in my opinion."

Jane looked taken aback. "Heaven, do you fancy him?"

Good question.

"I'm not sure." She rubbed the spot between her eyebrows. "He confuses me."

"You shouldn't have danced with him, especially in that scandalous fashion." Jane held Turi in place as he tried to lean over the window. "You two were practically hugging and became the talk of the evening."

"He isn't as terrible as everyone thinks. Sometimes he's serious and cranky, but other times, he looks fragile and vulnerable." And his lips were surprisingly soft, gentle, and deliciously wicked.

"The marquess? Fragile and vulnerable? He's a grinder."

"That's what I thought until I saw another side of him."

Jane put Turi on the seat next to her. "Well, I hope you don't see any other side of him."

~

EFFIE COULDN'T STOP THINKING about Tristan as she lay on the sofa with Pepper and Kettle.

Pepper had his head on her lap while Kettle was busy with a thorough cleaning of his glossy black coat and sharp nails while showing off his sense of balance and flexibility.

Tristan had stared at her as if she'd been the most attractive woman in the kingdom and he couldn't resist her, and she would be lying if she said she didn't find his look fascinating. That look alone had made her feel desirable and… powerful?

He was such a commanding man that having the power to make him ache for her was ridiculously heady. How vain of her. But admittedly, he was attractive, scary at times, but definitely attractive. He could also be cold, and she didn't understand his relationship with Rowan. He was a lovely boy but seemed terrified of his brother.

Did Tristan mean to become her suitor? She had no idea what she was supposed to do with that possibility.

"Darling?" Papa entered the library.

"Papa." She closed the book she'd been pretending to read and stroked Pepper's head. "You're early."

"I gather you visited Montcrest today." He had the same tone as that morning, and she didn't like it.

"Yes, well, not exactly. As I told you, I met with his young brother, Lord Rowan. He wants to learn everything about horses and animals."

There was no need to mention her second visit.

He sat in front of her. "And you didn't see Montcrest?"

"Briefly." She had no intention of receiving another lecture on how terrible Tristan was. She could draw her own conclusions. But while she was there. "Did you see Colin the other day? Did you go to Greenford?"

A corner of his eye twitched. "Of course I did. Why?"

Kettle stopped licking himself and stared at Father with his large eyes; one of his paws remained stretched out over his head.

"I heard you were in London."

"I visited Colin." He didn't sound confident, and she didn't believe him.

"Why don't you want to sell to Lord Montcrest?" she asked before he could press her on. "The land in Easthollow doesn't have any value, and the railway will help the people in a small town."

Papa stood up, hands clasped behind his back. "I don't want to help Montcrest get richer. His father was a ruthless man who didn't deserve his good luck, and I don't see why I should help his son. I helped them in a moment of need, and when it came to return the favour, the late Montcrest didn't show any mercy. He robbed me of the deal that would have let *me* expand my railway company. But no, he was too selfish to remember I'd fed him in a time of need."

She looked at him. "I can't believe it. You refuse to sell the land to Montcrest out of spite." A bitter taste filled her mouth. "Remember the truth is you didn't want to help them. I insisted. And you don't help someone in the hope they'll return the favour."

Sensing her distress, Kettle quietly left the armrest to jump on the top shelf from which he could keep an eye on the world and stay out of trouble.

"That's quite enough!" He paused, then exhaled. "I'm sorry, I didn't mean to be so harsh."

She straightened. "I don't want to meddle with your affairs. I'm trying to understand why you want to punish Montcrest for something he didn't do."

"Darling." Her father took her hand. The change from outraged to sweet was so fast her head reeled. "Trust me. Montcrest is the same as his late father. Ruthless, greedy, and conniving. His father used every dirty financial trick he knew to make money without caring about whom he was hurting."

"Again, what does Montcrest's father have to do with anything?" She slid her hand out of his. "He and his father aren't the same person."

"Montcrest learnt from his father. He'll stop in front of nothing. He regained his fortune and more, but it's not enough. He wants more. He'll never be satiated. And his grandfather plotted against the monarch!" The outraged tone was back. "Don't listen to anything he says and please don't visit him anymore."

Nothing Papa told her made her want to stay away from Tristan. "His grandfather was never charged with treason."

"Because he was a cheater."

She threw a hand up. "You have all the answers. But Rowan is a fine boy and a friend of mine."

"Who will become a remorseless man like his brother."

She gathered her patience. "Nothing you've told me so far has convinced me of Lord Montcrest's bad character. Quite the opposite, I must say."

"If Montcrest and his father had been gentlemen and played by the rules, the London and West Marches Railway would be mine! But no, the late marquess found some tricky way to secure the licence to build the railway." He put a fist on his chest. "That licence was mine. He stole it out from under me and his son was his accomplice. That's the kind of man Montcrest is."

She was still sceptical. From what she'd seen, every business deal involved one trick or another. Those gentlemen kept stabbing each other in the back. Papa was being resentful and unreasonable, only because he'd lost a deal.

"Surely, it wasn't the first business deal you have ever lost," she said, trying to make him see reason.

"No, it wasn't, but the Montcrests are traitors to the crown, and I don't deal with criminals." He fixed the knot of his cravat.

The situation was clear now. She folded her arms over her chest. "You're angry because a ruined, disgraced, and penniless man beat you at a business game. Had it been any other lord, you wouldn't have minded that much."

He worked his jaw. "Think about what I told you next time

you want to see him." He left the room and closed the door with a thud.

She must have struck a nerve.

Pepper raised his ears. Kettle jumped on the sofa again and put his soft paw on her arm.

"What would you do, Kettle?" She stroked his velvety head.

Kettle would do whatever he wanted, as he usually did.

fourteen

Tristan lay on the dirty floor of The Octagon after his opponent had punched his stomach hard enough to make him nauseous.

Pain throbbed through his body—a war drum symphony that meant peace to him. Around him, a dozen dirty fights were ongoing. Heavy feet stomped dangerously close to his head, but he didn't care.

When he reached that ecstatic state of calm, he didn't care about anything. He didn't care about George warning him to stop fighting, Winchester shunning him, Harris's hurt looks, or the avalanche of emotions Effie woke up within him, including shame.

He blinked, and the lights came in and out of focus. Shadows ran over him, and he wished to be one of them. He wished to join the darkness and be done with.

He'd tried to kiss Effie, and she'd put him in his place with a few words. One word, actually.

He deserved her rejection because, even though he wasn't as refined and sophisticated as his late mother would have liked him to be, he was aware a gentleman shouldn't put a lady in a compromising situation, and he'd done that more than once.

Especially if the said gentleman hadn't acted on attraction only.

Effie was beautiful, but he'd met plenty of beautiful women, and not one of them had made him lose his mind and control as she had. She was special but not because of her hazel eyes changing colour, her bright smile, or her glorious chestnut hair. Her kindness made her special. Her kindness towards him in particular.

She had no reason to be kind to him. Hell, he wasn't kind to himself. But she was kind to him, and he didn't understand why.

He shut his eyes as a man dropped next to him, brushing his shoulder. Shouts and thuds filled the stuffy air of the ring, but he was at peace.

He made a decision. Then and there, on the bloody floor of The Octagon, with his muscles screaming in agony, and his mind clear and free.

He'd decided to marry Lady Effie.

EFFIE GENTLY HELD the tiny paw of Turi, Jane's Pomeranian, as she bandaged it. The small dog was a perfect patient. He remained still, didn't try to bite her, and let her apply creams and bandages to his paw without crying blue murder. His mistress, on the other hand, had a flair for the dramatics.

"Is it serious?" Jane paced on the carpet in her sitting room, only to stop to caress Turi's head and start pacing again.

Her silk skirt flapped around her legs, distracting the dog.

Effie suppressed a laugh. She understood the deep bond between a human and an animal, and she wouldn't make fun of that. But Turi only had a scratch on his metacarpal pad. Hardly deadly.

Everything that happened to the Pomeranian was a cause of worry. Turi was one of her regular patients.

"The cut isn't deep, and while infections are a problem, I think

Turi's paw will recover soon. As long as he doesn't lick it too much and keeps the bandage on."

"Thank goodness." Jane sat on the sofa, the back of her hand on her forehead. "When he started limping during his morning walk, I thought the worst."

"Just make sure he doesn't lick the wound. I could wrap a towel around his head to prevent him from reaching his paw, but if he doesn't bother the paw, I would prefer leaving him free."

"Thank you so much, Effie. You're a godsend. My physician would never take a look at my Turi. He said something about a superior calling. And it seems veterinary doctors all live in the country, dealing with cows and pigs."

"I know. I started practising on farm animals, too." She packed her bag with gauze and disinfectants.

Jane hugged her. "I'll always be in your debt. How can I repay your kindness?"

"Do not worry. Besides, I don't have any official qualifications."

Jane waved an elegant hand. "Tosh. I don't care about that. You saved Turi's life."

That was an exaggeration that Jane repeated every time Turi had a minor illness.

"I'll check on him tomorrow." She closed her bag.

Making an animal and a person happy was her favourite thing in the world.

Turi licked her hand and wiggled his tail weakly. Likely, he wasn't sure if she'd done him a good turn or not.

"I feel terrible for not giving you anything," Jane said.

"Don't, please."

"But I want to return the favour." Jane winked. "I'm sure you'll be interested in a juicy piece of gossip."

"I don't follow gossip."

Jane gave her a conspiratorial look. "I happen to know something about your Lord Montcrest."

She moved the bag from one hand to another. "He isn't my anything."

Jane lowered her voice. "I saw how you looked at each other as you danced together. Be warned. Everyone did."

Effie's cheeks warmed. That wasn't completely untrue. "I haven't made up my mind about him."

Jane sat on an armchair and placed Turi on her lap.

Effie sat down as well and dropped her bag.

"My husband isn't fond of Montcrest. The late marquess was a harsh businessman."

"I keep hearing that, but what did he do?"

"I'm no expert in economics, but the late marquess was uncompromising for starters. When he wanted something, he never negotiated with anyone, but went after it with a vengeance, ruining many friendships. He pushed his workers to the limit, not caring about the consequences. He reduced the quality of his steel to sell more, and if he could find a legal loophole, he would exploit it aggressively. He was an expert in price wars. He would decrease the price of his product when everyone was increasing it, going against the market, and he wasn't above using trade secret thievery to get what he wanted. During the years he worked hard to rebuild his family, he made a lot of enemies."

"But is Lord Montcrest the same?"

Jane caressed Turi who fell asleep with his muzzle between his paws. "Everyone assumes he is. They worked together since Lord Montcrest was able to walk, so he must have learnt from his father."

"He is certainly a determined man." Menacing as well.

"People either envy him or are sour because Montcrest is doubling his fortune by the minute. His railway company is the most successful in the kingdom. The queen praised him. But people say Montcrest exploits his workers, as his father did."

She mulled the information over. Perhaps she was too gullible. The fact Tristan loved horses didn't mean he was a good person, and if he exploited his workers only for greed, then Papa might be right about him. Although she hadn't imagined his sweet, vulnerable side. He wasn't as harsh as people thought. He was trying to build a better future for the people living in that small town. A ruthless businessman wouldn't care.

"But that's not what I wanted to tell you." Jane leant closer. "Rumour has it he has a mistress, a powerful, famous lady, likely married, who helps him get what he wants."

Why was she surprised? He was titled, rich, and handsome and unmarried. A pang of disappointment stung her chest. Did he stare at every woman as he'd stared at her? How many women felt as special as she felt only because he seemed to adore her?

"A married lady?" she asked.

"She probably is." Jane nodded. "Apparently, Montcrest leaves his house at night often and heads towards Chelsea alone, on foot."

"Chelsea? What does he do there?"

"At its edge, the Duchess of Norfolk has a flat she also visits often. Maybe it's a coincidence. Maybe it isn't."

The Duchess of Norfolk was practically royalty. If there was one powerful lady in the kingdom after the queen, it was her.

"That would explain his success in his business as well." Jane kept stroking Turi. "The duchess is likely pulling strings for him."

"If that's true, then Lord Montcrest isn't different from his father."

Jane exhaled as Turi snored softly. "Alas, the more good-looking they are, the more deceitful. Except dogs, of course."

Except dogs.

fifteen

Maybe proposing to a lady shouldn't be treated as a regular business deal, but Tristan didn't know how to handle it differently. He had only one strategy he used for everything from business deals to personal relationships, and it consisted of a direct approach and clear conditions.

Admittedly, the strategy worked well for one, but not so well for the other, judging by his astonishing lack of friends. But he couldn't change overnight, and once he made a decision, he wanted to go on with it.

That was why he'd driven to Archer Hall to see Effie.

From his carriage, he stared at her house. How different it looked from his own now that he paid attention to it. It was all bright and cheerful with colourful bushes of peonies, pretty light green curtains, and outdoor vases of red geraniums. He found the house more intimidating than his own; it elicited too many emotions.

He exited his carriage right when she walked along the pavement towards him. He took that as a good omen.

He waited for her, ignoring the hint of worry rising in his chest and the visions of their kiss flashing across his mind. He was a marquess and a successful businessman. She was probably looking for a suitor. Her father would oppose, but if she agreed to marry him, he could push Winchester. It was logical for her to agree to become his wife. He was a good match.

Her smile was a little shy when she stopped in front of him, carrying her veterinary bag. "Lord Montcrest, are you here to see my father or me?"

"You."

"Is Zeus all right?"

"Yes."

"Good. Would you like a cup of tea?"

"No. I would prefer a walk." He offered her his arm.

She hesitated before taking it.

"May I carry your bag?" He stretched out his free arm.

"Thank you." She handed it to him.

They walked along the pavement towards a small park where lush trees swayed their green canopies in the breeze. Another good omen.

"What did you want to tell me?" she asked.

He should start with an apology for having touched her the other day, but he decided against it. Apologising before a proposal seemed the wrong way to begin a solid relationship. But on the other hand, she would appreciate an apology, and what she wanted was his priority.

"I thought about what had happened the other day."

She stiffened, gripping his arm more tightly.

"I'm aware I didn't behave like a gentleman. A gentleman would propose before taking liberties with a lady, and that's what I mean to do."

She gazed up at him. "Excuse me? You want to propose so you can take liberties with me?"

Damn. That had come out wrong. He should have prepared a speech. "Yes. No." He paused in the awkward moment. "I'm saying I want to ask you to marry me."

She stopped walking, her lips parting. "Why?"

"Because I want to." He understood too late he'd said the wrong thing with the wrong tone.

What he'd meant to say was that his biggest wish was to have the honour of marrying her because being close to her filled him with peace and hope.

His habit of economising on the words had prevailed over his good sense, which admittedly wasn't strong to start with.

The shock disappeared from her face, replaced by annoyance. "Just like you *wanted* to dance with me. But marriage isn't a polka. Things don't happen just because you want them to."

He bowed his head. "It came out wrong."

"No, it came out perfectly well."

"Effie." He straightened. "I need a wife, and you need a husband. The logical thing to do is to get married."

He should shut up. While what he'd said was true, it wouldn't appeal to her, especially told in that fashion.

"You're worsening the situation." She slid her arm out of his.

She was right, and he didn't know how to repair the damage. He was too used to speaking as a businessman.

"You should appreciate the fact I asked you first instead of going to your father."

She folded her arms over her chest. "For that *kindness* alone, I should marry you, which for you is only a business transaction."

"No." He exhaled, pinching the bridge of his nose. "I'm not making much sense, but I find you very attractive. More than should be reasonable."

He probably shouldn't have said that, either. Not in that dry way. He'd never felt what he felt for her ever before. The onslaught of emotions within him caused by her mere smile didn't make sense. That was why his attraction was unreasonable, but it sounded as if he didn't think she was beautiful, thus the attraction didn't make sense. His thoughts were all over the place.

He held up a hand. "I didn't mean that. You're incredibly beautiful."

Her eyebrows lowered over her blazing eyes. "Lord Montcrest, the conversation ends here. Thank you, but no, thank you." She snatched her bag. "As I said, marriage isn't a business transaction."

She turned around and walked away, but he wouldn't renounce her without a fight.

He followed her. "I didn't mean to offend you."

"But you did."

The words he wanted to say—that he loved her kindness and compassion; that, yes, he found her beautiful, but her beauty wasn't the only thing he liked about her; that she meant peace for him; that his troubled soul was quiet only when she was with him —remained trapped in a knot of emotions in his throat.

As angry as she was, she would reject him even after he said those words, and her rejection would hurt too much because it would come after he'd opened himself to her, after he'd made himself vulnerable to her. That wasn't the type of pain he was interested in.

He watched her leave him, aware he deserved her anger and the pain.

sixteen

The next day, as she was having breakfast, Effie was still seething after the absurd, confusing proposal of marriage by Tristan.

Seething was maybe a strong word, since she'd gone through a wide range of emotions in the past hours.

She'd been annoyed, offended, and incredulous. But then, worry for Tristan had crept through her thoughts, and finally compassion as well. She hadn't let him explain himself properly although his proposal had been one disaster after the other.

But maybe he'd wanted to say something else. Or maybe she should stop defending him. She had to judge his words and actions, and they hadn't impressed her.

Besides, after what Jane had told her, doubts bothered her. Did Tristan have a rich, noble mistress? Was he as brutal with his employees as his father had been?

Rumours were only rumours, and he might not be as terrible as they pictured him. Still, his words, said in the wrong moment and with the wrong tone, had irked her, which was hypocritical of her, considering she'd accused him of having a short temper. As a result, she'd slept poorly, and her mood was foul.

"What is it with you?" Papa asked, sipping his morning tea in the sunroom.

"Is it so evident?"

He gave her an affectionate smile. "You're easy to understand for me. Just like your mother, you wear your heart on your sleeve. What is it?"

No, she didn't want to discuss Tristan's proposal. Papa was already prejudiced against him; he would challenge Tristan to a duel, or something similar.

"Just annoyance that will go away as soon as I take a walk."

He tensed a little. "Where are you planning to go?"

"I don't know. Maybe I'll go to Farringdon. There's a new park I would like to visit."

He put down his cup of tea, and maybe she was too sensitive that morning, but she could swear he shivered.

"Why don't you go to see Colin? There's a train leaving in a couple of hours from Victoria Station. The girls will be delighted to play with their favourite aunt, and the day is beautiful."

She chuckled. "I'm not their favourite aunt."

"You will be if you bring them the almond cake Cook baked yesterday." He squeezed her hand. "Take a day for yourself. See your brother and nieces. Leave London. It'll do you good."

A day immersed in Nature with her brother and nieces was a strong temptation compared to busy London.

"Maybe you're right."

"I usually am."

"I'll go to Greenford then. The country will be a welcome change from the city. I'll take a walk in the forest with Colin if he's free. It's been a while."

He nodded, tension leaving his shoulders. "Excellent." He rose and kissed her cheek. "I'll see you at dinner, or tomorrow if you decide to stay with Colin and come back in a day or two." He stared at her with hope.

"Honestly, are you trying to get rid of me?"

"Of course not, darling. But if you need to spend the night in Greenford, I can only be happy for you."

"I'll think about it."

He kissed her cheek again and left, humming a tune.

An hour later, Effie was in the hallway, ready to go in her travelling cloak and leather boots. The footman opened the door for her when the butler arrived.

"My lady, this has just arrived." Doyle handed her a message.

She didn't pick it up immediately, fearing it was Tristan, but she exhaled when she realised it was Rowan, politely inviting her to the inauguration of Tristan's latest locomotive at Aldersgate Station, which ironically was close to Farringdon, her original destination. Her sour mood melted like sorbet in the sun.

The boy didn't deserve her bad temper, and she wanted to make him happy. Although she wasn't ready to see Tristan again. The thought sent a fresh wave of doubts through her.

"Change of plan, Doyle," she said. "Instead of Victoria Station, I'll go to Aldersgate Station, and I would like to send a message to Lady Vaughan."

~

"You look awfully tense, if you don't mind my saying," Jane said as she and Effie walked towards Aldersgate Station.

"I'm just tired. I didn't sleep well."

"Because of what I told you?" Jane asked. "You're disappointed by Montcrest, aren't you?"

"He proposed," Effie blurted out before she could stop herself. Perhaps she needed to tell someone.

A gasp came from Jane. "He did not! What did you say?"

"I refused. Between what you told me and his proposal, which was too close to a business deal, I wasn't convinced." But she wasn't convinced now about her reasons for rejecting him.

They stopped in front of the station under the dark shadow of the building.

Train stations were growing all around London at an alarming speed, and maybe that was the reason for the barren, uninspiring façade. No ornaments or clever design, but instead it was designed as if the architect didn't care about beauty and elegance. It was only a square, boring pile of bricks that made her sad for some reason.

Things happened too fast in London, and beauty was sacrificed for speed. Like a hasty, practical marriage proposal.

"I didn't want to be the cause of your refusal," Jane said. "After all, he's a marquess with a solid financial situation. A good match. Rumours would follow you everywhere if you married him, though."

"That doesn't worry me. I just want to find a gentleman who understands how important practising veterinary medicine is for me, respects my choices, and doesn't treat me like a broodmare."

"My, my. You've been reading those suffragettes' pamphlets again."

"No, I just want a proper gentleman."

Jane touched Effie's shoulder briefly. "I think you'll have more luck finding a dog with those qualities."

"So, you think I should have accepted his proposal? I thought you disapproved of him."

Jane hooked her arm through Effie's and resumed walking. "I would have left him to wonder about my answer for a while, instead of giving him a quick, flat rejection."

"What's the difference?"

"That you would have kept him on pins and needles. Something a man like him hates."

"I don't want to be cruel."

Jane sighed. "You'll never understand how things between a man and woman work."

They walked up the short flight of stairs to the main hall of the station. The inside was less disappointing with its soaring ceiling and Grecian columns, but it was so crammed with people she could barely see anything else.

They made their way through the excited groups of well-dressed ladies and gentlemen, a band of musicians, food vendors, and journalists. The thick smell of a coal and oil engine was the same as in any other train station.

"So many people." Jane craned her neck. "Where's your friend?"

"Over there." She led Jane towards platform number one where Rowan was standing next to a shiny locomotive blowing steam.

She smiled when Rowan spotted her and ran towards her.

"Lady Effie." He removed his flat hat and bowed. "Lady Vaughan. Thank you for coming."

Jane shielded her eyes with a gloved hand from the light coming through the glass ceiling. "We wouldn't have missed it for anything in the world. Is that the new locomotive your family is inaugurating?"

"That's her." Rowan stretched out an arm towards the shiny black machine. "Tristan said I could ride with the machinist for the first stretch if I wanted to."

"Wonderful." She rose on her tiptoes to see past the crowd of passengers, onlookers, and dignitaries.

Tristan should be close.

A part of her wanted to see him soon; another part wasn't so sure. Only Tristan could make her so confused. Her pulse gave a kick when a group of men parted, revealing him. As if summoned by her stare, he turned towards her, and their gazes locked.

She didn't mean to stare at him, but his eyes had a magnetic quality she couldn't dismiss. The glint in them wasn't hard to interpret; it was sheer, pure longing, and her pulse spiked in reply.

He weaved through the crowd towards her, moving with

predatory menace. A little shiver went down her neck the closer he walked.

Rowan stopped smiling when Tristan stood next to him.

"Lady Effie. Lady Vaughan." Tristan gave her another intense stare she found difficult to hold.

"What a beauty you have there, Montcrest." Jane pointed at the locomotive.

Tristan took a moment before angling towards her. "She isn't just beautiful but also strong and determined. She's special."

Jane looked puzzled. "You'll get great satisfaction from her."

His harsh mask slipped for a moment, and he showed the same fragility as he'd revealed the night of the ball.

His long eyelashes fluttered down. "One can only hope."

Effie's face warmed, but this time it wasn't anger.

Rowan broke the spell. "May I go on board?"

"The train should leave in twenty minutes," Tristan said, returning to be his usual controlled self. "But if you want to go now and take a tour, the machinist will let you in."

Rowan let out a whoop. "Thank you." He went to hug Tristan but stopped awkwardly midway before stepping back from him.

Tristan moved as well as if to hug him back, but between Rowan's indecision and Tristan's stiff moves, nothing happened.

"Ladies, I'll see you later." Rowan bowed quickly before rushing towards the locomotive.

Steam crept out from underneath the machine and wrapped around Tristan's legs, giving him the air of a supernatural being emerging from the shadows.

"Lady Effie, I need a word in private if you have time," he said, bringing her back to the less ominous present.

Jane gave her a shocked, wide-eyed stare. "Do you want to go?"

The sooner she dealt with Tristan, the better. Also, she might clarify some of her doubts. "I do. Will you be all right here?"

"Do not worry about me. I'll stay here and wait for the machine to..." Jane waved. "To start."

Effie followed Tristan to a quiet corner at the end of the platform. The station was crowded, but his presence never failed to be imposing as if he used more space than he needed.

He clasped his hands behind his back. His dark coat enhanced his broad shoulders and the golden hues in his hair. "I understand I didn't express myself properly the last time we met."

She fought the urge to avert her gaze, but she didn't want to appear more intimidated than she was. "I won't lie. Your words confused me."

"That wasn't my intent." He swallowed a couple of times. "What I meant to say is that I find it difficult to focus on my work because I keep thinking about you. Something you said, something you did, or the way you smiled keeps intruding in my mind. My thoughts are stuck on you, and I'm not complaining. Quite the opposite."

She shifted her weight, unsure about what to say or think. He was the first man who had made plain his interest in her, and she would be lying if she said she didn't find that exciting.

"I like your happiness and your kindness. I like how expert you are in veterinary medicine. I like you when you talk about anything. I like *you*." He raised a hand slowly, his eyes widening and darkening with longing.

If she didn't want to be touched, he was giving her plenty of time to step back, but she didn't mind his touch after what he'd said.

Her chest rose and fell quickly as he trailed a finger along her jaw. If she was confused earlier before he touched her, she was now completely lost. He possessed an aggressive charm hard to ignore. His confidence and his looks attracted her attention. But a marriage required something more than a pretty pair of eyes and a strong charm. She wanted to know him better.

Still, a little shiver ran down her back and caused her toes to curl.

He sucked in a breath and stared at her with the same intensity as the other day. Whatever he did, he did it completely and without compromises. She was at the centre of his world for now, and it felt wonderful.

He traced the curve of her cheek and brushed it with his thumb. A little sigh left her. The touch was as light as that of a moth's wings, but she felt it through her body with a strength that shook her. Desire radiated from his touch, and she was tempted to see how deep his desire was.

"Effie," he whispered, his voice husky and low. "What I'm trying clumsily to say is that I—"

Whatever he meant to say was cut off by a thunderous blast. An orange flash flickered.

The ground quaked, causing her to totter. Smoke filled the air with its pungent smell, and a force shoved her back. He wrapped his arms around her and went down with her on the hard platform, taking the brunt of the impact.

She bumped her nape against his arm. He groaned in pain. Dust and pieces of metal rained around them. The air seemed to be scorching as if someone had opened the door of a blast furnace.

At first, a buzz was the only noise in her ears. She blinked, but smoke caused her eyes to water. Then screams and thudding footsteps overwhelmed her. Tristan's body weighed her down, and the fear he might be dead made her gasp.

"Tristan." She raised his heavy head, and his blond curls fell over her hands.

He blinked slowly. Dust rained from his hair, and a cut on his cheek bled. His top hat was nowhere to be seen.

"Tristan?" She patted his cheek.

He didn't seem to have heard her.

"Please say something." She cupped his face.

He gazed around and blinked again. "Are you hurt?"

"No. I don't know. What happened?"

"Rowan!" He shot up with impressive speed. He staggered on his feet and made a gagging sound.

"Tristan." Speaking scratched her throat.

He went to run in the middle of the chaos of smoke and dust but skidded to a halt and turned towards her. "I have to go. I must find him."

She propped herself up on her elbows. "Go. Don't worry about me. I'm fine."

"I must find him." He looked confused and hurt.

She waved him away. "Go."

He hesitated a moment before racing away into the smoke.

She lost sight of him a moment after and regretted having told him to go. She should have asked him to wait for the smoke to settle. Loud wails sounded all around her, but she couldn't guess from whom. The station was a hazy blur of smoke and orange flashes.

She staggered to her feet and waited for her head to stop spinning before walking towards the spot where Jane had been. Pieces of metal littered the ground, and the air was thick with the smell of burnt wood and coal.

An explosion. The locomotive's boiler must have exploded. Her brain was finally working again.

The moment the realisation dawned on her, so did fear.

Rowan. Jane. All those people.

She walked along the platform gingerly. "Jane? Rowan?" A coughing fit caused her to shake.

Her voice got lost in the midst of dozens of other yells and voices. She stopped moving, not knowing where to go. Her eyes watered as the smoke stung them, and a bitter taste filled her mouth. Between the dust and smoke, it was impossible to see anything.

She wasn't sure for how long she wandered aimlessly through the devastated platform, but her legs grew tired.

"Effie!"

She sobbed when Jane came out of nowhere and hugged her.

"You're safe." Jane wrapped her arms around her shoulders,

shivering. She was covered in dust. Her gown was ripped in places, and her hair was thoroughly dishevelled. Aside from that, she seemed unhurt. "We need to leave." Her voice sounded incredibly low and shaky.

Effie shook her head, running her tongue over her parched lips. "Tristan and Rowan."

"Please."

Effie searched the devastated platform as the dust started to settle. People were lying on the ground in different positions, limbs at impossible angles or missing altogether. A wave of nausea caught her at the thought that one of those people could be Tristan or Rowan.

"I can't leave them here."

Jane closed her hand firmly around her arm. "We'll only be a hindrance, and Effie, I can't stay here a minute longer. Please."

Police officers and the fire brigade rushed to the platform. Those standing were shoved and jostled. A pair of firm hands grabbed her shoulders. She screamed.

"Madam," an officer shouted, "you must leave. Now!" He pushed her towards the exit none too gently.

Tears blurred her sight as she let Jane drag her onwards, but the smoke was not the cause of them.

seventeen

If Tristan stayed in the hospital without any news on Rowan for two more minutes, he would go mad. He sat, stood up, paced, and sat again in the bright white corridor of St. Bartholomew's Hospital.

Rowan had been in the operating theatre for over an hour, and no one had told Tristan anything. A nurse had attended to the bump on his head and bandaged it, but boxing routinely in The Octagon had strengthened his body. His head ached, but he would survive.

The coming and going of nurses and doctors into the theatre had stopped a while ago, and the part of the hospital where he stood was quiet.

He had no idea how many people had been injured in the blast. Hell, he hadn't seen Effie either after he'd found Rowan unconscious on the platform. He'd sent his footman to search for her, but even that front hadn't brought any news so far.

Debris covered his clothes and filled his nostrils with the smell of smoke and fear. They would stay with him forever. He leant against the wall and sucked in a deep breath, cursing himself for having agreed to take Rowan with him, only because he'd wanted to build a good relationship with his brother.

He'd done such a great job.

"Tristan."

His heart stopped as he heard Effie's voice. She was running towards him. Her cheeks were pale, and white dust covered her Prussian blue gown, making her look as if she were wrapped in a starry sky. No cuts or blood marred her.

Acting on pure instinct, he met her midway in the corridor and pulled her into his arms to make sure she was safe. Selfishly, he needed more than ever the sense of peace only she could give him. He released her immediately, lest she feel uncomfortable.

"How are you? I'm sorry I had to leave." He fought the impulse to touch her face. "After the doctors arrived to take Rowan, I couldn't find you. I was sick with worry."

"I'm fine. Don't worry about me. I went home briefly. Then your footman told me you were here, and I came immediately." She searched his face. "Your head."

"It's nothing."

"Rowan?"

He cleared his throat past the swell of emotions blocking it. "They're operating on him."

She clamped her hands over her mouth.

"He's mostly fine," he hurried to say. "Or so I thought. When I found him, his ankle was broken, but other than that, he didn't appear to have any major injuries. But he's been in the theatre for too long, and nobody tells me anything."

"The surgeons are overwhelmed. Injured people keep arriving. Maybe they're busy with other patients as well."

He glanced at the set of double doors opening to the theatre. "I can't lose him. I shouldn't have let him close to that damn machine."

"You didn't know what would happen." She brushed a curl of hair from her cheek. "I thought the boiler exploded, but while I searched for you on the pavement, people started to talk about a bomb."

"A bomb." He wasn't sure how that made him feel. Right now, only worry for Rowan dominated his emotions.

If it'd been a bomb, then either the Fenians or the Russians were responsible.

"It was a miracle that Rowan was far from the locomotive when it exploded," he said. "He'd been about to get onboard when he spotted a friend in the crowd and walked away from the engine."

Rage swelled. If he'd been at The Octagon, he would have boxed until he dropped on the floor.

"If it was a bomb, what a vile thing to do." Her shoulders shook. "And for what?"

Seeing her so distraught, he couldn't contain himself. "You're fine, aren't you?" He cupped her cheek and studied her lovely face.

A dark bruise offended her cheek, but the shadows in her eyes bothered him the most; they weren't as bright as usual.

"I'm fine. But I was scared..." Her bottom lip quivered, and he hated seeing her crying.

He held her, and she rested her head on his chest. "I was scared, too. Mostly for Rowan."

"When the explosion hit, I thought the worst. I thought I'd lost you."

In the middle of the storm of emotions troubling him, the fact she'd worried about him brought him a ridiculous amount of relief.

They held each other tightly until a new group of nurses hurried along the corridor, rolling down a stretcher. He let her go, missing her softness immediately.

He handed her his handkerchief.

"Thank you." She wiped her cheeks. "Rowan was so happy to get on the locomotive."

"I should have told him not to go. Our father died when

Rowan was still a child. But before that his mother had the brilliant idea of running off with her lover. I'm what is left of our family, which isn't much."

"Rowan's mother left him?"

He almost regretted having told her that. She had the uncanny ability to make him lower his guard by simply staring at him. "Father did everything in his power to contain the scandal. We haven't heard from her ever since. I did my best to find her, but with no results. And now he's injured."

She put her hand on his and squeezed it. "Don't blame yourself for the deeds of wicked people."

But he was one of those wicked people.

Controlling his voice was hard. Too many emotions to handle at once, and he was used only to pushing them down. "I've been too busy to spend time with him. And now this." He raked a hand through his hair.

"But you obviously love him. That's what matters."

"I beg to differ. What's the point of loving someone if I can't show it?" He wasn't thinking of just Rowan.

"You're showing it now."

"I'm not so sure. I'm not sure of many things."

The doors opened, and a white-coated doctor came out. Tristan gazed away from her eyes filled with compassion.

"Lord Montcrest," the doctor said.

Tristan stood still, his breath flushing out of his lungs.

The doctor's face was unreadable. "Lord Rowan is in his room. He should be awake now. We had to set the bone and remove shrapnel from his leg. The surgery went well."

"Thank goodness," Effie said.

Tristan exhaled, but then the doctor's words sank in. "Is he out of danger?"

"Yes, granted that no infection sets in. Lord Rowan might have problems walking though," the doctor said. "Time will tell. Sometimes the healing process goes smoothly, and no lasting damage remains."

"I want to see him now." He didn't sound polite to his own ears.

"I would like to come as well." Effie gave him a pleading glance.

She had no idea how much comfort her presence brought to him.

"Very well." The doctor led him to a room where the smell of chlorine couldn't cover that of blood.

Rowan lay in a white bed with his leg propped up on a tall cushion. He smiled weakly when he saw Tristan. A large bruise covered half of his face; the other half was as bloodless as the bedsheets.

He took Rowan's hand and was glad to find it warm. Surprisingly, Rowan closed his shaky fingers around his hand, too.

"How do you feel?" he asked.

"Tired." Rowan smiled at Effie, blinking slowly.

"We were worried about you." Effie held his other hand.

"I didn't have time to be worried." Rowan tried to shift the pillow. "Everything happened so fast."

He helped him up. "You'll get better soon."

Rowan gave another slow blink. "I feel peculiar."

"I bet you do." He was used to the sight of blood and injuries. As absurd as it sounded, he enjoyed the bruises and wounds on his flesh. But Rowan's heavily bandaged leg disturbed him, even though no blood was visible.

He exchanged a glance with Effie.

She mouthed, "Laudanum."

Rowan sagged on his pillow. "You don't have to stay here if you don't want to," he drawled.

Tristan poured a glass of water from the pitcher just to have something to do. "I never do anything I don't want to, and you aren't fine."

"I would like to sleep now." Rowan faced the wall.

"Of course." Effie caressed his head. "I need to go home as well. I went home quickly to see Papa, but he was out. He's probably home now, and he'll want to see me."

Tristan's heart tightened as Rowan fell asleep. He escorted Effie out of the room.

"I'll come back tomorrow," she said, touching his arm.

"Thank you." He wasn't sure why panic caught him right now. Rowan was alive, and Effie didn't have a scratch. The bloody locomotive would be rebuilt. Yet he was shivering with fear. "Your presence here means a lot. I know you don't approve of me, but I'm grateful you put aside your dislike for me to come. Rowan needed to see you."

"You make it sound quite dramatic. I don't dislike you, and I care about Rowan very much."

"I'm grateful for that as well."

"Are you going home? Do you want to come with me? My coachman can drive you there."

"No, I'm staying here with Rowan."

She squeezed his hand for a long moment, and he loved the feeling of her soft fingers on his skin. "I'm sure Rowan will be all right."

Oddly enough, he believed that, too when she said it.

eighteen

A long, warm bath was the perfect cure for Effie's fatigue. The water was cold and inky when she climbed out of the bathtub. Every time she closed her eyes, the view of the smoky platform tormented her. But the horror of the day wasn't the only thing occupying her mind.

She'd caught another glimpse of Tristan's soul, and she was rather shaken by the experience. He'd been scared and worried sick about his brother. Not that he seemed less dangerous while in that state, but certainly more vulnerable. And his speech before the bomb had gone off had left a mark in her heart.

No one had ever been so honest with her and so shocking at the same time. She'd misjudged him. He cared about her. A lot. His proposal wasn't simply a business transaction for him; it was something deeper.

"You have another bruise here, my lady." Her maid applied comfrey poultice on Effie's calf. "You're covered in bruises. Shall we send for Dr. O'Neil again?"

"Don't worry." She tugged at the lapels of her dressing gown, staring at her reflection in the mirror of the vanity.

A couple of bruises marred her forehead, and a small cut sliced her chin. But what struck her was how pale she was. The day had drained her.

"It must have been terrifying, my lady." The maid's voice broke.

"I can't complain. I'm in one piece." She patted the maid's hand. "I'm just tired now."

"The bed is warm and ready."

"Have you sent my message to Lady Vaughan?"

The maid nodded. "Lady Vaughan will see you tomorrow."

There was a knock on the door.

"Effie?" Papa said in an urgent voice.

The maid had barely time to open the door before he rushed inside. "My lord," she said.

"There you are." He squeezed Effie in a tight hug that made her sob.

The maid left the room quietly.

"I'm fine, Papa." She rested her head on his shoulder and inhaled the familiar scent of his cologne.

"I was terrified." He quivered. "When I returned home and found your message, I went to the hospital but didn't find you."

"You must have missed me by a minute. I went to St. Bartholomew's to visit Rowan. He got injured."

He paled and sat on a chair. "Seriously?"

"A broken ankle that would probably make him limp, but he was lucky." She shivered as the vision of Rowan lying in the hospital bed flashed across her mind. "They had to remove shrapnel from his leg, poor boy."

"Why were you at Aldersgate Station?" He took her hand in a firm grip, and an accusatory tone slipped into his voice. "I thought you were in Greenford, visiting Colin and the girls."

"I changed my plan at the last minute. Rowan asked me to go with him to the inauguration of Montcrest's new locomotive. The boy was supposed to be with the machinist during the maiden voyage. It was a miracle he wasn't onboard when the bomb went off."

He breathed quickly. "You could have died or been injured, too. Why didn't you listen to me and stay away from Montcrest?"

"I told you I didn't want to disappoint Rowan. He's a sweet boy."

"Yes, but—" He pressed his lips hard and faced the fire. "You shouldn't have been at the train station."

She understood his anger to an extent. No one could have known a bomb would have exploded.

"I was so scared." He held her, crushing her again. "I could have lost you. What a tragedy. It shouldn't have happened."

"I'm fine. Truly. Others weren't so lucky."

Including Tristan. The incident had troubled him deeply, and she wanted to be close to him. No matter what Papa said.

AFTER A NIGHT SPENT on a chair next to Rowan's bed and hours with the police, going home was a strange but welcome change for Tristan.

Harris had broken a strict code of conduct and hugged him so tightly he'd felt pain in his ribs. His valet, James, had nearly wept when he'd seen him. At first, Tristan had thought James's distress was due to the state of his dirty and crumpled clothes. But no. James had been genuinely concerned about his master, which should tell him something about how much his servants worried about him.

He'd never spared a thought about that before, but now he wondered if he should do something to show his appreciation for his servants' care.

After a hot bath and a few hours of sleep, he went to the dining room for breakfast, almost refreshed. Worry about Rowan turned the tea and scones into paper in his mouth. Effie had told him the incident wasn't his fault, but Rowan was his responsibility, and so far, he'd done a poor job at keeping him safe.

"My lord." Harris brought a fresh pot of tea. "Mr. Fleet wishes to see you."

He nodded. He couldn't avoid seeing George, and on the bright side, his friend wouldn't be here to lecture him that day.

"If you're too tired," Harris said, "I'll inform Mr. Fleet to return later."

His first instinct was to dismiss Harris's concern, but he changed his mind.

"Thank you, Harris, but I'm fine. I would like to see Mr. Fleet. I appreciate your concern, and I'm sorry if I haven't shown my gratitude."

Harris's expression reflected his surprise. "No need to apologise, my lord." He sniffled. "I'll be...I'll tell Mr. Fleet to come." He left, wiping his eyes.

George strode into the dining room, eyes wide with fear. "Tristan!"

"You're in time for breakfast—"

"I was worried." George hugged him, leaving him speechless. "I've just returned from Bristol. I sent a wire yesterday, but you didn't answer."

"I probably haven't seen it yet."

"How is Rowan?" Sheer fear cracked George's voice.

"At the hospital. A broken ankle and some bruises. He should be sent home this afternoon. It could have been worse."

"I want to see him."

"You will." He patted George's shoulder so the hugging would end. "Take a seat."

"Bloody anarchists. It was the Russians. They decided to bomb the station after one of them was given a seven-year prison sentence. Too short a sentence in my opinion." George sat on the chair next to him, looking worse for wear. "The locomotive?"

"Damaged but nothing that our engineers can't fix. The police informed me the explosion didn't go as planned. The device didn't employ its full energy."

"What would have happened if it had?"

He, Effie, and Rowan would be dead.

George poured himself a cup of tea from the buffet table and drank a few sips immediately.

"I reckon we'll be able to fix the machine in a few weeks," Tristan said. "A waste of time and money, but I don't care about that now. The important thing is that Rowan is alive."

George inched closer. "I'm starting to think there's more behind the bombing."

"What do you mean? They wanted to blow up the entire station in revenge. Pretty simple."

"Yes, but I can't believe no one knew about the attack." George took out of his pocket a piece of paper. "I always keep an eye on the stock market. Our competitors are earning a lot of money after the blast while our company is losing it. And guess who is earning more than anyone?"

Tristan read the short stock market report. "Winchester gained twenty thousand pounds in one afternoon."

"Indeed." George rubbed his forehead. "I mean to get to the bottom of this story. I promise."

"I don't understand. What does Winchester have to do with the Russians? You can't possibly think he's behind the bombing."

"He has been a thorn in our side from the beginning. First, he accused your father of cheating him out of a deal, although it was his fault. Then, he refused to sell Easthollow, even when we offered to share the railway with his company." George lowered his voice. "Then I saw him shaking hands with the Russian anarchists, and now a bomb conveniently goes off during the inauguration of our new locomotive model. It could be a coincidence, but we're businessmen. We don't believe in coincidences."

"Speculations." He folded the piece of paper.

"Speculations that make sense."

"Lady Effie was at the station. Winchester wouldn't risk her life."

George drummed his fingers on the table. "True. But as I said, I'll investigate the matter."

THE SMELL of chlorine pinched Tristan's nostrils when he entered St. Bartholomew's Hospital with George.

Yesterday, his nose hadn't worked properly after the blast, but now, the pungent scent reached his lungs.

"I can't believe Rowan almost died." George shook with either rage or worry. Maybe both.

"I hope he'll be able to walk normally again."

Grey sunlight added a layer of sadness to the hospital corridor. The shiny sunlight from yesterday had vanished, as if the sun hid in mourning behind the clouds.

Rowan lifted his head an inch when Tristan walked into the room. The mild disinterest in his face turned into an expression of relief the moment George appeared.

"Uncle George!" Rowan sat bolt upright.

George rushed past Tristan to hug Rowan. They held each other, crying together.

George kept repeating, "My boy."

"I was scared," Rowan said, resting his head on George's shoulder.

"So was I." George held him again. "We'll go home soon and do everything to make you recover as quickly as possible."

They kept chatting and comforting each other, laughing now and then.

He didn't get closer to the bed. He stood aside, again feeling as if he were intruding in a private moment. Rowan and George were a family, and he wasn't sure he was part of it.

nineteen

I f Effie hadn't known that Jane had been in the middle of an anarchist attack the previous day, looking at her now, she would never have guessed. Jane's cheeks were rosy, her hair perfectly styled, and her slender figure radiated authority when she entered Effie's drawing room. The satin ribbons on her hat fluttered around her head, adding a touch of elegance.

"How are you?" Jane took her hand.

"A few minor injuries, but nothing serious. It's Rowan I'm worried about."

"What a tragedy." Jane sat on the armchair. "I'm sorry for both Montcrest and young Rowan."

"You're the only one besides me who shows compassion towards Tristan."

Jane gave a little shrug. "The incident made me think. No one deserves to be killed like that. Now I think I was too harsh on him and his family. Also, my husband told me something else about Montcrest. Something I haven't told anyone."

"Tell me."

Jane waited for the footman to leave. "Years ago, when his family's financial situation started to get better, he worked in a warehouse for hours on end. One night, he was attacked as he was returning home."

"What?"

"I'm not sure why, but he ended up in hospital and remained there in a state of prolonged unconsciousness for a few months."

"Oh no." She'd heard of those uncommon cases when a patient remained in a deep sleep and woke up for no apparent reason.

"Some slanderers say the deep sleep damaged Montcrest's head, and that's why no lady wants to marry him, even though he's a good match."

She was about to cry. The more she learnt about Tristan, the more she understood him.

"Please don't tell him I told you this story. He wouldn't thank me."

"But I do." Besides, Tristan wouldn't be so open to her and tell her about his past.

"You're a doctor of sorts," Jane said.

"Thank you for that. It really cheered me up."

Jane waved dismissively. "Do you think Montcrest's brain can be truly damaged?"

"No. He can do everything like any other person. He can speak, move, and reason normally."

"Some might object to the last one."

"What I mean is that, physically, he's fine." Spiritually, perhaps not.

"But does the incident explain his cold temper? Lady Mabel thinks his brain doesn't work properly."

The anger she felt was quick. "Since when did Lady Margaret become an expert in brain damage? What does she understand about medicine?"

Jane looked taken aback. "I'm the messenger. Don't get upset with me."

"But you shouldn't repeat unfounded and potentially

damaging news. That's how rumours can destroy someone's reputation."

"I don't understand why you're becoming agitated."

She fought another comment on how dangerous rumours could be. They were Londoners' favourite pastime. But poor Tristan was targeted too many times.

"I simply wish you would stop listening to every piece of gossip you hear," she said diplomatically.

Jane gave her a sceptical look. "It's not my fault if people tell me what they know."

Effie sighed. Changing her friend's mind was a hopeless cause.

T RISTAN WAITED for the physician and the nurse to finish making Rowan comfortable in his bedroom at home.

The fatigue of the past two days and the worry had the surprising effect of silencing his nervous twitch although he wouldn't mind a visit to The Octagon just to forget about the world.

George fussed around the bed, straightening cushions and pulling the curtains. His red-rimmed eyes were a testament to his love for Rowan.

"All done, my lord." Dr. O'Neil collected his tools and bottles from around the bedroom. "I'll visit Lord Rowan every day and make sure the wound is healing properly."

"No sign of infection so far, right?"

"Not one."

"Lord Rowan will be able to walk normally, won't he?" George asked.

Dr. O'Neil hesitated. "The surgery was extensive, and the shrapnel damaged the bones, tendons, and muscles. But Lord Rowan is young and strong."

Too young to deal with such a terrifying situation. Tristan cursed again his decision to take Rowan with him.

George's clenched jaw proved the answer wasn't to his liking.

"I'm sorry I can't give you any guarantees.," Dr. O'Neil said.

George swallowed hard. "If you'll excuse me, Tristan. I need to..."

Tristan patted his shoulder when his friend didn't talk further. "Have a sip of that horrible brandy. It'll fortify you."

George kissed the top of Rowan's head and hurried out of the room, blinking. Rowan remained silent.

The doctor bowed his head and left with the nurse, and Tristan was alone with his brother.

He waited a few moments before going closer. Rowan's expression didn't invite a conversation. His deep frown was likely similar to Tristan's. Without the influence of the laudanum, Rowan's discomfort with him had nowhere to hide.

"Are you in pain?" he asked.

"A bit." Rowan leant back and stared at the ceiling. The harsh line of his jaw made him look older.

"I'm happy you're at home." He didn't know what else to say.

Rowan turned his head towards the window. "She didn't come, did she?"

"Who? Lady Effie? I'll send her a message if you wish to see her."

Rowan worked his jaw, looking surprisingly mature. "No, not her."

"I see." He sat on the edge of the bed and exhaled. "No, she didn't come, nor did she send a message."

"My name is in every newspaper. She must know."

An insult towards Charlene, Rowan's mother, remained trapped in Tristan's mouth. With effort, he didn't voice his thoughts.

He swallowed the bitter taste in his mouth. "Yes. She must know."

Rowan turned on his side, as much as the injured leg allowed him, and pulled up the cover.

"Rowan—"

"I'm fine. You can go."

Everything he wanted to say—that Charlene would never come back, and Rowan had to accept it; that hoping someone as shallow as Charlene would change was a waste of time; that Rowan should stop thinking of her—seemed wrong. But he couldn't give Rowan false hope, either.

"You'll tell me if you need anything," he said instead.

"It sounds like an order. As usual."

"I didn't mean to give you an order."

"I want to be alone, please." Rowan's tone didn't leave room for a reply.

He and Rowan had more things in common than he would have imagined, so he rose and headed for the door.

Harris entered the room before Tristan could exit. "Lady Effie is here. She wishes to see you, my lord."

"Would you like to see her?" he asked Rowan.

"No." Rowan didn't turn around.

"There will be other occasions," Harris said diplomatically before Tristan could speak.

"I'll tell her you send her your regards," he said.

Rowan didn't acknowledge him.

When he went downstairs to see Effie, warmth stirred in his chest, a combination of relief, desire, and happiness. Until he saw her bruised face.

He wanted to hold her again and trail his lips over the blue bruise until it vanished. Before the incident, he liked her spirits and light, but now the urge to protect her overwhelmed any other sentiment.

"Tristan." She flashed a feeble smile. "How's Rowan? May I see him?"

"Physically, he's recovering, but he isn't in the mood to see anyone. Not today at least."

She lowered her shoulders. "I understand. Well, I won't disturb you further."

"You never do. I'm always happy to see you."

Her smile was full and genuine.

They both stood there for a heartbeat or two.

Effie broke the spell first. "I'd better go home anyway. I didn't leave a message for Papa to tell him where I was, and he had a fit yesterday."

"He must have been worried."

"Yes, because I changed my plans at the last moment. He thought I'd gone to visit my brother in Greenford, but then I received Rowan's message and decided to go to see the famous locomotive."

That caught his attention. "Your father had no idea you were at Aldersgate Station?"

"None. It was quite a shock for him. I've never seen him so upset."

"I can imagine." He needed to talk to George. "Let me escort you to your carriage." His heart gave a kick when she slid her arm through his.

Her cheek brushed his shoulder as they walked down the steps to where her carriage was parked. For a split second, he imagined walking out with her at his arm as his wife. There wasn't anything he wanted more than to be next to her and make her happy. A dream, for now.

He helped her climb into the carriage. "I hope we can talk soon."

"We will." She parted her lips as if wanting to add something else, but then she closed them.

"What?" he prompted.

"I care about you, Tristan. Please do not believe I don't."

His next breath cleansed his body from sadness as if he were breathing mountain air, instead of London's fumes.

"You have no idea how happy I am to hear that," he whispered.

"No, I think I do."

She waved when the carriage rolled forwards, and happiness stunned him so hard he stood there on the pavement until the carriage turned the corner.

twenty

A week had passed since the incident, and Effie hadn't seen Tristan once, even though she'd visited Rowan regularly. He'd been busy with his company after the financial disaster caused by the bombing. For reasons she didn't understand, the incident had caused him to lose money, aside from the material damage caused to the locomotive. He'd been either out of the house or locked in his study with Mr. Fleet and other investors.

She hoped to see him that day when she visited Rowan so she could talk to him.

The footman helped her don her coat in the hallway as Jane made sure the carrier with Kettle was properly shut.

"Thank you for coming, Jane."

Jane petted Pepper. "Don't mention it. I'm always happy to see your pets, and Turi loves them, too."

The Pomeranian showed his short but pointed teeth at Pepper and growled at the carrier where Kettle was hissing.

"Kettle doesn't like being locked up." Jane jumped when Kettle let out a long, high-pitched meow.

"It's for a short trip. I'm sure Turi, Pepper, and Kettle will cheer Rowan up."

"Are you going to see Montcrest again?" Papa walked into the hallway. "I need my coat," he said to the footman who nodded.

"Not this again. Rowan desperately needs some company. He's rather blue after a week in bed, and his leg bothers him."

"As long as you don't spend time with Montcrest." He put his hat on. "And don't go around without letting me know where you are."

"I'm not a child," she said dryly.

Right then, Kettle let out an ear-piercing wail that made everyone jump.

Papa shook his head. "Kettle agrees with me. Please, Effie. Anarchists keep bombing London."

That was true. She kissed his cheek. "I won't be late, and I won't go anywhere else."

The drive in the carriage was short but uncomfortable. Kettle meowed, Pepper wiggled his tail like a windmill, and Turi scowled at everyone like an old matron annoyed by rambunctious young people.

They drew a collective breath when they climbed out of the carriage. Kettle was the only one still complaining, howling like a trapped banshee.

"Nearly there, Kettle." She cooed, but the cat was beyond comfort.

They didn't need to ring the bell. Kettle informed the household of their presence.

Harris opened the door, his surprise clear as he looked at the cat carrier that was making such racket. "What is this, my lady?"

"It's Kettle." She forced a smile. "A surprise for Lord Rowan."

"I'm afraid the surprise has been spoilt." Harris led them to the drawing room. "Lord Rowan is here." He winced when Kettle increased the volume of his lamentation.

"Lady Effie. Lady Vaughan." Rowan stood up from the armchair, using a crutch.

"We brought you company," Jane said over Kettle's wailing.

Turi wriggled out of her arms and ran about the room, scoffing.

"Don't stand up for me." She put the carrier with Kettle on the floor.

Pepper tried to sniff Turi, but the Pomeranian barked in annoyance.

Rowan's eyes brightened. "Thank you. What a treat."

"I hope so," she said under her breath.

The moment she opened the carrier, Kettle stopped crying, which was an improvement, but he didn't dash out as she'd expected.

Rowan offered his hands to the dogs. Turi licked it immediately, but Pepper didn't come near him.

"Pepper is quite shy." She stroked his head.

"He's beautiful." He used his crutch to walk to Pepper and stretched out his arm.

Pepper sniffed his hand, twirling his tail. Kettle didn't leave the carrier yet, but the hard glint in his eyes promised retribution. Instead, Turi seemed to be in a race, running around the sofa.

"Turi," Jane called him. "Be quiet. I don't understand his behaviour. He's usually very calm."

Wasted breath. Turi was too excited to listen, and his enthusiasm was contagious.

As Pepper walked around the room, trying to imitate Turi, Rowan observed him. "He limps."

Effie scolded herself inwardly. How couldn't she have thought about that? "Pepper was born with a lame leg. But as you can see, it doesn't bother him. He won't be a hunter, but he's my friend like Kettle, and he's sweet and loving."

The smile vanished from Rowan's face as he used his crutch to follow Pepper. "We have something in common."

Jane snatched Turi from the floor, stopping his wild race, and exchanged a glance with Effie.

"I'm sorry, Rowan. I didn't think Pepper might upset you."

"Oh, no. I'm not upset. I understand him. He makes me think."

"About what?"

"He doesn't complain, does he?" Rowan lowered his gaze. "He does his best. I've been quite upset in the past few days."

"Understandably so," Jane said.

He scrubbed the back of his neck. "I wasn't very nice to the people around me."

Effie could only imagine what Rowan was going through. "I'm sure your brother and your servants understand. They all love you."

He nodded and caressed Pepper again. "There's a lot to learn from animals."

The setter repaid the attention enthusiastically, licking Rowan's hand. Turi wanted to be part of the party and joined them, licking Rowan's hand as well.

Rowan giggled. "They tickle me."

She laughed. "You're already friends."

"That was easy, and what about—Hey! He's gone." Rowan tilted his head towards the carrier. "Kettle isn't there."

They turned towards the carrier.

"What? I didn't see him leaving it." She searched around, a thousand thoughts going through her head. "Kettle? Come here."

Jane huffed. "I think it was Turi. He distracted us. Kettle could be anywhere."

Effie searched under the sofa, behind the curtains, and on the shelves, but there was no trace of the black cat. Worry set in her stomach. What if he ran in the street? Or if he got stuck somewhere? He was so upset that he might have gone anywhere to feel safe.

She put a hand on her chest.

"Lady Effie, don't worry. We should split up to look for him," Rowan said. "Lady Vaughan and I will search the next room."

"Won't you get tired?" she asked.

"I'll use both crutches, and the physician told me I need to move." He hopped to the other crutch and employed both of them. "My foot won't touch the floor."

"You may want to search the corridor and the stairs while we search the ground floor," Jane said.

"Yes, I'll do that."

As Rowan and Jane headed to the next room, she found Harris in the corridor.

"Do you need anything, my lady?" he asked.

"I lost my cat. Have you seen him?"

Harris looked alarmed. "A cat? Roaming freely? I thought he would stay in the carrier."

"I couldn't leave him there for long. The plan has always been to let him out once here, but he vanished."

Harris dabbed his forehead with a handkerchief. "I'll go downstairs and ask the servants to help."

"I'll go upstairs." As she went up the austere dark stairs, a black tail flickered through her field of vision. "Kettle!"

She followed the tail. The scoundrel sped up and rounded a corner as if to say, '*serves you right.*'

"Come here, Kettle. I'm sorry I kept you in the carrier." She chased him down a corridor until he disappeared into a room.

"Kettle. You naughty—" She came to a grinding halt as she bumped against a hard wall of muscles.

"Effie," Tristan said at the same time as she said, "Ouch!"

He took her elbows to steady her. "What's happening?"

Kettle slipped through their legs like an eel and vanished again in the blink of an eye.

"Is that your cat?" Tristan gazed around.

"Kettle! Come here." She clenched a fist. "I don't know why I bother calling him. He never comes. One could spend hours trying to find the perfect name for a cat. All wasted."

He smiled. "Good morning, by the way."

She smiled back. "My apologies for the intrusion. I thought my pets would cheer Rowan up. The situation was perfectly under control a moment ago."

"I think he's gone to the library. Come."

"Perfect," she said, faking a calm she didn't feel.

Her feeble optimism took a vicious blow when she entered the library. The room had a high ceiling, tall shelves, and dark nooks as far as the eye could see. Searching for Kettle would be like searching for the proverbial needle.

"It'll take ages to find him." She slouched her shoulders.

"Where's your optimism? At least he won't escape from here." Tristan closed the door behind them. "Kettle, come here."

She glanced at him. "Never underestimate what a cat can do. Cats are superior creatures, I tell you."

"It's worth a try."

They walked down the aisle between two shelves offering dozens of great places for a cat to hide, climb, and observe without being seen.

"The bruise is almost gone." He searched a half-empty shelf. "I'm glad."

"My cheek is still tender."

"I hate seeing that bruise on you," he said in all seriousness.

"It was nothing. Your cut was worse. Did Dr. O'Neil check it?"

"No need. It's fine." He searched over a shelf, closing the conversation.

If he didn't want to be pestered about the cut. Fine. She wouldn't insist. She crouched to check the floor. "Kettle! Please."

Not even a hiss could be heard.

She walked on, stopping every time a shadow flickered. At the end of the aisle, they turned to the next one.

"You've been busy." She checked the space behind a vase.

"Repairing the locomotive proved to be a longer and more expensive affair than I'd thought." He tilted his head up towards the top shelves. "Thank you for keeping Rowan company. He isn't in a good mood, is he?"

"I don't blame him. He can't walk without crutches and seems rather lonely." She paused in the middle of the section on botany. "If I may say something."

"You don't need my permission."

"Can't you find the time to be with him? He needs you."

"I tried, and he asked me to leave. But I'll try again. You're right. I spend the evenings with him, but I guess it's not enough, and to be honest, he doesn't speak much when I'm with him."

"Why?"

He gave a little shrug, but she wasn't fooled. The way he lowered his eyelashes belied his pretended nonchalance. "He's intimidated by me."

"I can't imagine why."

A corner of his mouth quirked up before he turned serious. "I think that's Kettle. Over there!" He made a dash for the other end of the aisle.

She caught the view of a furry ball darting away. "Kettle!"

They both skidded to a stop on the polished floor at the end of the aisle. She gazed around. Pots of rhododendrons, marble busts of ancient philosophers, and a couple of armchairs crammed that corner. No black cat.

"He was there." He turned around, an incredulous expression on his face. "He vanished."

"Welcome into my world."

He exhaled, hands on his hips. "That's why I prefer horses. Obedient and easy to train."

"No need to be harsh on cats. It's not a cat-astrophe." She laughed, but he didn't crack a smile. "Oh, come on. It was a silly joke, but you could smile. You really work too much."

"Sorry if I'm not *feline* happy today."

She stared at him with her mouth open. "My goodness. Have you just made a joke?"

"I do work too much."

They both laughed. To her surprise, that was the first time she'd heard him laugh with abandon. His face transformed from cold to warm in a moment. He looked more handsome when the worry lines on his brow smoothed.

"Two adults beaten by a cat." He kept searching. "He can't be far."

"I'm sorry about your locomotive." She followed him down another aisle, this one on husbandry. "I hope they find the thug who put the bomb at the station."

He didn't say anything, but his mood changed again.

"May I ask you something personal?" she asked. "Very personal and intimate."

"Yes, although I'm surprised you're interested in my personal, intimate life."

"I am since your proposal."

He cast her a glance before checking under the shelf. "Ask away."

"I heard gossip of you meeting your mistress in a flat close to Chelsea."

He flashed a crooked smile. "A mistress. Interesting. Gossip is only that—hearing something you like about someone you don't like."

She waited for him to add something else, but he didn't. So which part of the gossip was fabricated? The mistress, the flat in Chelsea, or everything?

"I do like you," she said.

He spun towards her with such speed she feared he might have pulled a muscle. "Do you now?"

"Yes, but let's get back to the question. What do you mean?" she said.

"That you shouldn't listen to gossip. It never gets anything right. I don't have a mistress."

That was a relief and yet another proof of how unreliable

gossip was. She'd scolded Jane for listening to gossip, but she'd done the same.

"Please don't believe everything you hear about me." He opened and closed his fist. The skin on the knuckles was cracked, and a joint was swollen.

"What happened to your hand?"

"Boxing."

"Don't you use gloves?"

He pointed at a corner. "He's over there," he whispered. "He isn't moving. I think he's run out of steam."

She followed his gaze. Kettle was perched over a copy of *The Nine Lives of a Cat: A Tale of Wonder* by Charles Bennett.

They both laughed.

twenty-one

Tristan winced as Effie pressed a cloth on the bleeding slashes on his hand. Another day, another cut she had to take care of. The only thing that changed was the location. Now they were in his drawing room.

Apparently, grabbing Kettle was the worst thing he could have ever done. When he'd started to gather the cat in his arms to take him downstairs, the feline had reacted with speed in his limbs and murder in his mind. It'd taken but a moment for his sharp claws to leave a clear message on Tristan's hand.

"I'm so sorry." Effie applied more disinfectant to the cuts. "Kettle was stressed and tired, and he doesn't know you. You scared him."

"Another creature scared of me. Great."

"Well, Kettle isn't usually sweet," Lady Vaughan said, facing the window.

"Thank you, Jane." Effie glowered at her.

At least Pepper and Turi were sympathetic. As Tristan sat on an armchair, the dogs were curled on the floor while Rowan had the wild panther half-asleep on his lap. Kettle was the picture of innocence, purring softly as Rowan gently stroked his fur.

"Kettle seems to like Rowan." Tristan flexed his fingers. They were a bit stiff after his last session.

"Kettle isn't afraid of Lord Rowan." She bandaged his hand. "Cats have their favourite people, and there's nothing we can do about that."

Rowan smiled. It wasn't the carefree, boyish smile he'd shown before the incident, but it was better than nothing.

"Thank you for bringing Turi, Pepper, and Kettle here," Rowan said. "It was fun—" He fell silent, and the weak smile vanished. "I didn't mean to make fun of you, Tristan."

"I didn't think you were."

And just like that, Rowan returned sad.

Tristan exchanged a glance with Effie, wanting her to notice how quickly Rowan's mood changed when he was around.

"You're welcome," she said. "The most difficult part is taking Kettle home in the carrier. You can turn around, Jane. I've finished with the bandage."

"Please." Lady Vaughan let out an exaggerated breath. "Can't we leave him here? He certainly knows the house."

"I'm afraid it's not possible. Kettle would try to return home on his own, and I don't want him to wander the streets for hours."

Tristan was concerned when Effie lifted Kettle to wrestle him in the carrier. If he tried to put his hands on Kettle, he would get hurt again.

Somehow, she slid the furry fury into the carrier with surprising dexterity, and the following loud feline wails sent goose pimples all over his skin.

As usual, he escorted her to the carriage. Turi jumped inside quickly and sat on the squab as if wanting to demonstrate how proper pets should behave. Pepper required his help, not managing to leap, and Kettle was inconsolable.

"Thank you for everything you do for us," he said once they were all inside the carriage.

"My pleasure."

Despite the noise coming from the carrier, he stood there. He hadn't finished his marriage proposal. "Can I see you tomorrow in private?" he asked as Kettle meowed at the top of his lungs.

"What did you say?" She tilted her head.

"I asked if I could see you tomorrow in private!" he shouted, but Kettle chose exactly that moment to fall silent. Cursed feline.

The entire city must have heard him.

The footman and the coachman turned towards him. Lady Vaughan's stunned expression would have been comical if he weren't utterly embarrassed. Then everyone gazed at Effie.

She cleared her throat. "Of course. I won't have Kettle with me." She laughed nervously.

"Thank you."

The wailing started again. That cat hated him.

He stepped back from the carriage and signalled for the coachman to go.

She waved at him as Kettle kept protesting about his imprisonment.

He returned inside with a heavy heart, despite the laughter he'd shared with her. Usually, when he made a decision, he didn't go back to it. He only went forwards. But with Effie, he kept wondering what he had to offer aside from his title and fortune, which she didn't seem to care about. He wanted her to be his wife, but he wasn't sure he was the right husband for her.

But then again, he didn't want to live with the doubt of what could have been between them. There was also the possibility that she would run for the hills the moment she learnt his supposed mistress was a dirty, illegal boxing ring.

The warmth of the blazing log fire welcomed him when he stepped into the drawing room. Rowan tottered on his good foot, almost losing his balance as he stood in front of the flames.

"Careful." Tristan steadied him, taking his arm.

"Thank you." Rowan slid his arm out of Tristan's grip and leant on the crutches.

"Are you going upstairs?"

"Yes."

"I'll help you."

"There's no need."

"Rowan." He regretted the commanding tone. "Why are you frightened of me?" He'd asked that question a few times, but he would keep asking it until his brother answered.

"I'm not." Rowan walked towards the door, using both crutches.

"Then what is it?" He followed him.

"I'm tired."

He followed him up the stairs in silence, just to make sure his brother didn't fall. And that pretty much was the only thing he could think of to help his brother.

He held the door open for him. "I think we need to talk."

Rowan sat on the bed. "Why now? Because I might not walk ever again?"

"Because you could have died, and I was bloody scared."

Rowan lifted his gaze to him, his mouth hanging open. "You were scared?"

"To death. I thought I'd lost you." His voice cracked, and for the first time in his life, he didn't hide his fear.

"You barely know me," Rowan whispered.

That was true. And it was his fault.

"You're my brother. We can spend some time together and get to know each other better." He stretched out his arm towards Rowan.

"Do you really mean that? Or do you just pity me?"

That was something he would say. The similarity with Rowan didn't please him in the least. His darkness was contagious.

"I mean it with all my heart, and it's not pity, but compassion." He'd learnt something from sweet Effie.

For a moment, he thought Rowan wasn't going to shake his

hand, but then he slipped his hand into Tristan's and sealed the deal.

He couldn't stop a smile. "I'll let you rest now. You had a busy afternoon."

Rowan nodded. "Thank you."

When Tristan closed the door, he realised that interaction with Rowan had been the first one he hadn't treated like a business deal.

twenty-two

The thought of talking with Effie again didn't help Tristan relax. And that day, he would rather be in The Octagon than in a carriage with George, as nervous energy had tormented him since the incident. But George wanted to confront Winchester, convinced the earl was involved with the anarchists.

"Honestly," Tristan said as they drove to Archer Hall. "I think you're exaggerating. Winchester can't be involved in a conspiracy with the anarchists."

"Just because the police haven't found any evidence yet, it doesn't mean he's innocent."

"It certainly means he's more likely to be."

"I spent the last week searching for evidence," George said with the intensity he reserved for important business deals. "And I got confirmation of Winchester meeting the Russians often. I must talk to him."

"Winchester is a pain in the arse. But a murderer? No."

"I spotted him close to the anarchists' seat. I saw him talking with them." George raised a finger for each of his points. "He earned thousands of pounds after the bombing. What further proof do you need? What does an earl have to do with those people and their extreme political ideas?"

"Fine. Let's say you're right," he said. "How do you plan to make him tell the truth without any evidence?"

George didn't flinch. "I simply want to confront him, one gentleman to another."

"Is that your plan? Great. That will do the trick."

"Let me lead the meeting."

Tristan didn't add anything else. He had enough problems to deal with between the reconstruction of his locomotive, his feelings for Effie, and Rowan's recovery. Winchester could wait, but if talking with him helped George drop the subject and focus on more urgent problems, then so be it.

Effie was another matter. She'd rejected him twice, but he wasn't too proud to try a third time. If he could talk to her without hiding his feelings, she would listen to him.

"I hope you'll support me," George said when the carriage stopped.

"I always support you." His voice softened.

George smiled fondly at him. "You know, when I play Ludo with Rowan, I feel sorry that you and I didn't have the opportunity to share the same experience, playing together and laughing at silly things."

"We were too busy surviving." But he would be lying if he said he hadn't thought about that either.

"Yes, but..." George gazed around as if searching for inspiration. "Having fun with Rowan is so easy. When I'm with you, we discuss money and business deals, and it's always been that way. Perhaps we should change."

He shifted on the seat, not sure he wanted to remember those dark days and how things had been different. "You helped Father and me get back our fortune."

"Is it that important, though?"

Tristan didn't answer. Because if the answer was 'no', his whole life would unravel like a threadbare hessian carpet. They couldn't change the past. And that was it.

George exhaled. "You always clam up when we discuss something deeper than money, and they say I'm the grumpy one."

"Let's focus on Winchester, shall we?"

An uneasy silence settled between them, and he did nothing to break it.

The butler let them inside and showed them into the drawing room. He fought a smile at the books on veterinary medicine scattered on the table and a rubber ball under a chair. There were plants everywhere, the portrait of a setter hung askew, and the scent of cinnamon lingered. Despite Winchester's cold hospitality, the room was warm and cosy.

If anything, Tristan found odd the fact Winchester had agreed to see them.

"Montcrest." Winchester gave a stiff nod of his head. "Fleet."

"My lord." George's tone sounded strained. "Thank you for seeing us."

"You didn't give me much choice." Winchester gestured at the armchairs. "You said it was a matter of the utmost urgency. Take a seat. If this visit is about Easthollow, I'm afraid you're wasting your time. I haven't changed my mind about selling it."

Tristan was about to say something, but George wanted to lead the meeting.

"No, my lord. Easthollow is the last of our problems," George said. "I'm more interested in knowing about your involvement with the anarchists."

Winchester worked his jaw. "Excuse me?"

"You were seen in the company of the Russian anarchists days before the attack at Aldersgate Station," George said.

"Aren't the Montcrests those who have a history of high treason?" Winchester asked with a snarl.

"Take that back!" Tristan shot up.

Winchester rose as well. "How dare you come here and throw accusations?"

"Do you deny having met the anarchists?" George insisted.

Winchester clenched his fists. "That's none of your business."

The door opened, and Effie stepped inside. "Papa, I heard voices, and I was worried—" She gazed from her father to Tristan and closed the door behind her.

"My lady." George bowed.

Tristan bowed his head, too, wishing she weren't there to witness his short temper.

"Perhaps you shouldn't be present during this conversation." Winchester waved her off.

"Why?" George asked before Effie could talk. "Are you afraid of your daughter's reaction at knowing her father is involved with the anarchists?"

"What?" She let out a half chuckle. "Nonsense."

"George," Tristan said.

"I'm not involved with the anarchists!" Winchester shook a fist. "Fleet is suffering from a delusion."

"Will you deny having met the anarchists in front of your daughter?" George asked calmly. "You told Lady Effie you'd visited your son in Greenford the day I saw you with the anarchists. You lied because you didn't want her to know you'd met with them."

"I don't understand where you're going with these accusations." Winchester's voice rose.

Instead, George's voice was cold and low. "Let me explain it to you. You ordered the bomb planted at Aldersgate Station."

"This is absurd!" Winchester reddened.

Effie gasped. "How can you accuse my father of something so despicable?"

Tristan rubbed his temple. He shouldn't have listened to George. They didn't have a shred of evidence against Winchester, and he didn't believe the earl was involved with the anarchists to start with. "George, we should go."

"No," George said.

"You're making a fool out of yourself," he said, moving his lips as little as possible.

"I want the truth. Winchester wanted to destroy our company, and he ordered the anarchists to bomb our locomotive."

"That's a lie." Effie shook her head.

Tristan took George's arm and gritted out, "We should leave."

"Tell the truth." George shrugged himself free and stepped closer to the earl. "You almost killed your daughter because you didn't know she was at the station. You thought she was safe and miles away from London, but no, she was so very close to the danger."

Tristan regretted having given that information to George.

Winchester lost his composure. "Nonsense."

"How afraid you must have been." George lowered his voice. "When you discovered that your daughter was at the station. Did you imagine her body torn apart by the bomb?"

"George!" he said as Effie gasped.

Instead, the earl went awfully silent.

"What a torture for you to think that your daughter was dead because of you."

"Enough." Tristan seized George's arm and yanked. "You're crossing a line."

"You must leave." Winchester's voice lacked the anger it should have. He shivered, but Tristan doubted it was rage.

George didn't move. "Have you already forgiven yourself? Do you blame yourself for the casualties? Tristan's brother almost lost a leg because of you. And for what? So you could earn a few pounds? Was it worth—"

"The bomb wasn't supposed to kill or hurt anyone!" Winchester shouted.

Silence dropped. Only the sound of the grandfather clock chiming loudly in the room.

"Papa?" Effie put a hand on her chest. "What did you say?"

Surprise caused Tristan to stand still. He kept his hand around George's arm.

Winchester ran a trembling hand through his hair. "I didn't order anything, and I swear, I'm not involved with the anarchists. I only..." He took a deep breath, closing his eyes for a moment. "I heard about the possible plan of planting a bomb on one of Montcrest's locomotives to blow it up when no one was around, but it was supposed to be a rumour."

"You didn't think to warn the police?" Tristan released George's arm; anger spread within him like fire on dry grass.

"It was a rumour, nothing more." Winchester's voice quivered. "And the attack wasn't supposed to be aimed at people. No one should have been hurt."

"My brother could have died." He could barely control the intense twitch in his muscles. Had he been in The Octagon, he would have found a partner and boxed until he collapsed. "Effie was there."

"I know!" Winchester shook with rage. "That proves I didn't take the rumour seriously."

"But you didn't know I was at the station," Effie said in a shaky voice. "You thought I was somewhere else."

"Effie." Winchester took her shoulders. "Trust me. I didn't think the anarchists were seriously planning a bombing."

"You didn't think!" His breath came out in quick pants. "Your duty was to warn the police, or me. You should have told me." Darkness spilt in his vision, and his pulse drummed in his ears. "All those people...you could have avoided the tragedy."

"I regret not having taken the threat seriously." Winchester regained some of his composure. "But what happened isn't my fault."

George shook his head. "I don't believe you. I think you heard about the rumour and understood Tristan's company would be damaged and decided to stay quiet for that reason, not because you didn't think the threat was real."

"No, dammit!" Winchester closed his fists. "I would never do anything like that."

"I don't believe you." Tristan was shaking with rage, too. "I've been kind to you so far. You refused to talk to me. You rejected my offer, and I made a new one. Not anymore. My brother might not be able to walk without a limp for the rest of his life. You put my brother's life at risk. You almost killed Effie. I won't forgive that." Pulse drumming in his ears, he strode out of the room and didn't wait for a footman to pull the door open. He ignored his carriage as well and walked along the pavement. If he didn't go to The Octagon now, he would have a fit.

He ignored George calling him. Even Effie called him, but he kept walking.

twenty-three

After Tristan stormed out of the house in a cloud of rage, Effie stood still for a while in the drawing room. She wasn't sure when Mr. Fleet had left.

Papa sat on the sofa, his elbows resting on his knees.

With legs seemingly made of lead, she walked over to him and sat next to him. "Papa."

Talking hurt her throat.

"I swear I had no idea." He rubbed his face hard enough to redden the skin.

She swallowed a few times, trying to understand what had just happened. "You lied about visiting Colin."

He nodded.

"How did you get so close to the anarchists to hear rumours about their activities?"

"Many of the workers in my steel factory are Russians and share some ideas with the anarchists. Their representative meets me on a regular basis. We often discuss workers' rights. Not every anarchist uses bombs. The majority believes in peaceful protests. One evening, I met him at this club, which happens to be the place where workers from every part of London meet. There were violent anarchists among them, and I heard their plan. And that's all."

She put a hand on his arm. "Why didn't you warn the police?"

"Even you accuse me!" He stood up. "I hear rumours about riots and organised, armed strikes every week, and they never come true. There aren't only Russian anarchists in London, but also Fenians, Luddites, and anti-monarchists. If I went to the police every time I heard about a possible threat, I would live at the police station, and the police would no longer take me seriously."

"But a bomb is another matter, and you certainly were concerned enough to suggest I go to Colin's."

"I was simply relieved that you wouldn't be in London just in case."

She wrapped her arms around herself. "That doesn't make your situation better."

He rubbed his face again. "I didn't stay silent on purpose to punish Montcrest. Did I benefit from what happened? Yes. But I didn't think, not for one moment, that the threat was real. When it comes to your safety though, I'm extremely careful, but I didn't seriously believe a bomb would have exploded. I would have warned the police otherwise. If you don't believe me, then we don't have anything else to discuss." He shot up and walked out of the room.

"Papa!"

He ignored her and slammed the door shut behind him.

She sagged on the sofa. Papa sounded honest, but at the same time, he had his responsibility and had profited from the tragedy. She'd been at Aldersgate Station. The horrible scene was still fresh in her memory. And Rowan had risked dying.

What worried her the most was Tristan. He'd been furious when he'd left, understandably so. She hoped he wouldn't do anything reckless.

～

It was past two in the morning when Tristan returned home from The Octagon. Even to his standards, he'd overdone it that night.

He'd been knocked out twice by hitting the floor with his head, and while his face didn't show the signs of his fight, the rest of his body was a map of bruises and sore spots. Painful bumps had swollen on his knees and back. His ribs hurt, too. Breathing hurt. Thinking hurt. But a couple of thoughts kept swirling in his battered mind.

Winchester had known about the attack and done nothing to stop it. Effie and Rowan could have died.

He'd played a fair game with the earl, always honest. Not anymore.

He'd made the mistake of underestimating him and paid the price.

During the years he'd spent working with his father, he'd learnt a few dirty financial tricks. It was time to use them.

He dragged himself up the few steps to the front door, guilt and pain weighing him down. George was right. He should stop going to The Octagon. His addiction to pain wouldn't end well. Sooner or later, something would happen to him. A punch too strong, an opponent too violent, a fatal mistake, and he would be permanently damaged or worse. But what was the alternative? Opium wasn't healthier than The Octagon, and liquors didn't attract him.

He chuckled at his own pathetic excuses. Guilt often came after a session at The Octagon. It would go away, as many other things did, and the cycle would start again.

He rang the bell to his house, but to his surprise, George welcomed him. Although 'welcomed' wasn't the right word.

"Where's Harris?" he asked, annoyed that George had seen him.

George stood there staring at him, battered and bruised as he was, with his mouth hanging open. "Bloody hell."

He brushed past him into the warm entry hall. "What have you done to Harris and my footmen?" He staggered on his feet.

George held him up. "I sent them to bed hours ago. Harris wanted to stay up, but I convinced him to retire. Your servants don't have to pay for their master's foolishness. I'll fetch Dr. O'Neil myself."

"No need." Besides, the doctor would give him opium, which would numb the pain, and Tristan's work would be pointless.

"You aren't well."

"I am. Trust me."

George helped him up the stairs, seemingly more in pain than Tristan, judging by his strained expression. "When will you bloody stop?"

Had it been any other situation, he would have told George to mind his own business.

Staring into the dark eyes of the man who had been with his family for decades, he didn't find the courage to lie. "I don't know. I don't think I can."

The conversation was nothing new. But George would usually lose his temper and tell him to go to hell, and Tristan would ignore him and carry on with his miserable life.

But that night, George's expression softened with pain and pity. "I must apologise. I didn't mean to make you suffer like that when I decided to confront Winchester."

"The way I am isn't your fault."

It was the first time he'd had a normal conversation with George about his addiction.

"I promised your father I would protect you." George's voice cracked. "I'm not protecting you."

Tristan gathered his strength to squeeze George's shoulder. "You helped me build an empire."

"That's not the same thing."

"You're getting sentimental. You must be tired." He leant against the wall, surprised by how easy talking with George was.

Not that he was opening himself completely, but he wasn't as cold as he usually was.

He noticed a piece of black fabric on George's head. "What's that on your hair?"

"What?" George touched his head until he found the piece of fabric. "Oh, this." He showed him an eye patch.

"Is there something I need to know?"

George smiled. "I played pirates with Rowan. He asked me if he was going to have a wooden leg like Long John Silver. I told him I would buy him a parrot, and one thing led to another."

He laughed. "You're really good to him."

"He's a great boy." George wiped his eyes. Rowan was a delicate subject.

"Why don't you find a bed and sleep? I want to see Rowan, then I'll collapse in my bed."

"We should talk about you."

He shook his head. "Not now. I'm tired."

George sniffled. "If you can manage on your own."

"I can. Go. Take the blue room. I'll see you tomorrow."

George nodded and patted Tristan's shoulder.

When he was alone, he took a moment to collect himself. He seemed to feel everything too deeply those days. Effie was the reason for the constant turmoil inside him. Her happiness was like an earthquake cracking his defences and making him vulnerable to every emotion.

He opened the door to Rowan's bedroom and entered as quietly as he could. The crutches were propped against the wall, and Rowen was asleep with a thick cushion under his foot.

Rowan might not be able to walk without a limp ever again, because Winchester hadn't done the right thing. He was as guilty as those who had planted the bomb.

The gas lamps in the corridor lit the bedroom, but there was enough light to make out Rowan's head.

Tristan pulled the quilt up to cover his brother's shoulders.

"You're back." Rowan's sleepy voice came from under the layers of covers. "You've been gone for hours. Uncle George was worried."

"I didn't want to wake you up."

"I sleep lightly these days."

"Why?"

"My foot hurts and itches."

Tristan sat on the edge of the bed. "I'm sorry."

Rowan rolled on his back. "The physician said it's normal. It means the foot is healing. Not your fault."

"It is. And I'm sorry for having been a terrible brother."

Rowan was silent for a long time, and Tristan didn't expect him to contradict him. "You're busy," Rowan said in a grumpy voice.

"That's not an excuse. I'll try to be different from now on." If he couldn't change his addiction to The Octagon, the least he could do was be a better brother.

Rowan slid a few inches down the covers and gazed away.

"You don't believe me," he said.

Rowan didn't answer.

"You know you can tell me everything. I won't get angry. I promise."

"All right." Rowan's voice came muffled.

Tristan wanted to talk more, but Rowan was tired, and it was the middle of the night. Maybe he couldn't always have what he wanted.

He caressed Rowan's head until the boy fell asleep again.

Yes, from today, he would change.

He would change many things.

twenty-four

A few days had passed since the horrible meeting with Tristan, Papa, and Mr. Fleet, and Effie hadn't made up her mind about her father.

She was playing with Pepper, throwing a ball in the garden, but her mind kept drifting off. When she'd visited Rowan, Tristan had never been there. She hadn't talked much with Papa, either. He kept professing his absolute innocence, but at the same time, his company was flourishing at an alarming speed, and he'd insisted she'd gone to Greenford on the day of the attack. It was hard to forgive him.

Pepper dropped the ball at her feet when loud voices distracted her.

"...supposed to do now?" That was Papa.

"An urgent meeting..." That was Lowe, Papa's secretary and factotum.

"Yes, because if I ask him nicely, he will stop." Papa shoved the French windows open and paced on the porch. The luscious evergreen bushes didn't soften the view of her furious father. "I would have more luck asking the tsar to behave."

She walked over to him with Pepper at her heels. "Papa, what happened?"

"Nothing you should worry about." He strode inside and headed upstairs.

She chased him. "Papa."

"It's a serious matter, Effie. Leave it to me."

"Oh, no." She stepped in front of him, blocking his path to his study. "No more secrets. I think they did enough damage to us. Tell me what's happening."

He entered the study, and she followed him.

"Papa." She used the stern tone she reserved for Pepper. "After what happened with Montcrest, I think you owe me some honesty."

Lowe exchanged a nod with him before closing the heavy oak door. "Lord Montcrest is acquiring your father's company."

She'd expected something more shocking. "I don't understand. How?"

"He has the shareholders in his pockets." Papa fidgeted and raked a hand through his hair. "I don't know exactly how he's doing it, but I know why. He's chipping away pieces of my company like a filthy rodent."

"Is it legal?" she asked.

Lowe spread his arms. "Unless he intimidated or blackmailed the shareholders, forcing them to sell their shares to him, which isn't the case, yes, it's legal, unethical but legal."

"He's going to kick me out of my own company!" Papa roared.

"That's not possible, my lord." Lowe didn't sound confident. "You still hold your shares."

"That's his plan. Mark my words." Papa gripped the back of the chair. "Once he finishes, he'll be the owner with me, and he'll drive me mad until I sell the whole lot to him."

A vision of Tristan's furious face flickered through her mind. His rage had screamed revenge. And now he was exacting it financially.

"Even if he buys the company, he won't ruin you, will he?" she asked.

Papa's pale face answered. "He'll never stop." He breathed hard and sweat glistened on his face. "He's a vindictive bastard, like his father." He loosened the collar of his shirt, but his breathing remained raspy.

"Well, you exacted your revenge against Montcrest by refusing to sell him Easthollow," she said. "All because you thought his father was unfair to you."

"Refusing to sell a piece of land isn't the same thing as what he's doing!" Papa gritted his teeth.

She was about to suggest he talk with Tristan when he let out a strangled groan.

He put a hand on his chest and dropped to his knees.

"Papa!" She rushed to his side.

Lowe pulled the door open. "Doyle! Send for the physician. Lord Winchester is ill."

"Papa." She crouched next to him and helped him lie down.

Awful choking noises came out of him, and his eyes watered.

"Breathe." She unfastened the collar of his shirt and caressed his cheek. "Please, breathe."

Effie didn't understand anything about finance, but she understood bad news. As Lowe had shown her, in a short time, Tristan had indeed threatened her father's company with the sheer power of his money.

In the drawing room, she stroked Pepper's and Kettle's heads as she waited for Dr. O'Neil to finish visiting Papa.

That was one of those medical occasions when her knowledge of veterinary medicine was useless.

Lowe sat on a chair, reading the newspaper. The only sign he was worried about Papa was his frequent glances at the door.

Pepper licked her hand gently, and Kettle stared at her without blinking as if he wanted to force happiness into her.

"My lady." Dr. O'Neil entered, his smile strained. "Your father is resting now."

She held her breath. "Was it the heart?"

"No, it wasn't."

She exhaled. "I thought he was having a heart attack."

Lowe sagged as well. "Thank goodness."

"He suffered from a strong moment of panic, which can mimic a heart condition. I prescribed valerian root and passion-flower tincture to help him rest. He's in no danger now, but he must rest and reduce his activities."

She nodded. "Thank you, Doctor."

After the butler showed the doctor out, Lowe asked for his coat.

"My lady, give my regards to His Lordship. I'll be more useful in the office, trying to contain Lord Montcrest's damage."

"Of course." She loitered in the hallway, still torn between justifying Tristan and condemning him.

She entered Papa's bedroom. His hair had turned grey seemingly in a few hours, and his skin had an odd green tone that worried her.

"Papa." She took his hand.

He didn't turn towards her.

The curtains were drawn tightly, blocking the sunlight. Only a couple of lamps were lit.

"I'm so glad it wasn't the heart. You gave me such a fright."

He swallowed hard before he sat upright and shoved the cover aside.

"What are you doing? Dr. O'Neil said you must rest."

"I can't. I have to see my banker and talk with my solicitor. If I do nothing, Montcrest will steal the chair from underneath me."

She put a hand on his arm, surprised to find it quivering. "The situation can't be so dramatic. Your work can wait. Lowe is taking care of everything. You need to recover."

"If I don't intervene, we'll be full of debts by tomorrow. My bank accounts will be frozen. I won't be able to withdraw a penny. That's how dramatic the situation is. I underestimated Montcrest. I swear I didn't want the anarchists to blow up his locomotive. I had no idea..." He wept, hiding his face in his hands. "You have to believe me. I would never do anything so vile."

Effie had never seen her father weeping. Not that their family had gone through hard times or close losses. Quite the opposite. Her brothers and sisters were married and had children. Mama hated London, but she and Papa cared about each other deeply. They were a happy family, and seeing Papa so distraught broke her heart.

When she hugged him and let him cry, her chest clenched for him.

She didn't understand finance, but she understood Tristan a little, and she needed to see him.

twenty-five

The house was in turmoil the next morning as Effie tried to have breakfast in the sunroom. She'd believed that Papa had overreacted about the situation of their finances, but he'd been right.

Tristan's aggressive attack was quickly bringing her family to its knees. Papa's bank accounts had been frozen overnight. Letters of complaints from business associates kept pouring in like confetti at a wedding. The footmen were talking about searching for new employment. A maid had already left, and even Doyle was worried. In the midst of the chaos, Papa was deeply asleep, thanks to one of Dr. O'Neil's sleeping potions.

She had no time to waste.

Tristan's revenge had to stop before her family was completely destroyed. Her father would have another fit once he woke up. She would find something to bargain with if Tristan listened to her.

After changing into a dark green morning dress, she slid out of the house almost without anyone noticing.

The crisp air turned into mist around her mouth, and a strong gust of wind slammed against her chest as if it wanted to shove her back home.

Her determination wavered. She might not be able to make Tristan see reason. Perhaps she was overestimating her influence on him, but they understood each other a little. He wouldn't be completely unsympathetic to her pleas.

She walked at a fast pace along the pavement. Her determination kept floating up and down with each step. But the closer she walked to his house, the less frightened she felt. She wouldn't leave his house until she spoke to him.

Harris didn't look surprised to see her when he opened the door. "My lady." His tone was apologetic.

"Is Lord Montcrest receiving calls? Please."

Harris must have pitied her because he showed her to the drawing room and exhaled. "Please wait here, my lady." He loitered. "His Lordship is a good man. Please, my lady, don't believe he isn't."

"I know his heart. I do."

With another sigh, he left her alone in the room that smelled of beeswax. Maybe it was Papa's suddenly uncertain financial situation, but the austere furniture and heavy drapes seemed to close in on her.

She paced between the Italian dark silk sofa and a sophisticated Louis XVI-style table, needing to steel herself for the imminent confrontation.

"Effie." His deep voice sounded calm and composed, the opposite of how she felt.

Despite her state of agitation, a shiver ran down her back upon seeing him again in all his masculine charm. He was the same, yet he'd changed.

His facial muscles were more defined. Well, all his muscles were more defined if the way his jacket stretched across his shoulders was any indication. But the tension in his neck enhanced his dark-circled eyes.

"I'm not surprised to see you here." From his flat tone, she couldn't understand if he was glad or annoyed to see her.

"Thank you for seeing me." There was no point in not being polite. Attacking him immediately wouldn't end well.

He stretched out an arm towards the sofa. "I guess the reason for your visit has to do with your father."

"You guessed right." She ignored the seat. "Please, Tristan, stop. We can't take any more of your attacks. My father is the shadow of himself. He had a fit yesterday. I thought he was dying of a heart attack."

He remained deadpan. "He's responsible for a bombing."

"He isn't a murderer. He should have gone to the police, yes, and he didn't do it, but not because he wanted to hurt people. That's what you refuse to understand."

"His action, or in this case, inaction, has consequences."

"You've punished him enough. You've made your point. Stop."

His icy blue eyes didn't show any mercy. "Rowan might not recover the full use of his left leg. Tell me, Effie, what's the price of a boy with a permanent limp?"

"I'm sorry about Rowan. I'm devastated by what happened to him." She shook with emotion. "My heart breaks for him. But being ferocious to my father won't change anything."

"The police don't want to prosecute him. Someone must teach him a lesson."

"Someone who? You?"

"Yes!" His upper lip curled up in a snarl.

They stared at each other, their breathing uneven.

"What do you want from me? What can I do to convince you to stop?" she asked. "Name your price."

He didn't answer.

She took a step closer, desperate to cause a reaction from him. Anything. Even anger would be better than his coldness. "I'm ready to give you anything you want to make you stop."

"What? Money? I don't need it." Deep lines appeared on his brow.

"There must be something. You've always liked me," she added in a clumsy attempt to remind him he'd wanted to marry her. He was supposed to listen to the woman who would be his wife.

Perhaps she wasn't so different from her father. She was using his feelings towards her to get something in return.

His frown deepened. "Yes, but what does that have to do with anything?"

"Well..." She tried not to lose her composure as she racked her brain for words. "Surely, you can think of something you would be happy for me to do for you." She winced inwardly. That sounded as convoluted as her messy thoughts.

"I want to marry you. You know that."

She straightened but hesitated before talking. "Then you can have me."

The offer had slipped out of her mouth before she could think it through. It came out wrong like everything else she'd tried to say in the last five minutes. Although why not? He'd shown interest in her. He'd wanted to marry her. If she could use that to save her family, she would.

Finally, his cold mask cracked, and emotions slipped through. His sapphire eyes widened, and she could swear a light blush coloured his cheeks. Had she shocked him? She forced herself not to lower her gaze or to shiver.

"You don't mean it," he said, lacking his usual confidence.

"I do." She jutted out her chin. "I would do anything to make you stop this absurd revenge on my father, and I know you have plenty of money. I don't have much to offer aside from myself."

He had the decency to lower his gaze for a moment.

"So here I am." She stepped closer. "You can have me," she said again, sounding more confident after seeing his composure crack.

A tendon in his neck ticked. "What do you mean exactly? Are you proposing a marriage?"

"No." She didn't hesitate in her answer. Nothing good would come from a marriage born under duress. "I propose..."

Now her confidence wavered. Her offer was born on the spur of the moment, and the details were rather blurred.

What exactly was she offering? To become his mistress? No, that wouldn't suit her. Besides, he'd told her he didn't want a mistress. Then what? A single night of passion? She doubted that would be enough for him. A month, perhaps, or a week.

"I'll provide for you once I finish with your father," he said with shocking honesty when she didn't add a word. "You don't have to do this. You'll never starve."

"I don't want your charity."

"There's nothing wrong with accepting charity. I did it."

She should be more careful with her words. "I want you to stop torturing my father."

He straightened, gaining a few inches of menace. She had never negotiated a deal, and she was competing with a honed businessman in a field where negotiation skills were everything. Great plan so far.

"No marriage, so you want to be my mistress." He looked puzzled.

That made two of them.

"No." She wrung her hands but stopped quickly; the gesture would make her look weak.

He gave the slightest shake of his head. "What do you offer then?"

"A short affair." That sounded sensible.

"How short? Are we talking about a month, a year, or what?"

She forced herself not to fiddle with her hands. "A week." Even more sensible. But she was overestimating herself. Her body for a week might not be so valuable to him.

"A week." He folded his arms over his chest. "And what are we going to do during that week exactly?"

Did she really have to spell everything out for him?

She waved a hand. "It's clear, I suppose."

"No, it isn't. I have no idea what you have in mind. What am I allowed to do? What am I *not* allowed to do?"

"Well…" She searched around for inspiration, but the rural painting on the wall and the cherubs on the ceiling didn't offer much.

"Be specific."

Curse him. She needed to sit down. Her legs were quivering.

He sat in front of her on the armchair, his elbows on his knees and his intense stare completely focused on her. He didn't look less intimidating because he was sitting, and now she understood how a gazelle had to feel in front of a hungry lion.

She cleared her throat. "We can sleep together during that week."

"Every night and day of the week?" His voice lowered, and she didn't find it unpleasant.

"Yes," she said. "I mean, seven days."

"Seven days, not necessarily in a row."

"Yes."

"Seven days of us in bed together."

Said like that, it sounded rather improper, because it was. But in for a penny, in for a pound. "Yes."

"What can we do in bed?" His tone was challenging now. "Can I have you anytime I wish?"

She shifted, not sure what to say. "I don't have a lot of experience, so answering this question can be difficult."

She knew *something.* Things she'd learnt from books, friends, and horses, but she'd never tried anything.

He pinched the bridge of his nose. "You don't want to do this. It's obvious. You're only desperate."

"I may be desperate, but I am offering you a deal. Take it or leave it." She wouldn't be treated like a child. She was a woman capable of making her own choices, even though she had a vague idea of what those choices implied.

He studied her, drumming his long fingers on the armrests.

She wondered if he had the same warrior-like expression whenever he negotiated a deal.

He stretched out his hand. "We have a deal."

"You stop bothering my father right now, and I'll be your mistress for a week, and we'll do things I'm comfortable with," she said, not taking his hand.

"No, the deal was that we slept together for seven days."

She didn't see the difference. "Yes." She stretched out her hand, but it was his turn not to shake it.

"And if we do only things you are comfortable with, we'll hold hands all the time and nothing else."

"Are all negotiations so complicated?"

A corner of his mouth curved up. "Worse than that, but never as pleasurable."

She huffed. "I mean, we will, of course, do the deed. No, I won't be specific," she added in a rush when he opened his mouth. "Let's say we'll see each time what we choose to do."

"It's not much of an assurance, and the whole deal is rather vague, but I'll take it for now." He offered his hand again.

She shook it, feeling the hardened skin on his palm.

"When do we start?" He released her hand immediately.

"Tomorrow evening at seven, but you stop harassing my father today."

He leant back in the seat, his eyes darkening with desire. "Consider it done."

twenty-six

After Effie left, Tristan stood in the drawing room alone, pacing slowing next to the bay window. He couldn't believe what had just happened. The shock from her proposal had left him speechless. While she'd talked, he'd experienced a wide range of emotions, from scepticism to confusion and incredulity.

He'd agreed to the most absurd deal of his life with the woman he wanted the most. But his desire for Effie wasn't what had made him agree with her nonsensical offer. She was suffering and desperate, and while he would never let her starve or miss anything, he understood why she didn't want his financial help. He'd taken for granted she would have accepted his money. Her determination to refuse him had been like a slap to his face. His father had often said that arrogance was the enemy of a good businessman.

He'd accepted her deal also because he'd got what he wanted. Winchester had been punished for his lack of action. Effie had won.

A chuckle shook him. He doubted she would go through with the deal. Tomorrow at seven, she would ask him to forget the whole affair; she would tell him it was a mistake, but he wouldn't resume attacking her father. There was a limit to his malice.

Still, he couldn't stop smiling as he thought of her eyes ignited with determination and her cheeks flushing at each one of his questions. She was fierce when she wanted to be, and he loved it.

It was time to call back his dogs for sweet Effie.

WHAT ON EARTH had Effie done?

She wasn't sure she had an answer. After she'd left Tristan's house in a hurry for no reason, a deep sense of relief had washed over her...for about two seconds. Then an equally deep realisation of what she'd agreed to do had dawned on her with the strength of a freight train.

She paced in the library, unnerving Kettle to the point he retreated somewhere. Even Pepper was annoyed by her nervousness and left her alone.

"There you are." Jane's voice sounded from behind her.

She jumped and put a hand on her throat. "I didn't hear you coming."

"I gathered that." Jane hugged her. "I'm sorry about your father. I heard about his ordeal."

"He'll recover soon. I'm not sure I can say the same thing about his finances."

"Rumour has it that Montcrest is behind the attack." Jane removed her fine white gloves, one finger at a time. The white and lime gown she wore would be appropriate for an elegant tea party at Gunter's.

"For once, the rumour is true." She paced again. "I went to see Tristan to ask him to stop his attack."

"I thought you would. So? Did he see reason?"

"Yes, he did." She tried to sound confident.

Jane frowned, sitting on the sofa in a froth of satin. "How? He looks like a dog with a bone. He never lets go. What did you tell him to convince him?"

"I asked very kindly."

The frown deepened. "I don't believe you. Besides, you're terrible at keeping secrets. That's why I don't tell you mine."

"Do you tell mine to anyone?" She stopped in front of Jane, a hand on her hip.

"I won't be offended by your question because I know you're worried about your father." Jane pouted. "I'm interested in gossip, yes, but I don't blabber about my friends. So do you think he's going to stop?"

"It's early days. We'll have to wait and see if he agreed only to get rid of me or if he meant it."

That seemed to soothe Jane's doubts. "Don't be disappointed if it turns out he tricked you."

"I won't." She would.

Jane stood up. "There's something else I need to tell you." It was Jane's turn to pace. "You know I'm not as good as you are."

Ha! If Jane knew what Effie had done, she would change her mind. "What did you do?"

"Nothing too despicable." Jane flourished a hand in the air. "I asked almost every one of my acquaintances about Montcrest."

Effie dropped her arms at her sides. "Why?"

"I was curious to know about that mistress of his. I thought that, if she was the Duchess of Norfolk, then your father's problems would be more difficult to solve. It was for a good cause. Although I wouldn't mind knowing a juicy piece of gossip about the duchess. It would be useful."

She was curious despite herself. "What did you find out?"

"He visited Chelsea more often in the past weeks, a seedy area, which was disappointing. I don't think his mistress is the duchess." Jane closed the door. "He visits a disorderly house. He is a regular customer of the place."

"Oh." Words failed her.

She didn't know what was worse, a mistress or a disorderly house. No, surely a disorderly house was worse. Tristan's past was full of hardship. He should know that the girls working in a house of ill repute were desperate, starving, and forced to do things they didn't want to.

Jane put a hand on her shoulder. "Just one word. Syphilis. And the clap. So more than one word. My point is, stay away from him. Also, it seems he avoids Dr. O'Neil, likely because he doesn't want anyone to know he contracted a nasty disease."

She wrung her hands. "Jane, I have a confession to make, too."

THAT NIGHT, sleep eluded Effie. She'd agreed to have a tumble—more than one—with a man who frequented a disorderly house regularly. Ethical matter aside, she didn't want to get any contagious disease. On top of that, Jane's reaction to her confession had been discouraging. Her friend had pointed out the consequences of nasty rumours about Effie's closeness to the marquess, picturing an apocalyptic future that had terrified her.

The next morning, her appetite vanished.

She was alone, twirling her spoon in her cup of tea in the dining room, ignoring the slices of bread, porridge, and kippers. Papa was already in his study, working with Lowe. Dr. O'Neil's recommendations to rest had fallen on deaf ears.

She sipped her tea, but her stomach closed at the sight of the porridge. She couldn't withdraw her proposal, could she? Tristan would start attacking her family again. But she was going to lose her virginity—likely affecting her future chances of a good match—and she didn't want to get the clap as well.

Voices and footsteps came from the hallway in a worrying repeat of yesterday. She perked up. What now?

Papa opened the door, an astonished look on his tired face. "He stopped."

"What?" She shot up, heart pounding in her throat.

"Montcrest stopped attacking my company and even reversed some of his financial moves. That gives me hope."

Tristan had kept his word. She had no choice but to go through with her deal.

"How? Why?" Papa ran a shivering hand through his hair. "I don't understand."

"He isn't as heartless as you think." Although she wasn't sure he would have stopped without her intervention.

He hugged her, laughing in relief. "I can't believe it. I thought he was going to destroy me. Maybe you're right about him."

"But you must promise me you'll rest and follow Dr. O'Neil's instructions religiously."

"Yes, yes." He laughed again, and she would love to laugh with him, but while the news made her happy, anxiety formed a tight knot in her belly.

If she had to be completely honest, she found Tristan attractive, and he was clever and charming when he wanted to be. But she'd agreed to be his mistress under duress. Not exactly the romantic story she hoped for.

Too late now. The deal had been done.

<h1 style="text-align:right">twenty-seven</h1>

The evening arrived too soon for Effie as she started to get ready in her bedroom.

The news that Papa's finances were safe triggered a fresh flurry of activities in the house with Lowe going up and down the corridor, carrying stacks of papers, Doyle busy showing people into Papa's study, and more letters arriving every other minute.

In the midst of the chaos, a message for her from Tristan had been delivered to her without raising questions. He informed her he'd taken every precaution to protect her identity and keep her presence in his house a secret. She hadn't even thought about that.

Kettle had vanished again, annoyed by the commotion. Instead, Pepper had been so excited he'd dropped exhausted in her bed and slept soundly. She didn't even have the loving support of her pets as she got ready to see Tristan.

Her maid helped her don a fine Oxford blue gown with a silk overskirt and velvet rims. Her hair was styled in luscious curls, tied with silk ribbons matching her gown.

She wanted to make an impression, as silly as it sounded. Why she was putting so much effort into getting dressed, she had no idea. He would remove every item of her clothing five minutes after she arrived. The thought shouldn't be thrilling, but it was.

When Jane arrived to accompany her, she was as ready as her anxiety allowed, officially to go to the opera with her friend. Jane would leave her alone in Tristan's house, and then a cab would drive her home later. Simple plan, with lots of complications.

In the carriage driving her to Tristan's house, Jane stared at her from the opposite seat with disapproval. "Are you sure this is a good idea?"

"No. But I'm not going to be his mistress. This deal is different. It's something more civil." If she kept repeating that, she would believe it.

"Since I'm your accomplice, I want to make sure nothing terrible is going to happen to you."

"Tristan would never hurt me." That much she knew.

Jane took her hand. "I promised to help you, and I will. But think about your reputation."

"Not again."

"It doesn't matter how kind Montcrest is to you. Your chances of finding a good match will be gone the moment people gossip about you and him. Or worse, you'll become a spinster and not even a respected one."

A choking sensation got caught in her throat. If that future was the price for saving her Papa, then so be it.

"Nothing will happen if nobody knows what I'm doing. We have an arrangement to make my visits completely secret. He will have the back door left open for me, and no servants will be around. I'll enter without anyone knowing it."

Jane huffed. "Do you trust him? Even if he doesn't talk, one of his servants might."

Surprisingly, she trusted Tristan. He might be ruthless but was an honest man. "I do. I can't let him ruin my family."

"He will ruin *you*."

She pushed that horrible possibility out of her mind.

"I'm not simply talking about your reputation," Jane insisted. "You aren't the type of lady who doesn't care about an occasional tumble. You care deeply. I'm worried about how you will feel afterwards. You'll believe you're in love with him."

For some reason, Jane's words bothered her. A tumble wasn't enough to fall in love. If anything, his vulnerable side—the one he kept hidden—was a better reason to fall in love.

The carriage came to a stop in front of Tristan's house.

She inhaled deeply, smelling her cinnamon perfume mingled with London smell of burnt coal. "I need to go."

"Send for me if you need anything."

"Thank you."

"Thank you my foot." Jane rested her chin on her fist. "Anything can happen to you when you are alone with him."

She blew out a breath. "You're exaggerating. But I appreciate your concern."

"If you get hurt because of him, he'll get hurt because of me."

Tristan wouldn't hurt her. She was sure of that. But her pulse raced faster when she left the safety of the carriage.

"Do not worry. I'm perfectly safe."

"You're my best friend," Jane whispered. "The only person who never judges me or talks behind my back. I've never told you how much I care about you."

Effie hugged her. "Thank you for your support."

Jane patted her back. "You should carry a knife, just in case."

With those last reassuring words, Effie entered Tristan's house.

twenty-eight

Tristan fixed his white bow tie in the mirror again and straightened the silver forks on the table. Not that they needed to be straightened. Harris had made sure the silverware were each set at the perfect distance between each utensil and the plates.

Being alone in the dining room was a novelty. Usually, there were at least three or four people, even when he ate on his own. Harris and a footman would always stand next to him, ready to serve. But he'd promised Effie discretion. The table had been set before her arrival, and the food was warm and ready to be served.

He paced the entry hall until a knock on the door stopped him.

He wasn't ready. Perhaps he should call the deal off and let Effie be free of him.

He opened the door and she swept into view, taking a shy step inside. His breath caught. Her capelet was open on the front, showing her Oxford blue gown. It had a plunging neckline and a fitted bodice that emphasised her curves and lovely eyes. The diamond studs on her lobes and silver silk slippers made her look like a spectacular winter starry night.

Everything about her was spectacular, from her luscious chestnut curls to the way the top of her breasts lifted with each breath. Her lips looked glossy and plump, and her cheeks showed a delicate blush he found irresistible.

She quietly entered and shut the door. "Good evening." Her voice sounded small.

"Welcome."

As they stared at each other, he'd never felt as small and insignificant as in that moment. She was all golden light and brightness while he belonged to the shadows.

"Follow me." He led her into the dining room, with its soft candlelight and intimately set table.

She gazed around before tugging at her capelet. He rushed to help her and take the soft garment off her naked shoulders.

"Thank you." She handed him her purse as well.

He didn't know what the hell to do with them, so he laid everything on a stuffed chair, turning his back to her to collect himself. "I trust you didn't have problems coming here."

"Not at all."

The swish of fabric came. He faced her again. "The soup— What the hell are you doing?"

She was unbuttoning her dress. The sleeves already sagged down her arms.

She stopped, staring at him with unblinking eyes. "I'm getting ready."

"For what?"

"For...you know." Her face flamed red.

"For hell's sake." He released a breath through his teeth. "I'm not an animal."

He buttoned her up and pulled up her sleeves, making a mess. The satin was slippery, and the damn buttons were small and covered in silk. Not to mention that he caught a glimpse of her corset, which threw kerosene on the fire of his passion. If she undressed in front of him, he would kiss her and send for the vicar to marry her.

"You don't have to remove your gown."

She frowned in concentration as she finished buttoning her gown. "I don't understand."

He stretched out an arm towards the lovely table. "I want to have dinner."

"Before we go to your bedroom?"

"No." He held a chair for her. "There will only be dinner tonight."

Her frown deepened.

"I'm serious. Just dinner," he repeated. "I'm not going to touch you." As much as it pained him.

"I don't understand." She sat down, head tilted up to stare at him.

"I want to have a nice dinner with you. That's all." Although from that position, standing behind her, he had an enticing view of her décolletage.

His fingers itched to stroke her creamy skin.

He served the soup, being careful not to spill anything. During his family's hardest years, he'd learnt how to cook and serve. For the first time in his life, he was grateful for that.

She shifted on the stuffed chair. "But..."

"Yes?"

"I thought you wanted to have a tumble," she whispered the last word.

"I do. More than anything. But we can spend some time together first and be civilised about our deal."

"I think it's a great idea."

From her shaky voice, he didn't understand if she meant that.

He watched her from his chair when she picked up the spoon as if it were a weapon.

"It's not poisoned," he said.

She let out a chuckle. "I'm nervous."

"So I gathered." He took his napkin. "Enjoy your dinner."

She tasted the soup and paused. "It's delicious." She sounded as if she expected the opposite.

"Windsor soup. My cook's speciality."

"My compliments to your cook." She took small spoonfuls, pausing often.

"You don't need to stand on ceremony here with me," he assured her. "If you're hungry, enjoy the dinner. You don't have to impress me. You already have." He didn't mean to sound so solemn, but he was nervous, too.

She smiled, and her whole expression changed. She relaxed her posture and enjoyed larger spoonfuls of the soup. The crackling of the fire filled the silence, and he wondered again if he should call the deal off and just have dinner with her.

He poured her a glass of wine, and she sipped it, half-closing her eyes.

"Papa told me you reversed some of your financial actions recently," she said, drinking more wine.

"I'm a man of my word." He shared a long stare with her and was glad she didn't cower.

"Thank you."

"I did it for you, certainly not for him. But you made me realise I was going too far. Still, I don't believe in your father's innocence."

"That's the whole point, isn't it?"

"Yes."

A hint of sadness greyed her voice, and he regretted having brought up the subject. She helped herself to a slice of roast beef with asparagus and boletus porcini, another Cook's masterpiece. She nodded when she tasted them.

"You like mushrooms," he said.

"Love them, and these are exceptionally good. We often searched for mushrooms with my siblings in the country." She let out a little moan when she drank the wine. "This wine is wonderful. What is it?"

"A rare Château Latour 1890 from Bordeaux. Those vineyards had a very cold spring in 1890, but the weather in autumn was excellent, not too cold, and not too dry, which resulted in the best vintage in over three decades. It has a strong..." He chuckled. "You probably don't care about these details."

"Quite the opposite. I don't understand anything about wines, but I'm an expert in what I like. And I like this wine very much." She took another sip. "Perfection, especially with the meat and mushrooms. What were you saying?"

"Château Latour is a powerful wine, rich and full of flavours, with cassis and leather notes."

Her smile became wicked. "That's how I would describe you."

"I wouldn't complain. I would be afraid you might use other adjectives."

"No, I think I changed my mind about you." She stared at him for a long, intense moment before returning to her dinner. "And which wine would I be?"

"A Gewürztraminer. It's sweet with rose and peach notes, but one has to be careful because sometimes it stings."

She laughed, a full, rich sound that made him laugh, too. "Now I'm curious to taste this wine. Do you have a bottle?"

"I do." He rose and left the room, careful to close the door behind him. He entered the drawing room and rang the bell. His butler arrived a moment later.

"My lord."

"A bottle of our best Gewürztraminer."

Harris left. Tristan waited for him in the corridor. His butler had likely guessed who the secret guest was, but he'd promised Effie discretion.

Harris returned with a chilled bottle of wine. "My lord."

"Thank you." He was about to leave but paused when Harris smiled. "Is something the matter?"

Harris shook his head. "I'm glad to see Your Lordship happy."

"Do I look happy?"

"Very much, my lord."

He pondered Harris's answer, not sure about what to say. "Thank you."

Harris's affection was something he would never take for granted again. So far, he'd dismissed his butler's concern. Not anymore.

Harris bowed his head. "You're most welcome, my lord."

When Tristan entered the dining room, Effie was halfway through her roast beef.

"Here we are." He poured her a glass, releasing the sweet fragrances of the wine. "We should wait before drinking it to let the wine breathe."

"The scent is lovely."

He placed the plate with cuts of cheese next to her. They were supposed to be for later after the dessert, but they would taste great with the wine. "Try it with these."

"I didn't expect such royal treatment." She bit into a piece of cheese before sipping the wine.

"As I said, I'm not an animal."

"I know, but the deal was clear, and I thought you wanted to do the deed as soon as possible. Heavens, this wine is delicious." Her cheeks were flushed.

"We agreed to seven days of being in bed together. So tonight's dinner doesn't count."

She remained silent for a moment before she burst out laughing. "You're a skilled negotiator."

"I learnt the trade one battle after another. And I would never make you uncomfortable."

"Well, tonight, I'm very comfortable." She popped into her mouth another piece of cheese.

He poured himself a glass of wine and watched her going through the dessert with gusto.

"Do you miss living in the country?" he asked.

"Very much. I could do whatever I wanted there, but then Papa remained alone in London after my elder siblings got married, and I decided to keep him company. As the youngest daughter of thirteen children, no one supervised me in the country. I mean, our governess and nanny were so busy they didn't control me as they should have. My sisters and I loved running around without shoes. Papa hated that, but Mama said it was good for the feet. In fact, I have strong feet." She kicked off her shoes and wiggled her toes. "I can pinch people with my toes. Do you want to see it?"

He lowered his glass, perplexed. She had always been bubbly and talkative, but her speech was now a little slurred. The two empty glasses of wine in front of her pointed at the obvious, although the glasses hadn't been full to start with, and she'd been eating while drinking.

He put down his glass. "Are you used to drinking wine?"

She laughed. "Of course. Mulled wine, every Christmas."

Bloody hell.

She went to fill her glass again, but he stopped her.

"Let's stop drinking wine for now."

She pouted. "But I want another glass. I haven't finished the cheese."

"What about some fresh air?" He rose and helped her out of her chair.

She staggered on her feet. "Fine, but I'm not putting my shoes on."

"Lovely." He held her by the waist and led her to the set of double doors opening to the garden.

The fresh air carried the scent of the honeysuckle and wet soil. London contributed to the bouquet with the smell of coal.

She sighed and sagged against him. "It was a little warm inside. This is better." She snuggled closer to him, triggering a shower of shivers down his back.

"Yes, much better."

They went down the short flight of stairs to the paved path. The starry sky was generous with its silver light, and the fresh breeze was heavy with the scent of the flowers.

"Do you feel sick?" He caressed the top of her head.

Her eyes looked droopy. "Not at all. But my head is a little light."

"I'll take care of that, too."

He walked along the paved path through the flowerbeds. The movement and the fresh air should help her feel better. He would ask for some strong herbal tea as well.

Her soft body pressed against his. She probably wasn't aware of what she was doing. Certainly, she had no idea of the hot turmoil her casual closeness ignited inside him. Guilt stung him because he was enjoying a gift she didn't mean to give him.

"Do you still want to marry me?" Her voice came muffled.

"Yes, although you don't know everything about me. If I learnt something about myself and you in the past months, it's that, while I still wish to marry you, I might not be the right person for you."

She raised her big eyes to him. "Why? What big secret are you hiding?"

"If I told you, it wouldn't be a secret."

She exhaled. "If it's your visits to the disorderly house, I know everything about them."

"That's interesting because I don't know anything about them."

"You can tell me the truth."

He helped her sit on a marble bench under a willow tree. "I don't go to a disorderly house. That's the truth."

"So you lied about having a mistress. She's the Duchess of Norfolk, isn't she?"

He just about suppressed a laugh.

"Effie." He took her chin gently, wanting her full attention.

"As I told you, I don't have a mistress, least of all the Duchess of Norfolk."

She leant into his touch. "You seem honest."

"Because I am. I barely know the Duchess of Norfolk."

"So what's this big secret?" she asked.

"Something darker than a mistress and dirtier than a house of ill repute." He caressed her chin. Her skin was so silky that not kissing it required all his control.

She frowned. "You don't gamble, don't attend opium dens... what can it be?"

"Nothing worth mentioning."

"At least I won't get the clap."

He laughed, his belly hurting. "I don't carry diseases." Not in his body, at least. "You have nothing to worry about."

She rested her head on his shoulder, and he wrapped an arm around her waist. They stared at the stars in silence. He hadn't stared at them in years, yet they'd patiently waited for him.

"May I ask you something else?" she asked.

"By all means."

"Is it true your father mistreated his workers?"

He sighed. "At the beginning, Father wasn't careful with his employees. Yes, he was brutal, which started several arguments between us. It took a while, but he changed his way of dealing with the workers."

"And you?"

"No. My workers are well paid and enjoy two days off every week, and I pay for their medical bills."

"Wonderful!" Her surprise pleased him.

"And while we're talking about my father's business, no, he didn't use any tricks to get the infamous deal your father complains about. He simply made a better offer. Your father believed my father wouldn't pursue the deal, showing gratitude for the fact he'd helped us in the past. Winchester didn't take the deal seriously. That's all."

She snuggled closer to him. "I believe you."

"I'm glad to hear that." He smiled. "How's your stomach?"

"I'm not going to throw up. My head is less light, too."

"Good. I'll have an herbal tea brewed for your head. It works better than any hair of the dog."

"I'm full of hairs of a dog."

He released her, smelling her scent on his jacket. "I'll be right back. Stay here."

"I'm not going anywhere."

Those were the most wonderful words he'd ever heard.

twenty-nine

Effie wasn't drunk. Although she'd never been drunk, so she wasn't sure what being drunk felt like. But aside from a headache and a sense of fullness, she was fine.

She wiggled her toes on the pleasantly cold grass in Tristan's garden lit by the stars. What an odd night. She'd expected Tristan to bed her quickly, grunt, and leave, as the horses did. Instead, he'd been nothing but kind to her, and she'd enjoyed one of the best dinners of her life.

He seemed sad. Whatever his dark secret was, it tore at his soul, and she was sorry for him, even though he'd tried to destroy her family.

"For you."

He returned with a steaming cup on a tray. And maybe she was a silly, sentimental woman, or maybe the wine was affecting her, but the gesture cracked something within her.

She wished people saw how kind he was.

She took a sip of the tea. The scent of lemon and bay leaves filled her senses. There was a hint of honey and vanilla as well. Everything Tristan had given her to drink or eat tasted delicious and sophisticated.

"This is really good," she said.

"I like good food."

"Why are you so kind? I offered you myself, and we agreed on a deal, but you aren't taking advantage of it." She put the mugs on the armrest to cool.

He sat next to her. "I told you why."

"Or maybe you don't fancy me as much as you told me."

His eyebrows shot up. "Excuse me?"

The wine had untied her tongue, and she wanted to tease him. "It's a reasonable doubt. You can be honest. I won't be offended."

"Let me be completely clear." His expression was hurt. "I have never wanted any woman as much as I want you. That hasn't changed, and it's not going to change even after this deal is over." His voice had a husky quality that stirred something in her chest and lower.

For a split second, a vision of him lying on top of her and whispering those words in that voice filled her mind. And heat flickered again.

She was curious to see what type of lover he was. One didn't grow up on a farm without learning a thing or two about mating habits. She'd seen it all. Well, almost. And her sisters had often talked about their experiences at night when they'd been supposed to be sleeping. Some lovers weren't generous and didn't care about their partner's pleasure. Others were caring and gentle.

She found it difficult to place Tristan in one of those categories. He was both dominating and caring at the same time. But her sister Mary had told her that men could be completely different in bed from how they behaved in their everyday lives, and she had never understood what that meant.

"I shocked you," he said not without kindness.

"Surprised. No one has ever told me anything like that."

A sad smile tugged at his lips. "I'm glad to be sensible and sensitive enough to understand how special you are."

"I feel dizzy all over again." And hot.

"When you're ready…" He gently took her hand and opened her palm by caressing her fingers. "When you want it too…" He planted a soft kiss in the centre of her palm, lingering enough to make her feel his velvety lips. "I'll show you exactly how much I want you. Until then…" He closed her fingers over the kiss he'd left on her palm.

Her whole body trembled; it was an explosion of warmth and excitement.

A tingle waltzed on her skin. The spot he'd kissed pulsated as if the kiss were alive. She'd never felt so beautiful and desirable.

He caressed her closed hand before releasing it.

"I might be ready now," she whispered.

He traced the curve of her cheek with a fingertip, sending another quivering shot through her. "Not tonight. When you are completely yourself."

She did feel peculiar, and he stared at her with too much desire for her not to burn with excitement.

"We have time." He stopped touching her, and she nearly begged him not to.

The tingle intensified and became an insistent pulse that turned into a nagging feeling. She wanted him to kiss and touch her. Her whole focus was on the sensations he might give her.

That wasn't how she'd expected the night to go. She'd thought he would have bedded her, and then she would have looked forward to leaving him and forgetting about the whole thing.

Her wishing to be touched and kissed by him hadn't been an option.

She sipped the tea not to say something she might regret, and the tea was indeed excellent. Her head cleared, too.

"Better?" he asked.

"Yes. I'm afraid tomorrow I'll have a terrible headache." A breeze cooled her skin, making her shiver.

"No, you won't. Drink plenty of tea, and you'll be fine." He stood up and gave her his hand. "You should go home."

She didn't want to go home. How confusing. She took his hand, and together they walked back to the balcony.

"Don't your feet hurt?" He held the door for her.

"No. I have strong feet." She wiped her feet on the rug before putting her slippers on.

He was gallant enough to help her don her capelet. "Are you warm enough?"

"It's a bit chilly. But I don't mind. It helps with my head."

"I'll hail a cab for you." He escorted her downstairs and to the street.

No servant was around, as he'd promised. He helped her into the cab, his sapphire eyes capturing hers. They no longer were cold or distant but ablaze with care and longing, and she felt their warmth.

"Is there something you want to tell me?" she asked, sitting in the cab.

He sucked in a breath and parted his lips, but then he shook his head. "Good night."

"You can tell me anything." She meant it.

His sad smile returned, and for some reason, it pained her. "Get warm and sleep well."

She kept staring at him as the cab drove on. He stood on the pavement, engulfed by the shadows, but she could swear his eyes were glowing.

thirty

Tristan had been right. The next morning as Effie was sipping her morning tea in the sunroom, no headache bothered her. But something else did—a combination of regret, a vague sense of guilt, and a good dose of longing.

Before last night, she'd never considered her feelings for Tristan. But he'd stirred a certain desire in her. A desire that didn't want to leave her, thanks also to a sense of curiosity and tenderness. The good wine had nothing to do with her desire because she was well and sober after a surprisingly restful sleep.

The sunlight didn't hurt her eyes as she'd feared. But her thoughts jumped around, as Kettle did when he was nervous.

Jane came right after she finished her quick breakfast. Her stomach wasn't upset, but her appetite wasn't great.

After Doyle served a fresh pot of tea for Jane, they were alone in the bright sunroom.

"How do you feel?" Jane searched her face, likely for signs of a lie or a disease.

"I'm fine. You don't need to worry."

Jane folded her hands on her lap, as if gathering her patience. "He behaved, didn't he?"

"Tristan was nothing but a gentleman." She couldn't completely remove the disappointment from her voice.

"So you don't have to see him again. It's done."

She opened her mouth and closed it again. They hadn't discussed their next meeting. She would remember that, wouldn't she? Was the deal done and dusted? He'd told her that when she was ready, he would bed her, but that was rather vague.

She needed to see him and clarify the details. "I need to get ready to leave."

"To go where?" Jane looked shocked.

"A walk." She waved in the direction of London. "Somewhere."

Jane's shoulders lowered with a long exhale. "You don't fool me. Isn't it too early to see him again?"

"Perhaps yes, but I need to understand a few things."

"Effie, please, you must think about the rumours."

A flare of annoyance hit her. "You really should stop worrying about rumours and gossip. You know, all your accusations against Tristan, all the rumours you heard about him are false. He doesn't have a mistress and doesn't visit a disorderly house. Also, he doesn't mistreat his workers. Spreading lies is dangerous and unfair."

Jane looked flustered. The colour of her cheeks matched her red velvet gown. "I'm trying to help you."

"And I appreciate it, but I don't think that constantly listening to rumours or worrying about what people think brings anything good. And one shouldn't foment rumours that might prove to be wrong."

"I'm careful about what people say. Is that a crime?"

"Yes, if you make your decisions only worrying about rumours and not about what you want."

Jane scoffed. "I see you're in a foul mood." She rose. "Good luck with your endeavour. I don't think you need me." She headed for the door.

"Jane, please."

Too late. Her friend left without a second glance.

A few things Jane had told her about Tristan were true; others weren't. But that wasn't the problem. She didn't want to spend her life being careful not to start rumours about herself or worrying about what people would think.

Her deal with Tristan was dangerous, but rumours were the last of her problems. Her heart worried her more.

She chose a light purple gown with a lilac underskirt and a matching hat and heart pendant. In the country, there were few occasions to wear beautiful gowns, and she started to appreciate them. She wanted to look her best, lest Tristan think last night had worn her out.

No, she was lying. She wanted to see the hunger in his blue gaze again. He hadn't touched or kissed her, but she was already a wanton woman.

Harris didn't bat an eye when he let her in. Either he wasn't aware she'd been in the house hours ago, or he was a good actor.

"Lord Montcrest, please." She removed her gloves, pretending this was a perfectly normal call.

"My lady." He showed her into the drawing room and left.

He returned to serve tea.

"Is Lord Montcrest busy?" she asked.

"He's with Mr. Fleet. I don't believe it will take long, my lady."

"And Lord Rowan?"

"In the sitting room, my lady."

While she was there, she might see how Rowan was faring.

She went down the corridor and knocked on the sitting room door. "Rowan? It's me."

"Lady Effie." Rowan smiled. "I'm happy to see you." He was still using the crutches.

On a table, a shiny new copy of *A Textbook of Horseshoeing for Horseshoers and Veterinarians*.

She rushed to it. "This book is wonderful."

"A present from Uncle George. He said I'm going to be a great veterinarian."

"And I agree. How are you doing?"

His smile disappeared. "Dr. O'Neil has just left. He removed the cast. Do you want to see the wound? I know you won't faint. Harris became green when he saw it, and Uncle George was deeply upset. I would like to know your opinion."

"Of course."

He sat on a chair and uncovered his leg, revealing two long scars crisscrossed with stitches. "It's horrible, isn't it?"

"No. Considering what happened to you, the leg is healing well. May I?" She warmed her hands.

"Please."

She touched the scars and the flesh around them gently. "There's no swelling, and the bone seemed perfectly healed."

"That's what Dr. O'Neil said, but he didn't tell me if I would be able to walk again without crutches. What do you think?"

She hesitated before talking. The last thing he needed was false hope. "Animals are different, and they walk on four legs. Human anatomy is quite complicated when it comes to ankles."

"So I'll limp forever." He covered the scar.

"No, I didn't mean that. You're young and healthy. With time, the leg might work perfectly well."

He sagged back into the chair. "I hope it will when my mother returns."

That surprised her after what Tristan had told her. "Your mother is coming?"

He blushed. "I don't know. One day, she'll come and see me, and I don't want to give her a new reason to leave when she realises her son can't walk."

She took a deep breath not to let out a sob. Tristan hadn't told her the full story, but from what she'd garnered, the chances Rowan's mother would return were close to none.

She squeezed his hand. "A mother doesn't care about a bad

leg." She wanted to say more, that a mother would love her child unconditionally, but Rowan was a bright young man. He would understand she was listing all the qualities his mother didn't have.

"Why did she leave?" he whispered. "Was I such a terrible son—"

"No. I don't know her, but I know you. You're a lovely, clever young man, and any woman would be proud to call you her son. It's not you. She must have had her reasons, but they had nothing to do with you."

His eyes shone with unshed tears. "May I hug you?" he whispered.

"Of course, darling." She pulled him closer and held him.

He swallowed a few times as she patted his back. Her house had always been full of children, but her parents had never neglected them, no matter how difficult thirteen children were to handle. Yet Rowan had never experienced a mother's affection and likely a father's either.

The footman cleared his throat discreetly from behind her.

She was startled.

"Peter." Rowan wiped his eyes quickly, releasing her. "I didn't hear you coming."

"My lord, Mr. Trowbridge is here for your French lesson," Peter said.

"I'm ready." Rowan stood up and gripped his crutches. "If you want to see Tristan, he's in his study. You'd better knock and enter. When he's working, he forgets about the world." A hint of sadness laced his words.

"I will."

"Thank you." He gave her a shy smile.

"You're most welcome."

After Rowan left, she walked to Tristan's study and paused before knocking. The door stood ajar, and Mr. Fleet's voice came from the inside. So he was still there.

"Why did you change your mind? We were so close!" Mr. Fleet said.

"I made my point." Tristan sounded calm and composed.

"I don't understand you."

"I don't expect you to."

"Tell me what changed." There was the sound of a fist thumping wood.

"This conversation is pointless." That was Tristan.

They exchanged a few more words but too low for her to understand. And she was eavesdropping.

She was about to return to the drawing room when Mr. Fleet flung the door fully open.

He paused when he saw her. "Lady Effie."

She greeted him with a nod.

"Effie." Tristan smiled, brushing past Mr. Fleet and showing his dimples. His eyes lit from within, not with desire like last night, but with happiness. "Harris told me you were here. I'm sorry to have made you wait."

"I didn't mean to disturb you." She didn't know if she should leave or not.

Mr. Fleet shifted his gaze from her to Tristan. "How is Lord Winchester?"

"George," Tristan said in a warning tone. "I believe you are leaving."

"I believe I got the answer to my question. My lady." He walked along the corridor.

"Please." Tristan invited her to his study, and it wasn't as she'd pictured it.

The room was wide, filled with brown furniture, and flooded with light from the large windows. The smell of worn leather wafted from the books and chairs, and brass lamps were scattered around. She wanted to lie on the chair, put her feet up on the desk, and read a book.

"Did I interrupt something?" she asked.

"Yes, thank goodness." He crossed his arms over his chest, carelessly handsome. "I trust you feel well."

"The herbal tea worked wonders." In the bright sunlight flooding the room and in her very fine but tightly buttoned gown, coming here sounded like madness.

She should have stayed home and waited days before talking to him again, instead of chasing him like a lovesick girl.

"What is it?" He offered her a chair, but she didn't sit.

"I was wondering..." She would sound like a woman obsessed with him if she asked him when they were going to meet again. "I would love the recipe for last night's pudding, the one with the cherries on top."

Pathetic, but that was the best she could do without being prepared.

He gave her one of his *what do you mean?* looks. "You came here, first thing in the morning, to get the recipe for a pudding?"

"Yes. No, actually, I saw Rowan, and I would like to see Zeus." That was a better excuse, but too late.

"You don't have to come here to see Zeus and ask for my permission. You can go to the stables directly."

On second thoughts, that wasn't such a better excuse.

"Yes, well, thank you." She would be the first woman to have died of embarrassment.

He flashed one of the charming smiles he reserved for her only. "What did you want to tell me?"

She scratched her ear. Better to be honest. "We didn't discuss when we were going to see each other again."

"Are you eager to?" He tilted his head, and his golden hair caught the sunlight.

"Well...I'm busy, so very busy." She fiddled with her gloves. "I need to plan ahead."

His chest rose with a breath. "What about tonight? Dinner. No wine."

She pouted. "No wine?"

"It would be better for you."

A laugh almost escaped her. "So you still want to see me? I thought I bored you to death."

He stepped closer, and the wide room suddenly became a cupboard. "Why wouldn't I want to see you again?"

"I wasn't sure after I made a fool out of myself."

He took her hand, the one he'd kissed last night, and traced the heart line slowly with a finger. "I believe I was clear about my intentions."

A fluttery feeling started in her belly. "I wanted to be absolutely sure."

"Then let me repeat them again." He kept caressing her hand. "I don't want anyone as much as I want you. You are the last woman who should doubt her charm." He placed her hand over his chest where his heart was thundering.

His heart pounded against her palm as if the heartbeat were a shout of longing. What was happening to her? She'd never felt so desirable as she did now. One word from him, and all her doubts about what was right or proper, vanished in a puff of smoke.

But it wasn't just that. Her pulse spiked as well when he was close. She'd always found him handsome, but now she noticed a sweetness about him that made his beauty special, more intimate.

"You didn't make a fool out of yourself," he whispered in a voice that promised all sorts of wicked things. "You were lovely."

A soft moan was the only thing she could produce. Great.

"I'll see you tonight then." He kissed her knuckles, and she couldn't stop a smile.

"Tonight."

thirty-one

Tristan met his valet's gaze in the wall mirror as he got ready for another dinner with Effie. A dinner that made him more nervous than it should. After she'd left him desperate to take her, he'd been too agitated to sit and work, and there was only one solution for his troubles. He'd gone to The Octagon.

James glanced at the large bruise on Tristan's ribs and winced but didn't say anything.

The last session in The Octagon had been intense. A blow to the head had left him dizzy and queasy. The stab of pain in his lungs every time he inhaled hinted he might have broken a rib or two. But the last thing he wanted was his physician preaching to him about changing his lifestyle. Or worse, a dose of laudanum. The pain kept his inner turmoil quiet and his mind sharp. Laudanum made him numb, and numbness was the feeling he hated the most.

Not feeling anything was the closest thing to death.

"My lord, you might want an extra layer for the..." James cleared his throat. "There are a few cuts on your back that might bleed, and you don't want to stain your shirt."

"You didn't have problems removing the stains in my other shirt, did you?"

James inhaled. "It was a challenge, my lord."

"Fine. Add another layer."

"Of course." James helped him wrap a large bandage underneath the shirt and the jacket.

In his fine tailored jacket, white shirt, and bow tie, no one would guess his body was covered in dark bruises and almost broken. His need for The Octagon had increased recently. He had to go more often, stay for longer, and feel more pain. After the incident at Aldersgate Station, the twitch tortured him.

"You're ready, my lord." James dabbed Tristan's jaw with a warm, wet cloth, removing the tiny traces of shaving cream. "If I may."

Tristan shot him a glare. "What?"

James swallowed a couple of times. "I know it's not my place, but you probably should see your physician."

"*Should*? I shouldn't do anything, and I don't want to have this conversation ever again."

James nodded, but he didn't miss his valet's exasperated expression.

He'd thought being with Effie would have calmed his temperament. But seeing her without the freedom to touch her as much as he wanted only made him feel more guilty and desperate.

The dining room looked pristine with the white tablecloth, the white lilies in the vases, and the white candles burning softly—a stark contrast with the constant dark anxiety raging inside him.

Harris was finishing arranging the terrine and dishes on the banquet table. "My lord, everything is ready."

"Thank you, Harris." He looked out of the window at the lanterns glowing in the garden. "You may retire."

The butler paused at the door. "Mrs. Newton prepared an arnica salve for your...condition."

Calling his addiction to The Octagon *'condition'* irked him; it made the situation weigh down on him with too much strength.

"I don't have any condition," he said.

Harris didn't flinch and left a jar on the table. "With all due respect, we're all worried about you."

"That's not what you're paid for."

"Some duties have nothing to do with our salary."

Pain stabbed him in the ribs, forcing him to control his voice. "I'm fine. Thank you. You may leave."

The disappointed look in Harris's gaze was another source of pain.

Harris left quietly, but his words lingered in the room like an unwanted guest. The other night, Tristan had promised he would change his attitude with his servants, but the damn twitch made him grumpier than usual. A headache bothered him as well.

His hand shook when he poured himself a glass of water. His household had decided to preach to him. He didn't need anyone's help, least of all the help of people who wouldn't understand what he was going through.

He grabbed the pot with the white salve. The scent of flowers tickled his senses. He opened the window and was about to lob the pot into the hedgerows when a hand touched his arm.

"Tristan?"

He spun around, startling Effie who leapt back. He hadn't heard her coming.

"I called to you, but you didn't hear me." She frowned at his hand gripping the jar. "What were you doing?"

He fiddled with his collar and put the jar on the table. "I was distracted."

She kept frowning. The beautiful lime and tea rose pink gown gave her an ethereal, sweet aura, like a spring fairy, which was exactly what he needed to silence his anxiety. And he would rather cut off his left bollock than scare her.

"Is everything all right?" A long chestnut curl bounced over the crook of her neck, touching her creamy skin.

He'd never been jealous of a curl of hair.

The temptation to wrap the curl around his finger to straighten it, only to see it curl again, was too strong. He gently rubbed the curl between his thumb and forefinger, feeling how silky her hair was.

"I don't feel like myself tonight." The small, vague confession cost him energy and control.

"Would you like me to leave?"

"No." He held out a chair for her. "Please stay."

She sat down in a swish of silk. "You look tense."

"I am, but don't worry about me." He poured her a glass of elder water. "I'm glad you're here."

She put a hand on his, right over his scratched knuckles. He could avoid being hit in the face and could hide his body, but the bruises and scratches on his knuckles were in plain sight.

"What happened to your hands?" she asked, her voice sweet and soft like her touch, but devastating like a blow.

"I box regularly."

She stroked gently the fresh bruises. "So does my brother Frank. He was a boxing champion at Cambridge. But I've never seen him with such angry bruises on his knuckles."

"It's nothing." He'd said that countless times to everyone who had shown concern about his health and bruises.

But that night, the familiar words left a bitter taste in his mouth. He could easily lie to Harris, James, George, or Rowan. He couldn't easily lie to Effie.

"I don't believe you," she whispered, still touching his hand. "I can recognise brutal trauma when I see it. You don't box with gloves, and bare-knuckle fights are illegal. But why would a marquess, who can do everything he wants, risk life and limb in an illegal fight?"

He stared at his glass of water, a sense of shame gnawing at him as never before.

"And then there was that cut I stitched," she continued. "Tell me the truth."

"There's nothing to tell." He didn't sound confident to his own ears.

All those people worrying about him were chipping away at his composure.

On top of everything else, the headache pounded at the base of his neck and sweat damped his back. His sight darkened at the edges with a pulsating black halo that made him queasy.

"Please, Effie, let it go."

But she didn't. She kept caressing his hand. "This is the first time you've said please."

"That tells you how much I want you to stop questioning me."

She closed her hand around his. "There's something else I recognise, something animals and humans have in common. Fear. The eyes of a scared animal are the same as those of a man. What are you afraid of?"

He couldn't breathe. The blow he'd received in the head was affecting him. He tried to take another sip of water, but the room suddenly became dark.

thirty-two

Effie stretched out her arm in an attempt to catch Tristan, but with no success. He dropped to the floor with a thud, face paling by the minute.

"Tristan!" She checked his pulse. It was very feeble.

She had no choice but to call Harris.

She rang the bell, but for good measure, she also shouted, "Harris! Help!"

The butler arrived in a moment. "My lady."

"Lord Montcrest collapsed."

"I'll send for Dr. O'Neil." He rushed out of the room and returned with a footman a minute later. They lifted Tristan up, taking him by the ankles and underarms. "Gently, gently. My lady, would you please open the door to His Lordship's bedroom? It's upstairs, the last one on the left."

"Of course."

They carried Tristan along the corridor and up the stairs, and the sight of his lolling head and motionless limbs made her catch a breath. For a moment, Tristan's bedroom distracted her in all its simple glory. Sturdy walnut furniture, no frills, and a bed so large it dwarfed the room.

They laid him on the bed not without effort, as Tristan was tall and broad.

Harris removed Tristan's bow tie. "I'll fetch some water."

"Yes, please."

As she waited next to Tristan, she spotted a new bloodstain on his shirt. What on Earth had happened to him?

Too worried to wait for Dr. O'Neil, she unbuttoned the waistcoat and shirt and lifted the undershirt, only to find a stained bandage. She removed it and gasped. Bruises at different stages of colouring covered his skin. Deep purple bruises, faded yellow ones, and cuts marred his torso around the cut she'd stitched.

"Good Lord." She shoved the layers of clothes aside, revealing more bruises on his chest, shoulders, and sides.

Not an inch of his skin was whole. She wondered if the outside was mirrored in the inside.

The bruise on his left side was too big and swollen not to have caused some internal damage. She gently probed the ribs, but the swollen area didn't allow her to feel the bones, and she wasn't a physician.

He stirred and blinked his eyes open. A flash of anger crossed his face. "What are you doing?" He didn't sound as angry as he looked.

"You passed out." She touched his nape. "My guess is that, before falling to the floor, you already had a concussion, and concussions and nervousness aren't a good combination. Your state must have exacerbated the dizziness, causing the fainting."

He gazed up. "Bloody hell."

"Harris sent for Dr. O'Neil."

"Damn." He rubbed his face.

"Hopefully, you can say more than profanities. I think we should send for the police as well."

"What?"

She gestured at the evidence on his body. "You were attacked. How many people beat you? Were they footpads? Did they rob you? Did they attack you in the past?" She clicked her tongue. "There are some nasty thugs around. You're lucky to be alive."

He exhaled through his teeth. "I wasn't attacked, and I don't want to see Dr. O'Neil."

"Your silly pride won't help you. Many people are attacked every day on the streets. There's nothing to be ashamed of."

"It's not pride." He propped himself up on his elbows, grimacing. "No footpad attacked me."

"Lie down, please. Your concussion seems serious." She put a hand on his chest, feeling the muscles as tense as ropes.

He rubbed his face again. "I don't need the doctor."

His face caught her attention. She leant closer and examined his perfectly healthy face. Aside from his pale skin, he didn't have any marks on his face. Odd. The footpads, who had attacked him, had beaten his torso into a pulp but had mercifully spared his face. No split lips, no broken nose or black eyes, and no scratches. Even bare-knuckles fighters got punched in the face.

"You don't have bruises on your face," she said.

"Exactly."

She was about to ask him what he meant when the doctor entered.

"My lord, Dr. O'Neil," Harris said.

Tristan threw a hand up. "Wonderful."

"What happened?" Dr. O'Neil eyed Effie. "My lady." He sounded as if he was unsure if he should acknowledge her presence or ignore her for the sake of her reputation.

"I'm fine." Tristan blew out another breath.

"A concussion," Effie said. "And a rib might be broken."

"Let me see." The doctor started to touch Tristan's head and nape.

Tristan shifted away from him. "I said I'm fine!"

"Tristan!" Effie shot up, fists clenched. "Enough with your attitude. You passed out, are covered in bruises, and have a bump on your head. Stop behaving like a petulant child and let Dr. O'Neil examine you."

Silence dropped in the room. Harris cleared his throat. Dr. O'Neil slanted a glance at Tristan.

"Your behaviour is irrational," Effie continued, ignoring his tense expression. "You obviously need medical attention and a scolding. Dr. O'Neil can provide the first, and I'll gladly give you the second." She turned towards Dr. O'Neil. "I'll leave the room, doctor. Perhaps that would make Lord Montcrest more comfortable. I doubt it will make him more sensible."

She walked out of the room with Harris without waiting for Tristan to say anything.

thirty-three

The moment Effie left Tristan's bedroom, she let out a shaky breath. Stubborn, impossible man. She was shaking from head to toe.

"That was brave of you, my lady," Harris said after he closed the door. "He needed a scolding."

She felt anything but brave. "When was Lord Montcrest attacked?"

"Attacked?" His striped eyebrows went up.

"Obviously, thugs beat him."

Harris clasped his hands in front of him. "His Lordship wasn't attacked."

"He said the same thing, which doesn't make any sense. How did he get those bruises? Although his face is strangely fine. I know he's involved in bare-knuckle fights, but not even illegal rings are that brutal."

He shifted his position. "I can't say more. His Lordship will tell you the whole story if he's ready to. Would you care for a cup of tea?"

"Yes, please."

Twenty minutes later, after a cup of excellent tea and nothing but silence from Harris, Dr. O'Neil called her.

"My lady." The doctor let her and Harris into the bedroom.

"How is Lord Montcrest?" she asked.

Tristan's jaw was so clenched she feared it might snap.

Dr. O'Neil glanced at him before speaking. "The ribs aren't broken, maybe badly bruised, but they should heal in a couple of weeks. The concussion will require a bit longer, three weeks perhaps. Every patient is different. I prescribed a balm to be applied to the bump and the ribs. Valerian for the pain, light food, and rest." He angled towards the scowling marquess. "If you can convince His Lordship to do so."

Tristan muttered something, but she ignored him.

"I can and I will. Thank you, Doctor. May I have a word with Lord Montcrest in private?" She waited for the butler and the doctor to leave before sitting on the bed next to Tristan. "The truth."

He looked as if he hadn't slept in weeks. "I told you the truth. I wasn't attacked."

"The second part of the story, then."

"It's not of your concern."

She thumped the bed. "Honestly, I have treated mules less obstinate than you are, and donkeys less an ass than you."

He worked his jaw. "You truly know how to make me feel better."

"I'm trying to help you, and before you say you don't need my help, let me tell you that you do. Or you wouldn't be in that bed now, looking like my grandfather after a bout of pneumonia."

He pinched the bridge of his nose. "You're going to despise me," he whispered.

"Not if you tell me the truth. I could never despise you." She put her hand over his, careful not to touch his bruised knuckles. "Trust me and tell me everything."

There was a long pause, and she feared he wouldn't say anything.

He lowered his gaze. "As you guessed, I box in an illegal ring."

The bedsheet covered the mess on his torso, but the sight of his bruises was well imprinted in her memory.

"How many times do you box?"

He lifted a shoulder. "When I want to."

"Why an illegal ring? You must be a member of some fancy gentlemen's club where you can box every day in complete safety. Why not go there and be safe?"

"Exactly." He opened and closed his hands. "A proper club doesn't give me the same thrill."

"I don't understand."

"Years ago, I was attacked by a group of anarchists. They beat me within an inch of my life."

She held his hand, feeling his tendons tense. She expected him to slide his hand out of hers, but to her surprise, he gripped it with his strong fingers. "I know about the incident."

"I spent months in the hospital in a deep sleep. After I recovered, for a long time, I was easily startled and scared of walking alone at night. I hated feeling so vulnerable and frightened. The wounds healed, but from that moment, something changed in me. I started boxing to learn to fight back, and I found that I enjoyed the pain. Now I need the pain. I crave it."

Her throat became dry as she tried to understand how anyone could enjoy the pain. "You go to this illegal ring not to fight but to let other fighters beat you until you feel pain?"

He nodded without looking at her. "It's called The Octagon and is under a house of ill repute. I guess that's why there are rumours about me visiting such a place."

She took a moment to ponder his words. What was she supposed to say to someone who enjoyed feeling pain? She had no idea such a condition existed. Addiction to pain wasn't any different from addiction to opium. Both of them led only to one end.

"I understand it's shocking," he said.

"Terrifying more than shocking."

His Adam's apple bobbed on a swallow. "If you don't want to see me again, I won't blame you."

"I've never said I don't want to see you again." She held his hand in both of hers. "But Tristan..."

He stared at the bed canopy. A tear welled in his eyes and refused to trickle down.

"Look at me."

He turned his sad eyes to her. He had nothing of the usual cocksure marquess who tossed orders around. He was a vulnerable soul, filled with pain and loneliness, but stubborn enough to refuse her help.

"You must stop." Her voice cracked as the possible outcomes of his addiction filled her mind.

"I can't."

"Yes, you can. One day, you'll be punched too hard, fall to the floor, and never get up again. One day, you won't recover from an injury."

He shrugged as if it didn't matter.

"Honestly, I want to slap you, but you would enjoy it." A sob broke free of her. "What will happen to Rowan?"

"He's a clever boy. He'll be all right."

"He lost his father. His mother abandoned him, and he still hopes she'll return one day. Of course, he won't be all right without you. I won't be all right without you."

A flicker of life lit his gaze. "You don't even like me."

"That's not true. I wouldn't be here."

"You're here because you're worried about your father and made a ridiculous deal with me."

"I'm here because I'm worried about you."

"Effie." He blinked, but that tear didn't want to slide down. "Quitting is more difficult than you think."

"I'll help you." She sniffled. "We'll find a way. Next time you feel the need to go to the ring, you'll send for me, and we'll be together until the need is gone."

He flashed her favourite crooked smile. "I don't think it's that simple."

"Well, you might want to show a more positive attitude for starters, instead of being so pessimistic. That alone would do wonders."

He gave her an elegant nod. "Fair point."

"In my parents' estate where I grew up, we had a cow who was frightened of thunder. Every time there was a storm, she would kick and hit her head against the wall. The poor thing hurt herself. So I stayed with her every time it thundered, holding her with a rope quite firmly. It took a while, but she overcame her fear of thunder and had never hurt herself since."

"Fascinating story, but—"

"No but." She'd had enough of his '*but*'s. "You must be hopeful. That's the first step. I won't let you destroy yourself because I care about you."

Finally, that tear spilt and rushed down his cheek as if in a hurry.

She cupped his cheek. "I care about you, Tristan."

Was it so important for him to hear that?

"Promise me you'll do everything to stop this madness." She brushed his cheek with her thumb. "Promise me."

Another tear slid down. "I feel no motivation to do so. There isn't anything in my life that excites me or makes me happy. Aside from you."

"That's a start, and I'm here for you. We'll find something that replaces hurting yourself, something safer. And you sound very ungrateful. Rowan loves you. Harris cares about you. I care about you. And frankly, I'm disappointed you don't find me exciting enough to make you stop."

He flashed his sad smile. "Another fair point."

"Good. What do I have to do to convince you? Shall I kiss you?" She meant it as a joke, but why not?

The change of his mood was immediate. His eyes brightened with attention, and blood returned to his cheeks. Even his lips became an intense pink, catching her eye.

Heat stirred inside her as his gaze dipped to her lips.

"Do you mean it?" he asked in a low voice.

"Yes. If a kiss will convince you to try, I'll kiss you."

"Another negotiation." He pressed his cheek against her palm.

"Negotiations seem to interest you."

"You interest me more." His eyes locked on hers, and she couldn't gaze away.

She inched closer, smelling his cologne mingled with the disinfectant the doctor must have used. He slid his long fingers to her nape with infinite tenderness, sinking them in her curls. A flare of heat made her dizzy as their lips became a feather apart.

"You must promise me," she whispered against his lips.

"Anything you want." He brushed his lips against hers in a gentle stroke that fuelled the heat inside her like a breeze on a fire.

She shivered at the contact. He repeated the gesture, light and gentle, until she moaned. When he pressed his mouth against hers firmly, sensation exploded below and spread through her body. With his hand on her nape, he guided her closer, and that was the only warning she had before his velvety tongue demanded entrance.

She yielded immediately and trembled again when he explored her mouth with slow lashes of his tongue. Her toes curled, and a fierce hunger reared its head within her. He kissed her faster but was always careful to make her feel everything, every detail of the kiss.

The heat of his expert tongue made her inner muscles clench

with anticipation. He kissed her thoroughly and desperately, his chest brushing hers.

He trailed his fingers down her neck to her breasts until he found her nipple. A breath rushed out of her when he teased her nipple with his thumb. Liquid heat pooled between her legs. Sweet sensations took control of her body, prevailing over reason, and she surrendered willingly.

If he weren't injured and tired, she would beg him to take her.

He broke the kiss slowly, scattering little kisses on her lips and chin and stroking her nipple. His breathing came out ragged, just like hers.

For a long moment, they didn't speak, but their hearts were having a conversation made of fast pulses and loud thumps. He touched his forehead to hers, his nose brushing hers.

"Are you going to stop boxing illegally?"

"Yes." He didn't hesitate.

A riot of sensations washed over her, from triumph to a sense of power that worried her, and sheer joy.

"Then stop. Please. You would make me so happy."

He held her face in his ruined hands. "I will. I promise."

She wrapped her arms around his neck and hugged him, careful not to hurt him. He hugged her back and buried his face in the crook of her neck.

She made a promise as well. She would care about him and help him along the way because leaving him alone wasn't possible. How could she have ever thought him cold and unfeeling?

He was the opposite. Tristan felt too much, cared too much. And she cared about him, too.

thirty-four

Be hopeful, Effie had told Tristan last night.

He felt anything but hopeful the next morning, still lying in his bed. At the moment, only shame filled him; it overtook the physical pain.

But he was a man of his word; he'd promised her he would stop, and he would do his level best to honour his promise. That didn't mean he was enthusiastic about the future although a future where Effie kissed him was worth fighting for.

He stared at the bed canopy and relived the kiss. Just thinking about her sweet lips made his desire sizzle; it was a fire so deep he felt it in his soul.

Pain lanced through him when he inhaled, and his head ached. Deep down, he agreed with her and with all those people who had pointed out the risks of his habit. He'd reached his limit in The Octagon.

The first times he'd gone there, a few punches had done the trick. Now he needed more violence to silence the twitch.

In the middle of everything that had happened last night, Effie's presence in his house was no longer a secret, and he blamed himself for that. Everyone, aside from Rowan, knew she'd met with him in secret. Her reputation was at risk, and it was his responsibility to keep her safe.

The door opened a few inches, and Rowan poked his head inside. "May I come in?"

"Yes." He pulled the cover up to hide his bruises.

Rowan manoeuvred himself with agility, despite the crutches. He'd learnt to use them well. "How are you?" His voice was guarded.

"Just a few bruises and a headache."

His brother sat on the chair next to the bed. "Harris said you need rest because one of your ribs might be broken."

"I'm fine, Rowan."

"What did Lady Effie say about your illness?"

He perked up. "What?"

"She was here last night. I saw her. I woke up because I heard loud voices, and she was speaking louder than anyone."

"Great." He rubbed his temples. Even Rowan knew.

"What happened to you?"

"I hit my head when I was boxing." That at least was true.

Rowan narrowed his blue eyes so similar to his. "Where were you boxing?"

"It doesn't matter."

Anger contracted Rowan's face. He gripped the armrests. "I'm not a child. You can tell me the truth."

"You don't need to know everything about me."

"You never tell me the truth." Rowan's cheeks reddened. "When Mama left, you told me she would be back. But she didn't come back. You said something must have happened to her, preventing her from coming back. And she still she didn't come back. When I mention her, you never say anything. But I'm not stupid."

"I've never thought you were."

"She will never come back, will she?"

Tristan felt a knot of emotion in his throat. Last night had started a change within him, and now he couldn't stop tearing up. He must have suppressed his emotions for too long because now they were exploding under the pressure of his control.

He put a hand on his ribs. "Can't we have this conversation another time?"

"No." Rowan stood up, balancing his weight on his good leg. "I want to hear from you that my mother abandoned me forever, and I want you to tell me what happened to you."

"What good would that do?"

"You owe me." A sob escaped Rowan. "For all those times you were away or were angry or too busy. Do you want to know why I'm scared of you? Because you never look happy! What can be more frightening than someone who's always angry and so sad?"

Maybe he was still recovering from last night's turmoil, but all his defences were gone. Rowan's words cut him deeply. Every emotion was as vivid as the pain he so much favoured. Whether he preferred the pain or this raw emotional onslaught was debatable.

"I worked a lot, and I'm sorry if I neglected you, but everything I did, every hour I worked, I did it for our family." He wouldn't deny being sad.

"No. You did it for yourself and your obsession with rebuilding our fortune."

"I care about our family more than you can imagine." His voice broke.

"Say it." Rowan's voice was icy cold, and Tristan wondered if he had the same tone when he was angry. "Say that my mother will never come back."

"I don't want to hurt you."

"Uncle George told me it wasn't his secret to tell, but he was also honest and said not to hope for her return. Why did she leave? Why? Because of me?"

"Hell, no!"

"Then why?" Rowan stomped a crutch on the floor. "Why?" He stomped the crutch again.

"She had a lover!" The harsh words came out of his mouth before he could stop. He should have been gentler. But then again, that could be said about everything he'd done.

They stared at each other in silent shock.

"I'm sorry," he said. "I shouldn't have said it like that."

Crying in earnest now, Rowan snatched his crutches and started to walk away, but he lost his balance and fell over.

Tristan shoved the covers aside, rushing over to Rowan, ignoring the pang in his ribs. "Let me help you up." He bent down and took Rowan's arm.

"No." Rowan shrugged himself free. "You've never cared about me because we don't share the same mother."

"That's not true. You're my brother. I love you."

Rowan wiped his face and tried to stand up but paused when he noticed Tristan's bruises and bumps, or at least those the bandage left visible. "Who did that to you?"

"I did." If his brother wanted the truth, then he would give it to him.

"What do you mean?"

"I box in an illegal ring to feel pain."

Anger returned quickly to Rowan's young face. "You do that on purpose?"

"Yes."

"I don't understand."

"Neither do I."

Rowan studied the injuries. "You could die."

He stretched out his arm. "Rowan—"

"Don't touch me!" Rowan scrambled up to his good foot and walked out of the room as fast as the crutches allowed him.

He slowly sat down on the floor, his back against the bed. He'd horrified and hurt his brother, and he couldn't blame Rowan. He was horrified by himself.

That realisation hurt him deeply, and it wasn't the type of pain he enjoyed.

thirty-five

The argument with Rowan kept worrying Tristan for the whole day.

He winced as he got dressed with his valet's help. Effie would be there soon, and he didn't want to spend another day in bed when the sun was shining. The more he lay in bed, the more dark thoughts gathered in his mind like stormy clouds.

"I've almost finished, my lord." James brushed Tristan's dark jacket and straightened it.

The valet was paying extra care, careful not to accidentally hurt him.

"Thank you, James." Tristan angled towards his valet. "I didn't mean to be harsh the other day."

James lifted a shoulder. "Nothing to worry about, my lord. I understand."

"Nevertheless, thank you."

James nodded, radiating happiness.

Once ready, Tristan paused in front of Rowan's bedroom and peeked inside. His brother was studying at his desk, hunched over a book.

He knocked. "Lady Effie is coming here today. Would you like to see her?"

"Maybe. I have to study. Uncle George should come soon, and I want to go to the stables." Rowan didn't turn around.

"We should talk." He stepped closer.

"When I'm not busy." Rowan made '*busy*' sound like a hiss.

A protest died in his mouth. He guessed he deserved the cold treatment. He must have said the same thing to Rowan countless times.

"I do care about you. I didn't prove it, but I'll do better in the future. I know I disappointed you, and I'm sorry."

Footsteps approached, and George appeared from the stairs. "Morning, Tristan."

"George." He hoped to avoid another endless discussion about his health and his passing out.

But George didn't speak. He put a hand on his shoulder and gave it a light squeeze. Tristan nodded, understanding what George meant. His friend was there for him.

George turned towards Rowan. "How's my favourite lad doing?"

Rowan's face transformed from serious to cheerful. "Homework. Maths." He waved a notebook.

"It's your lucky day. Maths is my favourite subject. I'll help you." George sat next to Rowan, and the two started chatting and laughing.

Tristan released his frustration with a long breath and walked to the door, but as he left the room, he caught Rowan watching him.

He went down the stairs one step at a time both because of the pain and because he didn't want Harris to send for Dr. O'Neil again if he fell.

"My lord." Harris waited for him at the base of the stairs, and Tristan was glad that the butler didn't hurry to help him. "Lady Effie is in the garden. I'll serve tea in the sunroom."

The thought of seeing Effie sent a jolt of energy through him. "Excellent." He missed the last step and slipped, but Harris was there to steady him with a gentle grip.

"Thank you, Harris." He clasped the butler's arm.

"I'm here for you, my lord, as always. I promised your late father I would watch over you."

Maybe it was the kind tone with which Harris said that, but Tristan had to blink to clear his vision. He'd been a cold-hearted bastard with his servants.

"I know, and I'm grateful for everything you do."

Harris smiled as James had done, a bright, wide smile of happiness.

They remained still for a moment, smiling at each other.

"Lady Effie is waiting, my lord." Harris's voice cracked.

"Thank you."

Effie stood in the sunlight amongst the bushes of tulips. She turned when he stepped outside. Her light yellow gown had a matching underskirt with a fringe rim that undulated every time she moved, catching the light.

Finally, a sense of calm eased the tension in his shoulders. "Effie."

She raked a gaze over him, a clinical gaze, not a ravishing one. "How are you?"

"Better. My head still hurts, and the ribs sting, but I feel more rested." Even his confusion started to settle, and the constant rage was quiet, silenced by the affection everyone around him showed.

She hooked an arm through his and started promenading along the path. "I thought about you a lot."

He sucked in a breath. "Did you? I thought about you, too."

"Oh, I thought about you, but I also did my research," she said, blushing. "Don't be disappointed. It's the scientist in me. I'm compelled to open a book to find answers."

"You could never disappoint me. The important thing is that

you thought of me." He fought the urge to kiss her. "Research on what?"

"Your case."

He angled towards her. "Am I a case now?"

"Medically speaking, yes." She released his arm to rummage through her pocket and fish out a notepad. She showed him a page packed with unreadable notes, arrows, and too many exclamation points. "I read about the case of a pig—"

"Excuse me?"

"Oh, shush." She waved at him, and he couldn't help but smile. "There was a special pig for competitions. He won twenty-two national pork awards."

"You're pulling my leg."

"No." She scowled. "He was a famous animal. They called him Mr. Barry, the envy of many farmers. Anyway, he too had trouble overcoming his fear of loud noises, which was an impediment to his competitions, and once again, he was cured with controlled restriction and by the owner keeping him company during a crisis."

"And?" He paused to watch the flight of two blue butterflies. He'd never noticed them in his garden.

"That would be something we want to try."

Her '*we*' brightened his day more than the sunlight.

"You want to tie me down," he said in a teasing tone.

She let out a nervous chuckle. "No, no. What an idea."

He pinned her with a glare, feigning to be outraged.

"Well, it's an idea." She closed the notebook with a snap. "I want to help you. That's all."

"And I appreciate it. Even though you've just compared me to a pig."

"Mr. Barry, a national champion."

He laughed but had to stop when the pain in his ribs became too sharp.

She wrapped her arm around his again. "I can't imagine how you must feel to enjoy pain and crave it."

He put a hand on his aching ribs. "I don't enjoy every type of pain. If I fall from my horse and hurt my back, I feel nothing but annoyance. There are moments when I become nervous, and restless energy torments me. At first, I thought doing something physically exhausting would help. It did for a while, but my body demanded something more each time. Something more intense. The relief lasted for shorter times." He lowered his voice. "My visits to The Octagon have become more frequent as of late."

Compassion softened her features. "I would like to see this place to understand what it's like."

"No. It's not a place for you. Once you see certain things, you can't forget them."

"I'm hopeful." She brushed his hand, sending a shot of desire down his back that wasn't completely pleasant. "If a pig made it, so can you."

"Thank you for the encouragement," he quipped. "I feel much better now."

She laughed, and he enjoyed watching her so carefree.

"Thank you." He squeezed her hand. "Your help means a lot, especially now."

"You look sad. Is something the matter?"

"Rowan doesn't want to talk to me." He followed two squirrels rushing up a tree. Again, another surprise. He didn't know there were squirrels in his garden. "He knows about me, knows I lied to him about his mother, and he didn't take it well."

"He's a sensitive boy. Give him time. Would you like me to talk to him?"

"I would be grateful. Mostly, I'm concerned about him."

"I'll do my best."

thirty-six

Effie had been too quick at offering her help with Rowan. Harris had told them Rowan had gone to the stables, and she'd been hopeful at first, thinking that talking with Rowan among the horses would be easy.

But the moment she stepped into the stable and saw Rowan's grim face, she doubted she could convince him to talk to his brother.

Balancing on one crutch, he was brushing Zeus's mane without enthusiasm. She glanced behind her. Tristan was talking with the stable master, his posture slacking now and then, likely due to the pain. No groom was close, so she and Rowan could talk undisturbed.

"Good morning, Rowan." She stroked Zeus's muzzle, and he replied with cooing, happy noises.

"Lady Effie. Zeus is in great shape," Rowan said.

"How's your leg?"

He set the crutch aside and stood on his own two feet. "I can put my weight on it, but not for long, and at night it hurts."

She handed him the crutch back. "Tristan told me you're angry with him."

His expression hardened in the same way Tristan's would. She hadn't noticed how similar the two brothers were when angry until now.

"I guess you know what he does to himself," he whispered.

"I'm trying to help him stop, and your help would be much appreciated."

He put down the comb and caressed Zeus's neck. "He doesn't need me. He never has."

"You're wrong. You mean the world to him."

"Then it has to be a very small world."

"Give him the chance to show you how much he cares."

Rowan took the other crutch. "He had many chances, but he never told me the truth about my mother. I'm tired of being treated as if I didn't exist."

"You're wrong. Tristan loves you very much. He didn't talk about your mother because he wanted to protect you."

"You're very good, Lady Effie, but I don't trust him. If you'll excuse me, I need to sit." He walked away, brushing past Tristan, who had just stepped into the stable, without sparing him a glance.

Dealing with animals was easier, which was curious since she couldn't share a conversation with them. Yet she understood a horse or a dog better than a human. Cats were a completely different matter, but Kettle could make himself clear when he wanted to.

Tristan joined her next to Zeus. The horse showed his delight by neighing happily and butting his head against his master's hand.

"Zeus adores you," she said.

"I wonder why." He kissed Zeus's muzzle.

"Because you show him your love."

He lowered his gaze. "No luck with Rowan, I guess."

"No. He thinks you don't care about him. I told him he's wrong, but he's hurting, and I believe it doesn't have anything to do with you."

"In a way it does."

A while ago, she would have mistaken his blank expression for disinterest, but she knew him better now. He was hurting, too, deeply.

She laced her fingers through his. "I wish I could be more helpful."

He drew in a breath at her touch, staring at her with his usual intensity. "You're more helpful than you think." His gaze dropped to her lips, and just like that, she was tingling all over, aching for his kiss.

She rose on her tiptoes and was an inch away from his lips before remembering where she was. The stable master was a few feet away, and the groom could appear at any moment.

"What am I doing?" She lowered her heels and stepped away from him.

He didn't take his gaze off her. "Now you know how I feel every time I see you."

She let out a nervous chuckle, her cheeks warming. "It's powerful."

"Trust me. I understand."

"I would really like to kiss you," she whispered.

He took her hand and gazed around, suddenly quick and agile. "Say no more." He led her towards the end of the stall.

"Where are we going?"

"Where I can kiss you without being disturbed." He paused before pushing a door open and released her hand. "You can either go or follow me." The hope she said *yes* rang out of his voice.

She'd made up her mind ten minutes ago. "Let's go."

Her heart raced when he showed a wicked smile. He held the door open for her and let her into a storage room filled with sacks of grains and stable tools. The smell of wood and hay thickened the air. Sunlight sneaked in through the gaps between the wooden planks of the walls.

He locked the door behind them, and the click caused a thrill to course through her. She shouldn't find being compromised so exciting.

"And now?" She pulsed and ached everywhere as he took her waist and lifted her, only to sit her on a worktable.

The effort must have hurt him, judging by how he grimaced for a split second. And that was the last rational thought she had before he pried open her legs and nestled between them with the confidence of someone who belonged there. She had time to draw in a deep breath as he cupped her face and kissed her hard.

Her legs tightened around him on pure instinct, and her back arched of its own accord. The tip of his tongue slid past her lips, and she didn't hesitate to open her mouth for him.

Anticipation urged her closer to him. She ran her palms over his chest without pressing too hard on his bruises, but his muscles tightened like ropes in reply. He slid a hand under her skirts and stroked her thigh.

In her past, there had been a few handsome boys living close to her house.

But she'd never, ever seen such intense desire for her in a man's gaze or felt such desire in a touch. Tristan's blue eyes burnt from the inside out for her only.

Even through her stocking, his warmth and strength reached her core.

He caressed her with devotion. His breathing quickened, but his caresses slowed. Each gentle stroke and brush of his lips against hers made her tremble.

His fingertips went up along her thigh and teased the garter. Then they trailed down, sending shivers through her body. Then up again towards her sensitive inner thigh.

Desire caused her to tense. The wait for him to touch her had a bittersweet taste. He paused and stared at her as if asking for her permission. She was bold enough to widen her legs a few inches.

He let out a groan of pleasure as he resumed his exploration.

But he had no intention of being quick. He traced the curve of her thigh, taking his time. Should she beg him or urge him to speed up? The combination of longing and slowness was difficult to handle.

"Please," she said, not caring about begging.

"Anything you want." He sounded rough and husky, and she loved it.

A gasp tore out of her when he finally headed where it ached the most. The fabric of her drawers chafed her skin all of a sudden, and the air was too hot. He rubbed a delicate spot on her inner thigh that surely hadn't existed until a moment ago.

He stared at her as he slipped past the opening of her drawers. Her toes curled. The touch was so delicate and small, but the pleasure was so strong that her head spun.

Every other sensation that wasn't Tristan's gentle touch vanished. Each stroke of his thumb sent goose pimples everywhere through her body. She wanted him to feel what she felt. So she slipped her hand between them, even though she wasn't sure about what to do.

"Guide me," she whispered. "Teach me."

"You're killing me," he said in all seriousness.

Without removing his delectable hand, he opened the falls of his trousers and gently slid her hand through. They both exhaled when she touched him. He showed how to stroke him while rubbing her. And suddenly the emotions were too much for her body. Between him touching her and she touching him, her skin became extremely sensitive and the temperature too high.

When he added another finger, she couldn't contain the burst of pleasure building up. She had barely time to clamp a hand over her mouth before a scream came out of her. He groaned deep in his throat, resting his forehead on her shoulder.

She sagged back, panting and wondering how she could lead a normal life after that monumental shift in her world.

He inched his hand out of her skirt, scattering kisses on her heated face. He wiped himself with his handkerchief, and she was too stunned and dizzy with happiness to offer help.

He kissed her again. Somehow, his musk was more intense than before.

"You're so beautiful I have no defence against you. Your kindness and brightness conquered every dark spot within me. I have nothing else to surrender. My heart is yours."

She didn't know how to reply to that, still reeling from the release. "Tristan, I'm yours."

He adjusted her skirts, exhaling. "I didn't plan for this. I didn't want you to experience this in a stable."

"I forgot we were in a stable."

"Still, I can offer something better if you want."

"I do," she said before she could think, but she didn't need to. "I trust you, Tristan."

He took her face and kissed her again with passion and determination, and she returned both of them because she wanted him as much as he wanted her.

She had no doubts about that.

thirty-seven

The thunder shook the night as Effie entered Tristan's house. After their passionate kiss in the stable, he'd asked her to come for dinner, and she'd accepted the invitation without hesitation. She hadn't thought about changing her mind. She'd made the decision, and that was it. No afterthought. Quite the opposite. She was eager to see him.

Their deal was still going on, and she couldn't be more pleased to fulfil it.

When she arrived, rain splattered against the windows of the dining room, distorting the view of the garden. The air was thick with his restlessness and the scent of white soup. Soft candlelight lit the room, but the atmosphere was far from calm. Tristan was pacing, raking a nervous hand through his hair. She didn't need to ask how he was faring.

She closed the door behind her, and he came to a grinding halt.

"Talk to me," she said.

"I know I'm ruining everything, but I want to go." His chest rose and fell quickly. "If you hadn't been coming, I would have left an hour ago."

"But I'm here, and you aren't going. Besides, your body hasn't recovered yet. If your ribs get punched again, they might crack and puncture your lungs." She hesitated to get closer, not sure how he would react, or if he wanted her closer.

"What triggered the need?" She removed her capelet, not waiting for him. "You were fine this morning in the stable."

"I don't know. I'm worried."

"About what?"

He raised his gaze to her. "You."

"Me? Why?"

"I fear I might lose you." His voice quivered. "Especially after today."

She ran to him. "I'm here. You aren't going to lose me."

"I can't control this fear." He drew in a few deep breaths. The hard lines on his face showed the battle he was fighting against his urge. "I want to go."

She took his hand. "Do you want to go somewhere else to distract yourself? Drury Lane, perhaps?"

He shook his head, gripping her hand as a drowning man would grip a rescuer.

"Music? We can easily find a concert in Covent Garden."

He turned his wild gaze on her. "Hit me."

"What?"

"Punch me." He pointed at his ribs, right over the biggest bruise. "Where it hurts the most, so you won't have to use too much energy."

"Tristan, don't ask me that."

"Just once." His pupils were dilated, and his breathing became uneven.

"I've never punched anything."

"It's not difficult." He took her hand and closed it in a fist. "Curl the fingers inwards and fold the thumb across the top halves of your index and middle finger to protect them." He touched her knuckles. "You hit me with your knuckles only."

"Tristan, I beg you. I can't do it."

"Just once." He sounded desperate.

She exhaled and withdrew her arm to get ready to punch him. He opened his jacket and spread his arms to make himself an easy target. A moment of silence passed. She punched him lightly.

"Harder," he said. "I didn't feel anything."

She tried again, feeling his hard muscles against her knuckles.

"Harder," he said again. "Don't be gentle with me."

"Tristan..."

"I need this." He was shaking. "I want you to be ferocious to me."

She released a shaky breath and tried again with more energy.

He scoffed. "Harder."

A flare of anger overcame her. "No!" She took a step back. "When I said I wanted to help you, I didn't mean by hitting you. You can't ask me that. I will *not* hurt you. And it's vile of you to ask me that. You must find the strength to fight this absurd craving of yours in another way, but I won't punch you."

His facial muscles tightened to the point his face transformed. The thunder roared, and a bolt of lightning limned his silhouette from behind.

"You promised," she said. "I trusted you."

Tristan strode past her and walked out of the room, leaving her alone with the storm and her failure.

Voices came from the hallway. A door was shut. Then Harris entered the dining room, his face as grim as the weather.

"I gather His Lordship decided to go, my lady."

A sob rasped her throat. "I couldn't stop him. I'm so sorry. How arrogant of me to think I could help him."

"Oh, dear lady." The butler crossed the room to stand close to her. "You didn't do anything wrong."

She cried in earnest. "But I didn't help him at all."

He touched her shoulder tentatively. "I beg to differ. He has made great progress since he spent time with you. I've been with the Montcrest family for almost fifty years."

She wiped her eyes. "Fifty?"

"I was thirteen when I started serving as a hall boy in this very house. His Lordship's grandfather was the marquess back then. I watched His Lordship grow up and went through the family's ordeal."

"Why didn't you leave?"

He poured her a glass of water. "The late marquess was a good man. He helped me when..." He straightened the plates and the forks. "I had a gambling problem."

Now she understood why Harris was so patient with Tristan. Gambling was an addiction, too.

He cleared his throat. "Another lord would have given me the sack and left me to my miserable fate. Not the marquess. He paid my debts and helped me get rid of that vicious habit. I owe him my life and dignity. I could never leave his son alone. Don't be discouraged, my lady. It'll take time, but with your help, His Lordship will get better."

She put her hand over his. "Thank you, Harris. You give me hope."

RAIN SLIPPED underneath Tristan's collar and down his neck. His suit was soaked through, and he was chilled to the marrow. Dawn was approaching with its cold light, and shivers caused his teeth to chatter.

He'd sent his coachman home hours ago and had wandered through London's streets since then, half hoping to be attacked by a footpad.

No such luck.

Still, the cold rain and the night's chill had a calming effect on his temper.

After he'd stormed out of his dining room and left Effie alone, he'd meant to go to The Octagon and lose himself. But Effie's words had haunted him and echoed in his mind without mercy, worse than his twitch.

It's vile of you. Absurd craving. You promised. I trusted you.

He'd been called worse things than vile, but the insult said by Effie had a deep, intimate effect on him. Try as he might, he hadn't been able to enter The Octagon. He'd wanted to go to the ring more than ever, yet his body had refused to move as if it'd reached a limit of pain and nonsense beyond which it wouldn't be pushed.

He'd sent the coachman home and walked under the rain all night, shivering and thinking, sometimes just shivering.

As a grey dawn rose behind the storm, a blushing light sneaked through the angry clouds.

He stopped at Effie's house. The warm yellow lights glowing from the ground floor were like a beacon. What he feared the most had happened. He'd dragged her bright light into his twisted world, and she'd put him in his place with her honesty. The least he could do was to apologise to her and hope she wouldn't tell him to rot in hell.

Not feeling very lord-like, he walked to the rear of the house and knocked on the back door.

A scullery maid opened it. "You can drop the—my lord!" She gasped and curtsied.

"I must see Lady Effie." He stepped under the door canopy to get a break from the pounding rain.

The maid twisted her apron. "My lord...this is..." She shouted over her shoulder, "Mrs. Young! Mrs. Young!"

"What is the meaning of this?" A tall woman with greying hair came into view. She fell silent upon seeing him. Her chatelaine stopped clinking. "Lord Montcrest. You're drenched."

He was growing tired of waiting, and shivering with cold didn't make him less irritable. "It's pissing down."

The maid and the housekeeper gasped at his oath.

"My apologies, but I need to see Lady Effie," he said again in a gentler tone.

"I beg your pardon, my lord, but this is most inappropriate," Mrs. Young said, seemingly petrified.

The maid nodded.

"Can we let Lady Effie decide?" He craned his neck to see past the housekeeper.

"Yes, of course. I was surprised..." Mrs. Young stepped back and forth. "Is Lady Effie up?" she asked the maid.

"She was served her breakfast in her bedroom a while ago. She didn't feel well enough to go down to the dining room."

"Send Rose to tell Her Ladyship that Lord Montcrest insists on seeing her now." Mrs. Young gave him a concerned look. "Would you like to wait here? Or perhaps you want to go to the drawing room?" She held the door open.

"Here is fine." He stepped into the anteroom to the kitchen, inhaling the scent of apples, tea, and fresh butter.

"Would you like a cup of tea, my lord?"

"No, thank you."

"Very well, my lord. If you'll excuse me." Mrs. Young hurried to the kitchen, leaving him alone.

Water pooled at his feet as he waited.

Voices came from the kitchen. Footsteps pounded, and then Effie appeared in a lovely light pink morning gown as beautiful as a fresh summer day.

"Tristan." She raked an assessing gaze over him as if searching for a bleeding wound. "Are you all right?"

"No." He brushed his wet hair from his face.

"What happened to you?"

A small crowd of servants gathered behind her, murmuring. His idea of knocking on the rear door had been a stupid one, but that wouldn't be the first or last stupid thing he'd ever done.

She cleared her throat. "Perhaps we should have a cup of tea in the drawing room. Please come through, so we can let the servants do their work."

He followed her across the kitchen, amongst the scandalised glances of the maids, footmen, and kitchen workers.

"You'll catch a cold in those wet clothes," she said, entering a warm room with large windows overlooking the glorious sunrise.

The early morning sun struggled to come through the clouds, but it was putting up a fierce fight against the bad weather.

A flurry of activities followed as a footman took his wet coat. The butler gave him a towel and stoked the fire without disguising his complete disapproval with a sour expression. When tea was finally served, he had the opportunity to talk to Effie.

"Do you need Dr. O'Neil?" she asked.

Steam rose from his clothes.

"No. I didn't go to The Octagon last night," he said, sipping his tea.

"Really?" A bit of colour returned to her cheeks.

"I walked in the rain all night." He wanted to say more, but those were words to be said when they had complete privacy.

Coming here like that had been a mistake. He couldn't expect to be left alone with Effie after such an entrance. The butler kept peeking inside the room, the footmen came and went every other second, and the voices from the corridor meant other servants were close. Not to mention Winchester might come in at any moment.

He put his cup down. "Forgive my rudeness. I'll go home now."

"You've just arrived."

"I'll see you later, I hope." He bowed low. "I shouldn't have disturbed you."

She followed him when he walked to the front door. "Tristan."

He took his drenched coat from the footman. "Yes?"

She glanced at the small army of servants hanging around. "I'll see you later."

thirty-eight

Effie hadn't found a free moment to see Tristan that day.

Pepper had suffered from a minor stomachache after having gobbled down some grapes he'd found in the garden. Kettle had brought a dead rat into the kitchen, causing Mrs. Young to have a fit. And her neighbour's dog had needed stitches for a minor cut.

She was about to finally leave her house when Jane walked into the entry hall, carrying Turi in her arms.

"Good afternoon." Jane's tone was cold. "I wouldn't have disturbed you if Turi weren't sick. Do you have a moment to examine him?"

"Of course." She removed her coat and resigned to see Tristan later. "What's the problem?"

"There's something in his mouth, again, and I can't remove it."

Effie put Turi on the table in the drawing room and opened his small mouth gently. A piece of red rubber was stuck between his molars. "Did he chew his rubber toy?"

"He did." Jane remained clipped.

"There's no need to be so cold." She selected a pair of small tweezers from her bag.

Jane squared her shoulders. "My best friend accused me of spreading lies."

"I only meant to say you shouldn't waste your life worrying about rumours since they usually turn out to be untrue or at the very least inaccurate."

Turi didn't like the intrusion of the cold piece of metal and started to move his head right and left. She had to hold his jaw while working with the tweezers.

Jane slouched. "I heard rumours about me after my visit to Montcrest."

"Really?" She grabbed the piece of rubber with the tweezers and snatched it off.

Turi worked his jaw as if he were chewing something, his upper lip curling.

"I would be happy if you were less worried about what everyone thinks. That's all." She petted Turi who was licking his lips and teeth. "Turi is fine."

"At least one of us is."

"What did they say about you?" She cleaned the tweezers.

"That I might have an affair with him." Jane's voice quivered. "I'm risking my reputation for no reason."

"Exactly my point." She snapped her medical bag closed. "Rumours can destroy people's lives."

"I think I understand now." Jane gathered her dog and headed for the door.

"Jane, don't leave like that."

"I need a moment alone but thank you. I mean it."

Effie rubbed her forehead. Perhaps she'd been bitter with her friend, but between her uncomfortable night and Tristan, her patience was spread thin. And it was only a matter of time before Jane got caught in a web of gossip, too.

By the time she entered Tristan's house, dusk crept over the streets still wet from the day's downpour. The rain had come and gone through the afternoon, and a red sunset bled into the sky scarred by dark clouds.

Tristan welcomed her in his study, pale and tense as if he'd just recovered from a serious illness.

"I came as soon as I could," she said, running to hug him.

"Thank you for coming." He held her close, his breath caressing her skin.

She released him to see his face. "Your visit took me by surprise."

He rubbed the bridge of his nose. "I shouldn't have come to your house like that. I'm sure I gave your servants something to chat about."

"You were very brave."

"Brave? Mrs. Young could be intimidating, I suppose."

She chuckled. "I mean brave not to go to The Octagon. When you left last night, I was angry with you, and I was certain you would have fought again."

He took her hand. "I shouldn't have asked you to punch me. I'm sorry. I wasn't myself."

"You were desperate, but you found the strength to stop yourself from going to the ring. I'm so proud of you."

"It was harder than I thought and draining." He touched his face again. "Look at me. I feel bloodless."

She wrapped her arms around him. His muscles were hard and tense, but his embrace was sweet and caring. He smelled of citrus and rain.

"What stopped you? Why didn't you go?" she asked.

"You stopped me. Your words tormented me until I had to listen to them."

She caressed his hair. The firelight hit his blond curls with red and golden hues. He closed his eyes as she tangled her fingers through his hair.

"I'm glad you listened to me," she whispered. "Do you believe now that you can leave this deadly need behind?"

He gave her a sad smile. "With your help, yes."

He traced her cheek, chin, and neck with a finger, his gaze lighting with a familiar hunger. Her spine wilted under his touch.

"I want you, Effie. I'll never grow tired of saying that."

Her reply was a sigh.

He kissed her cheek and the corner of her mouth slowly. "If you say yes, if you want to be with me, nothing will change. I'll propose anyway."

He didn't need that speech because she already knew that, and she knew herself well enough to get what she wanted. She wanted him.

"I say yes, Tristan. To you, to everything."

Tristan had found a new addiction.

Pain was nothing compared to his need to pleasure Effie. It was a longing so strong that it turned into starvation.

She had no idea how difficult it was to contain his desire for her.

Watching her bright eyes, flushed cheeks, and parted lips triggered a storm of emotions he had to rein in. Her '*yes*' filled him with hope and love.

Holding her hand, he led her to his bedroom, careful not to meet any servants. Before locking the door, he gave her another chance to change her mind.

"I won't disappoint you," he said. "But if you wish to leave, you have only to say it."

She shook her head. "Here is where I want to be."

The beast inside him purred in happiness. He locked the door and kissed her, feeling her soft lips under his. Ignoring the quick pang of pain shooting through his body, he gathered her in his arms and laid her in his bed.

That was where she belonged, in his bed, among silk pillows and soft candlelight, in his arms.

After bunching her skirts up, he caressed her lovely legs, and she rolled her hips, perhaps unaware of doing so. The sweet scent of her skin wafted from underneath the layers of silk covering her. Too many. He wanted to see her properly. He wanted to see if her whole skin was as pink as her cheeks.

He pushed her knees apart and filled the space with his shoulders. Alarm widened her eyes when he opened the slit of her drawers. He gave her a moment to realise what was coming, brushing her intimately. Her response was immediate. A ripple went through her, culminating in a soft moan.

The amount of pleasure he drew from that sound was ridiculous.

As she half-closed her eyes, he dipped his head. A jolt brought her hips up, and he had to put a hand on her thigh to steady her. He kissed her deeply again, feeling her sweet heat around him. Her legs hugged him tightly as he kept kissing her. She gasped, moaned, and writhed in a dance choreographed by passion.

When she shuddered, he scattered kisses to her inner thighs, making her feel the light graze of his teeth. He propped himself up on his elbows, needing to see her.

She was stunning. "Take your clothes off," she whispered her command, and he didn't think of disobeying it.

Her wide eyes stayed on him as he unbuttoned his waistcoat and shirt. His trousers slid down his legs with a yank of impatience.

"You're magnificent," she said.

Cool air touched his skin when he lifted his undershirt.

He even removed the bandage around his ribs but regretted it when worry lines appeared on her face.

"Oh, Tristan." She caressed his chest with her clinical touch, but it didn't last as she started to explore his body with curiosity.

He lay down, and her elegant hands on his chest left a path of fire on his skin. It didn't matter that her movements weren't expert; his body was turning into an inferno anyway. He trembled as she moved her attention south.

Each inch of him that she conquered brought a new ounce of light to his dark soul.

"I want..." The rest of her sentence was inaudible so low she talked.

"What?"

"I want to do to you what you did to me." She blushed a fierce pink. "Guide me again."

A stir of anticipation coursed through him like a bolt of lightning. He did as told and watched her as he gently led her down. He helped her when she dipped her head over him. When the velvety heat of her mouth closed around him, a primordial force stunned him. The sensation was too much, too intense, and too powerful.

Her soft tongue stroked him lazily, and her lips squeezed him. Like a lad at his first experience, the release came quick and merciless, intense, and absolute, like his love for her. He'd barely the time to move her away before he spilt.

She'd branded him for life. There would be no one but her.

Tristan's mouth brushed hers. It was a gentle touch but also a deceit because it hid all his passion underneath it.

He drove his fingers through her hair and kissed her deeply. She slid her hand between them, and he couldn't suppress a curse when she touched him again. His body was a rope taut with desire, and she easily undid him.

They tugged at her clothes together without talking, without explaining. Petticoats fell first, followed by her shoes and stockings. He paused only to caress her shapely legs and explore every curve and soft spot. How lucky he was to be able to touch her. Soft moans left her glossy pink lips as he touched her. He resumed undressing her and didn't stop until they were skin against skin.

She clamped her legs and arms around him, holding him so tightly that even the pounding of his heart became part of her. As did his soul.

"I'll wear a sheath," he said.

"All right." Pink spread across her face.

As he took the sheath out of a drawer, he gave her time to think about her choice once again.

She sat upright. Her lovely breasts bounced, and her taut nipples drew his attention. "I won't change my mind. I want you, Tristan."

He stretched out over her, propped on his elbows, and waited again. He would wait forever if needed.

She opened her legs further. "I'm yours, Tristan. There's nothing I want more than to be with you."

"You're going to kill me with your words." He ran a hand over her breast and rubbed her pretty nipple before sucking it into his mouth.

Her sharp intake of air made him smile against her skin. When she writhed and clenched her fists over the bedsheets, he lifted his head from her breasts.

He inched onwards as slowly as he could, watching her face closely for any signs of discomfort. Pain throbbed in his body, but he pushed it aside. The only good thing about The Octagon was that he knew how to manage the pain.

Then they moved together flawlessly as if they'd rehashed the movements for weeks on end. She followed his rhythm, undulating and arching with him. Their body had a conversation of mutual understanding easier than his attempts at explaining himself.

The feeling of her all around him was more intoxicating than any session at the ring, more satisfying than any end of a fight.

They stared at each other in the midst of their passionate dance. She was helping him even now, doing her best to follow him and making him feel safe. They found their releases at the same time.

She'd claimed his heart when she'd shown him compassion. She'd captured his body with her first kiss. Now she'd conquered his soul, fighting his need for the ring.

"I want to take an oath," he whispered, caressing her glorious chestnut curls. Her chignon had come undone between a thrust and a kiss, and he loved how her curls framed her glowing face. "I swear I want to marry you and spend the rest of my days with you. There will never be anyone else but you for me. I love you, Effie."

She pulled him down for a hard kiss he approved of. "You don't need to take an oath because I feel your words as fiercely as if you'd shouted them. And I'll be honoured to be your wife, my love."

He hugged her, shivering with happiness and hope. His heart burst with love, so much love he wondered how his body could contain it. In fact, he didn't want to contain it but spread it as much as he could.

thirty-nine

Tristan wasn't nervous to meet Winchester but not completely relaxed either.

He wanted to do his proposal right, and even though Effie had already agreed to be his wife, he would talk to her father, aware the conversation would likely end with a mutual *'go to hell.'*

He waited for him in the drawing room when she walked in, beautiful as always, in a pink gown with a tight bodice and roses embroidered along the hem. His chest became lighter.

"Papa is about to see you," she said in a low tone. "He isn't going to react well."

"I'm not here to ask for his blessing. I just want to inform him of my honest intentions."

She scrunched up her nose. "I'm not sure that is the right attitude."

"I'm counting on his gratitude for having stopped my attack on him." He fought the urge to kiss her.

She chuckled. "Definitely not the right attitude. Besides, you're behaving as he did when he believed your father would be grateful for Papa's help and leave the infamous deal to him."

"True."

She frowned, studying his face.

"What is it?"

"You're pale." She put a hand on his shoulder. "How do you feel?"

"Weak." He lowered his gaze. "And I hate it."

"I think you've never been as strong as you are now."

He opened and closed his hands. The cuts on his knuckles had healed, and even his ribs were better; he could breathe freely. But fatigue rode him hard.

"A gust of wind could break me. I don't feel strong at all."

"The first step is always the hardest, but you're doing so well."

"The next time it happens, I fear I might break." He brushed a curl of her hair from her cheek. "Maybe your idea of tying me down isn't so absurd."

"If you think it might help, we'll try it."

"Montcrest." Winchester narrowed his gaze at their closeness.

Effie smiled shyly, stepping back from Tristan. "I'll leave you alone."

The moment she left, tension snapped between them like a suddenly tightened rope.

"What's the reason for your visit?" Winchester sat on the armchair and vaguely gestured at him to take a seat.

"I'll go straight to the point."

"Of course you will."

He placed his arms on the armrests. "I want to marry Effie."

Winchester's twitching eyebrow was the only sign the news had shocked him. "Marrying her won't change the fact I won't sell anything to you."

He wanted to tell him he could keep that bloody piece of land and that marrying Effie wasn't a business operation. She was more important.

"I don't care about what you will or will not sell. My reason for marrying Effie has nothing to do with my business. I love her." He couldn't completely remove the frustration from his voice.

Winchester snorted a laugh. "You don't love anyone."

"I don't care about what you think. I came here out of respect and to inform you of my intentions."

"Good. Because you'll never marry my daughter," Winchester said in a too-confident tone.

"She wants to marry me as well. I'm not interested in her dowry. You can keep it."

"Money isn't the problem." Winchester stood up. His mouth twitched under his beard. "I'd rather not have my new son try to destroy me."

Tristan rose as well. "I stopped and even reversed my financial moves, and I did it only because I love Effie."

"Don't take me for a fool. You're still attacking me, Montcrest. Not as aggressively and openly as before, but you still are, and I'm still bleeding money."

"I'm not doing anything," he gritted out, doing his best not to show his surprise. "I am many things but not a liar. I'm not attacking you, Winchester. It must be someone else."

"What a coincidence! Two different people attacking me in the same fashion, in a short time. When you're ready to tell the truth, then maybe you'll be worthy of my daughter." Winchester rang the bell.

The butler arrived a moment later. "My lord."

"Lord Montcrest is leaving." He didn't wait for Tristan to say anything and walked out of the room.

Tristan exhaled. He guessed professing his innocence would be a waste of breath.

Effie walked to the hallway as a footman helped him don his coat. "How did it go?"

"Not well. But you know me. I don't give up. Ever."

"But is there hope for his blessing?"

He couldn't say he didn't care about Winchester's blessing because it would be a lie. He cared about her father's opinion only because she cared about it. "Someone taught me that there's always hope." He leant closer to kiss her, only to stop himself before the butler yelled bloody murder.

She blushed, her eyelashes fluttering. "That someone is very wise."

"And stunning. Very stunning." He touched the rim of his hat and winked.

❧

PEPPER BARKED at Kettle who was curled up next to Effie on the sofa in the library.

She raised her gaze from the latest issue of *The Swiss Archives of Veterinary Medicine.* Barks and hisses echoed off the ceiling. Now and then, a sharp claw or a white fang made an appearance.

"Pepper, stop this ruckus. There's enough space for everyone." She patted the empty spot next to her.

Pepper started to jump on the sofa, but Kettle hissed and hit his muzzle with a paw.

"Kettle!"

Pepper howled, outraged. The barking started again, along with hisses and the menacing glint of fangs.

In the chaos, she couldn't hear her own thoughts, much less read. She hadn't expected Tristan's proposal to go smoothly with Papa, but after his visit, Papa had left in a hurry without talking to her. She was disappointed. He should have found a few minutes for her and discussed the proposal.

Maybe her annoyance disturbed her pets. Growls and yowls were exchanged with lukewarm attacks. She was about to intervene again when footsteps approached.

"Effie!" Papa's voice echoed in the high ceiling.

The barking and hissing stopped.

She put a hand on her chest. "I didn't hear you, Papa."

"I'm not surprised. I called you, but you didn't acknowledge me." He sat next to her, taking most of the space on the sofa and ending the argument between Pepper and Kettle.

"I know what you want to tell me. I've waited for you all day." She put the magazine aside. "Tristan."

His expression hardened. "He had the cheek to come here and ask for your hand. Well, he didn't ask. He was merely informing me."

"Do you dislike him so much? I know he attacked you, but now the situation is different."

"No, it isn't." He rubbed his chest, and she worried he might suffer from another moment of panic. "I didn't tell you because I was too proud and didn't want to worry you."

"What?"

"He's attacking me again, chipping away at my company."

No, she wouldn't believe that. "I doubt that. It can't be him."

"It can't be a coincidence. Two people who try to destroy me financially in a short time." He scratched his beard. "Of course it's him."

She straightened her spine. "He isn't as cruel as you think. Quite the opposite. I mean to marry him."

"I will never agree." He meant it. His tone was implacable.

"Then I'm sorry because I love you, but I love Tristan as well."

He took her hand and stared at her as if she were a child again and being unreasonable. "He isn't the right man for you."

"Let me decide that. Please. You've always respected my choices."

"Marriage is forever. I don't want to see you hurt by a ruthless man who doesn't care about you."

"Papa." She squeezed his hand. "You're wrong."

"My lady." A footman entered, breaking the tension. "It has just arrived, my lady. A coach is waiting for your answer." He handed her a message.

"Who is it?" Papa demanded to know, releasing her hand.

She unfolded the piece of paper. Only a line from Tristan. *I need your help*. The breath flushed out of her lungs. He was going through another crisis. So soon.

"Tell the coachman I'll go with him immediately."

"What is it?" Papa tried to read the message, but she folded it.

"Horse emergency. I must go, or he might die."

"Effie—"

"It's important. I can't let him die. He's been under my care for a while." She kissed his cheek. "Don't be angry."

"I'm not angry. I'm disappointed."

That made her pause because it hurt. "I'm sorry, but I'm disappointed, too. You're behaving as stubbornly as Tristan did. He came here to talk to you and show respect, and you're using me to hurt him. But you're hurting me."

"It's the opposite. I'm trying to protect you."

"It's my life. I want to marry Tristan. Don't force me to do something drastic. And after the incident at Aldersgate Station, I confess I trust you less."

He blanched. "For the last time, I didn't lie."

"But you didn't change either." She left the room before he could reply.

She got her coat and climbed into the carriage in a hurry both because she wanted to see Tristan and because she was angry with her father. Her pulse raced as she thought of all the possible situations she might find Tristan in. If he'd been boxing again, he might have been risking his life.

What if he asked her to punch him again? No, he wouldn't, and she wouldn't do it anyway.

"My lady." Harris welcomed her with a concerned expression. "Thank you for coming. His Lordship is in such a state. He's in the small sitting room. He doesn't want Lord Rowan to see him."

"I'll do my best to help him." She handed him her coat.

"Bless you, dear girl." He widened his eyes in horror. "Apologies, my lady."

"No need to apologise." She touched his arm before running to the sitting room.

Tristan was pacing, his breath uneven and his pupils dilated. He'd dispensed with the jacket, and his waistcoat was unbuttoned. His rolled-up shirtsleeves showed his muscled arms.

"I'm here."

"Effie." He crushed her in a bear hug, wrapping his arms of steel around her. "I don't know what to do. I'm scared."

"Take deep breaths. I'll stay with you through it."

"Tie me." He shivered. "Unless you do it, I don't think I can stop myself from going."

She trembled with the force of his request. "Do you really want me to tie you down in your bed?"

"Yes." Pain laced his voice, and she nearly sobbed at his suffering.

She rang the bell and waited for Harris. "I need a long, thick rope."

Harris gazed from Tristan to her. "My lady?"

"Trust me. Please."

"Of course." Harris left, puzzled.

"You're very brave." She stroked Tristan's arm.

"I feel the opposite." His blond curls fell over his face, giving him a boyish look that made his pain more heartbreaking.

"Breathe."

He did as told, his chest rising and falling quickly.

Harris returned with the rope. "Would that be all right, my lady?"

"Perfect. Thank you, Harris."

The butler left again, but the worry lines on his forehead belied his mood.

She took Tristan's hand and went upstairs to his bedroom. He shivered as if he were freezing.

"The fact you sent for me is already a huge achievement," she said, but he didn't seem to hear her. "You should be proud."

He stretched out on the bed. "Please."

"As long as you're sure."

"Unless you tie me down, I'll flee the house."

She hoped she knew what she was doing. A thousand doubts assaulted her. She was applying methods used for farm animals to a human.

The idea was as unreasonable as it sounded. She swallowed a few times as she wrapped the rope around his wrist and tied it to the bedpost as if she were hitching her mare. She tied his ankles as well, checking the rope didn't bite into his flesh too hard.

Only one hand of Tristan was free, lest he feel too constricted.

Growing up close to farm animals had taught her the importance of well-done knots. She would have never imagined she would use that knowledge on the man she loved.

He tugged at the rope. "It's tight."

"Too much?" She moved to loosen the knots, but he shook his head.

"No. That's what I need."

She really hoped he was right. "I'll stay here with you." She sat on the bed and took his free hand, getting ready for a long night.

forty

Sweat dampened Tristan's neck and back as he lay in his bed. The bed where he'd had the best experience of his life with Effie.

She was next to him, reading a book out loud for him. She'd thought listening to a story might distract him, rather than lying and staring at the ceiling, and she was right. Her sweet voice narrating the story helped him focus on something other than his urge.

The need to go to The Octagon came in waves like a fever. Every time the urge overwhelmed him, he pulled at the rope, and its sharp bite gave him a jolt.

Effie caressed his hair while she read, and he closed his eyes to enjoy her touch better. He had no idea how much time had passed from the moment she'd tied him to the bedposts. To him, it seemed like a week.

"Do you need a drink?" She put down the book.

He nodded, his throat parched. "Don't let Harris come in here. I don't want him to see me like this."

"Don't worry."

When she left to fetch Harris, he pulled at the rope viciously and tried to untie himself. But Effie's skill with the knots could rival that of a sailor. He wouldn't untie himself, and to do what, anyway? He'd asked her to tie him down. He was where he wanted to be.

The fact she was so good with knots made him smile for some reason. He loved how resourceful she was.

"There we are." She returned, carrying a tray. "I have tea, lemonade, and water."

"Lemonade, please."

She helped him drink a cold glass of lemonade. Its pungent and sweet taste brought relief to his throat and his head.

"You're doing so well." She stroked his cheek.

"It doesn't feel like that."

"Would you like to eat?"

"No." He kissed her hand. "Would you read again?"

"Of course." She sat next to him and resumed reading.

He closed his eyes. The rope gripped his wrist and ankles as if telling him it wouldn't let him go. The choice didn't belong to him now, but to the rope. He had to relinquish control over his urge.

The thought gave him a sense of peace and lifted the responsibility of a choice from his shoulders. It felt liberating.

Effie caressing his hair made him breathe more easily, and her voice eased the tension from his body.

Effie gently caressed Tristan's hair as he slept.

She was surprised he'd fallen asleep, but fatigue, from fighting his craving, was probably wearing him down.

There was a soft knock on the door, and she slid off the bed not to disturb Tristan.

"Yes?" she whispered, pulling the door open a crack.

Rowan craned his neck to look past her. "Harris told me Tristan is sick."

"He is, but he's asleep now." She tried to block his view.

He shifted his position. "What ails him?"

"It's complicated, but nothing contagious."

His face tightened. "Does it have to do with him hurting himself?"

She wouldn't lie to him. "He's trying to get better."

Tristan mumbled something in his sleep, startling her. The door opened, revealing him tied with the rope.

Rowan sucked in a sharp breath. "You tied him down."

"Shush!" She slipped out of the bedroom and shut the door behind her.

"What are you doing to him?" His face transformed from that of a boy to that of an angry young man.

"He asked me to. I wasn't sure, but it's working. The rope prevents him from going to the fighting ring. He's being very brave. Making this decision was incredibly difficult for him."

Tears welled in his eyes. "I don't understand."

"He's forcing himself to get better. It's brutal, but he needs that. He wants to move on and leave that horrible habit behind. He's doing it for himself, you, and me, and he needs our support. Without us, he won't get better."

"Even without me?"

"Especially without you."

He wiped his tears quickly. "I didn't treat him well in the past few days."

"He loves you very much. What he's doing proves that. I'm sure he understands why you behaved as you did."

He lowered his gaze. "Is he angry with me?"

"Heavens, no." She put a hand on his shoulder. "He's angry with himself. Not you. Never you."

For a long moment, he didn't say anything, and she was worried he might not believe her.

He tilted his chin up. "When he wakes up, let me know. I would like to see him."

She kissed his forehead. "Of course."

forty-one

When Tristan opened his eyes, the pink light of dawn lit the room. Effie slept next to him, curled into a ball under the quilt. Despite his tight situation, he smiled at her beautiful face as she breathed softly. Her long eyelashes fanned over her cheeks.

He blinked the sleep away. His wrist and ankles were still tied. His arm was numb, and his fingers were a bit swollen. Aside from that, the bloody twitch bothering him was silent as if he'd just returned from the ring.

"Tristan. Oh, my goodness." She bolted upright, rubbing her eyes. Her hair was dishevelled, falling in messy curls on her shoulders. "I fell asleep and left you tied down. I'm so sorry."

"Don't worry."

"It's terrible. You must be sore." She undid the knots in two simple moves.

The moment the rope released its bite on his flesh, warmth flooded him. Invisible needles stung his limbs as blood flowed again. He opened and closed his fingers, grimacing at the pain.

"I'm so sorry." She rubbed his hand. "I thought you wouldn't have slept, thus neither would I. Instead, we both fell asleep."

He stared at her flushed cheeks, dishevelled hair, and wrinkled gown. He would give anything to wake up every day like that with her at his side. Maybe not exactly like that.

"I'm so proud of you." She held his hand against her chest.

He caressed her jaw with his knuckles. "Thank you."

She gave him a shy smile that melted his heart. "You did the hardest part. How do you feel?"

"I think the need will come back to claim me, but now I know I can defeat it. But I tell you, it wasn't a pleasant evening."

She rested her head on his chest. "If the urge returns, I'll share the moment with you."

He hugged her, ignoring the pain of his numb limbs coming to life again. "I owe you my life."

"Don't be silly."

"I'm not. Without you, it was a matter of time before something happened to me. Without you, I wouldn't have apologised to Harris and James for how I treated them, and I wouldn't have told Rowan how much I cared about him. I would have died in The Octagon. Will you marry me even if your father doesn't want me as his son?" He hadn't realised how frightened he was of her answer until that moment.

In his arrogance, he'd taken for granted she would have married him, no matter what. But she loved her family, and her father was an important figure for her. She might ask him to wait until her father came around or reject his proposal altogether.

She kissed his cheek, her eyes glistening. "I'm sure that once Papa realises you have nothing to do with this new attack on him, he'll agree."

Not the answer he wanted.

"But what if he doesn't bless our marriage even after that?" He caressed her back, wishing he could take her away and marry her now.

She tilted her head towards him. "Yes, I would marry you. I love you, Tristan."

He hugged her. "I was afraid you would say no."

"I don't care if the world is against us."

"So, am I better than Mr. Barry the pig?"

She giggled. "A true champion."

He laughed, his pulse spiking for once in happiness. Now he was sure he could beat any urge he had.

But before that, he would prove his innocence and make sure she had the happiness she deserved.

WHEN EFFIE RETURNED HOME, a valid story to explain her prolonged absence wasn't clear yet in her mind. She could claim the horse's illness had been a delicate one, but her father wouldn't fall for such a silly lie.

There was the chance he hadn't been informed of the fact she hadn't slept at home. Before leaving Tristan's house, she'd refreshed herself, and the housekeeper had brushed her gown. She would pretend to have woken up early and taken a walk. Or she could tell the truth, so he would have no choice but to agree to her marriage, but wasn't that vile?

She exhaled when Doyle opened the door.

"My lady." He took her coat and seemed about to say something, but he closed his mouth.

She sniffed the air. The smell of kippers and freshly baked bread coming from the dining room was missing.

"Is my father up?"

"He is, my lady." He sounded strained. "But he didn't have breakfast. In fact, His Lordship didn't sleep much."

She stiffened. He had to be furious with her. He must have waited for her all night, worried about her. Truth was the best choice, then. She would deal with the consequences of his wrath. Besides, she'd told Tristan she would be with him against the world, and she would keep her promise.

"His Lordship is in his study, my lady," Doyle said before going down the corridor.

The last time she'd been so worried about seeing Papa had been when she was thirteen and had saved a fox from being killed by him during a hunting party. She'd told him he was a barbarian, and he'd told her she was a spoilt girl. Then he'd apologised and promised her he would never hunt foxes again. She doubted their current argument would end so well.

Loud voices came from the study. Maids ran from one corner of the corridor to the other, whispering.

She stopped one of them. "What happened?"

"Something serious, my lady. His Lordship is quite preoccupied."

Effie paused before approaching the study, her hands clammy.

"How did this happen?" Papa asked.

"It's not that difficult, only a matter of money." That was Lowe.

They talked over each other, and she didn't understand what they were discussing although the situation seemed a repeat of what had happened weeks ago.

"...damn Montcrest." The thud of a fist against the desk came.

Tristan? She was about to knock on the door when it was flung open.

Papa came out and stopped in front of her. His hair was unkempt, and stubble darkened his chin.

He gave her a long glance, narrowing his eyes. "You were with him, weren't you?"

"What is going on? Why didn't you sleep?"

"It's him. Montcrest." He breathed hard. "He's started trying to destroy me again. He's taking over everything, hiding behind anonymous buyers. Someone says Lord Vaughan is helping him."

She regained her composure, feeling guilty she was relieved Papa's wrath wasn't directed at her. "No, it's not possible. Tristan is innocent, and I'm sure Lord Vaughan is, too."

Lowe exited the study, carrying a leather bag under his arm. He looked like he'd spent the night up, too. "We're ready, my lord."

"I'll be ready in a minute." Papa waited for Lowe to leave. "Tell me the truth."

She tilted her chin up. So be it. "He was sick, and I wanted to help him. And that's all. Nothing untoward happened, and I'm absolutely sure he isn't attacking you."

"Nothing untoward—" He fell silent and squeezed a fist. "If I weren't so worried about the disaster happening to us, we would have another conversation. You truly disappointed me."

Not this again.

"I'm telling the truth. Nothing happened, and Tristan isn't attacking you."

"How can you be so sure?" He raised his voice.

"Because he gave me his word."

He snorted a laugh. "Of course, we must trust the word of a liar. He's exactly like his father and grandfather."

"You don't know him!"

"I know enough!" He paused, only to suck in a breath. "He's an ungrateful, conniving scoundrel, just like his father, and you shall never marry him."

"Try me." She matched his tone.

"My lord?" Lowe called from the entry hall.

"We'll talk about him later." He walked away, staggering a little.

She stood in the middle of the corridor, stunned and shaking now that the confrontation was over. Tristan would never lie to her. He'd promised. He wouldn't. And he'd spent the night shivering in bed although that didn't mean anything. The whole attack on Papa could have been orchestrated by him without him leaving his house. But she didn't believe he was guilty.

She walked to her bedroom and sat on the bed, her legs shaking. Barking came from the hallway, and voices drifted. She sagged her shoulders, wondering what was next.

"My lady." A maid dropped a quick curtsy. "Lady Vaughan wishes to see you."

Oh, well. She waved a hand in agreement.

"Do you want to see her in the drawing room, my lady?"

"No, please ask Lady Vaughan to come here. I'm tired." Effie blew out a long breath.

She didn't have patience for Jane, but after what Papa had said about Lord Vaughan, she believed Jane might have some information.

Jane entered slowly as if walking on her tiptoes. Her hair was styled in a simple chignon, instead of the usual complicated braid. No pendants or plush silk sash adorned her plain dark gown.

Instant worry got Effie. "Is Turi all right?" She sat upright.

Jane lowered her gaze. "Yes. I didn't come here to talk about Turi."

"I think I know why you're here." She gestured at the stuffed chair.

"Are you angry with me?" Jane asked, ignoring the seat.

"No. Truly. Only tired."

Jane perched on the chair, looking like a scolded schoolgirl. "People are saying John is helping Montcrest do some financial tricks to ruin people, and that I'm their accomplice because I was seen entering Montcrest's house." She sniffled. "I promise we aren't doing anything. We would never hurt you or your family. Those rumours are lies."

"Oh, Jane. I never thought you were attacking us." She hugged Jane, holding her tightly.

"We would never do that. I don't understand how people could be so cruel."

She released her friend. "Rumours are cruel. They start like a breeze and turn into a hurricane, destroying everything in their path."

"You're right." Jane let out a sob, and Effie held her hand without saying anything. Jane had already heard enough.

"I'm glad you don't believe the rumours." Jane wiped her eyes with a lace-trimmed handkerchief. "That taught me a lesson, didn't it? I'll be quiet from now on. No more meddling with gossip. I'm sorry for having been unbearable the last time we spoke."

"Forgiven, forgotten, and I wasn't nice, either."

"And I hope you'll let me help you organise your wedding." Tears hung in Jane's eyelashes. "I was wrong to doubt Montcrest solely on rumours. But I trust you. If you like him, then he must be a truly exceptional gentleman."

"He is." She hugged her friend again, laughing with her.

The best way to protect Jane was to find who was attacking Papa, and she knew how to do that.

AFTER JANE LEFT, Effie washed and changed, getting ready to see Tristan again. He understood financial tricks better than anyone.

He could have easily instructed someone to do the dirty work for him, but she refused to believe that.

When she was ready and went downstairs, the house was quiet, but a tall stack of letters was piled on the sorting table in the entry hall, and the stuffy air pressed against her chest.

A sickening lump of worry crawled up her throat. Whoever was attacking her father had started slowly, only to unleash their full wrath now. But Tristan was innocent.

She didn't bother with a cab or a carriage and hurried along the pavement, ruining all the work her maid had done with her hair, but she needed the walk to clear her head.

Harris wasn't even surprised to see her again. He took her coat, beaming at her. "His Lordship is in his study."

"Thank you, Harris."

"My lady," he said when she started walking. "Thank you for

taking care of him. He looks tired, but his spirits are better than yesterday. I'm hopeful."

"I do care about him very much."

"So do I, my lady." His happiness was palpable.

She knocked on the study door with a trembling hand.

Tristan stood up from his chair and flashed a bright smile that caused her to hitch a breath. He was pale with dark circles around his eyes, but aside from that, confidence radiated from him as usual with a sweetness that was new to him.

"What a surprise. I didn't expect you so soon. You make my day perfect." He opened his arms, and she ran to him, suddenly desperate for his comforting hug.

He hugged her and scattered kisses on her face. "Is something the matter?"

She inched away from him to see his face. "Papa. Someone is attacking him again. I don't understand much of it, but he's convinced it's you."

His arms stiffened around her. "No. I promised you I wouldn't do it, and I kept my promise. Whoever is doing it isn't me. Did you think it was me?"

"I trust you. No, I couldn't believe it was you, but you might have an idea of who it is."

"Does your father have enemies? His role in the Aldersgate bombing might have reached other ears."

She stepped back from him, tired of the same argument. "He didn't have any involvement. He isn't a murderer."

"You know what I mean." He held up a hand.

She rubbed her forehead. "I don't know what to think."

"I've already started asking questions to understand who is behind the attack."

"Have you?"

"Your father told me about his problem the last time we spoke. I want to find the culprit." He took her chin gently. "What matters is that you believe me. I swear I don't have anything to do with your father's troubles."

"I believe you."

He took her face and gave her a soul-searching kiss that made her forget what she was doing. The kiss was an act of reclamation and gratitude for having believed him. She shivered as desire ignited so easily within her. The kiss became faster until they were running their hands over each other's bodies.

The sound of footsteps made them stop with a jolt.

She laughed. "It's easy to forget where I am when you kiss me."

"It's the same for me. I'll bring news soon." He kissed her lips again with a sweet, soft kiss that was a stark contrast to his previous one.

But that was Tristan. He could be both gentle and ruthless, and she loved both sides of him.

forty-two

An afternoon of enquiries at his gentlemen's club had brought little information to Tristan. Or rather, the lack of information pointed to one person. The person he'd suspected all along. He'd hoped he was wrong, but his fear had become real.

In his study, he waited for George to arrive after he'd sent for him. He flexed his fingers open and closed them. The night had left him tired and sore, but a sense of freedom made him breathe better. And more than freedom, hope. Hope for a future without him being a slave to The Octagon. A future with Effie next to him. A future of love.

George walked into the study, casting him a worried glance. "What's the hurry? Did something happen? Is it Rowan?"

"Rowan is all right." Tristan straightened, ignoring his stiff back. "I'll be brief and go straight to the point. You must stop."

George was clever enough not to insult Tristan's intelligence and ask him what he meant.

"Winchester deserves it. He's an arrogant coward who hides his insecurity behind his title."

"You can't—"

George raised his voice. "Winchester almost killed you and your brother!"

He thumped the desk but regretted it as pain bit him. "Winchester has his responsibility, but destroying him financially won't change anything, and I care about Effie. I care more about her than about getting my revenge."

The truth in his own words surprised him. At first, he'd agreed to stop his attack on Winchester only because he wanted to please Effie. But now, his need for revenge was gone, replaced by love for her and the wish to move forwards, have a family with her, and make her happy. He wasn't sorry for that.

George slouched his posture. "I'm actually happy to hear you've found someone you care about."

He stood in front of George. "Then stop the attack."

"I'm so angry with Winchester." George clenched a fist tightly. "I know I'm not the most reputable businessman, but I would never risk people's lives."

"I'm angry too, but you can't live on anger. Anger can only destroy, and I'm more interested in building."

The door opened, and Rowan entered. "Good evening."

"Lad." George's tone and expression softened.

Tristan rushed to offer him a chair, but Rowan waved him off.

"I don't need it." Rowan swallowed, propping himself up on the crutch. "I heard the conversation."

George exhaled, composing himself. "A conversation that wasn't for children."

"Crutches or shrapnel aren't for children, either, or so Dr. O'Neil said, yet here I am." Rowan walked to George. "And I'm not a child. Lady Effie is a fine lady. She doesn't deserve your anger."

"I'm directing my anger towards her father," George said. "I don't want to hurt Lady Effie."

"She'll get hurt as well." Rowan tapped his crutch to touch his bad leg. "As it happened to me. I agree with Tristan." He glanced at him, and there wasn't a trace of fear or anger in his face. "Innocent people get hurt when you attack someone only for revenge. If you didn't learn that after the bombing, then there will be other boys like me."

George glanced everywhere but at Rowan. "I have nothing to do with the bomb. That was Winchester and the anarchists."

"I want you to stop hurting Lady Effie," Rowan said with determination.

He squeezed Rowan's shoulder and was surprised when he didn't recoil. His brother smiled at him, and a quiet conversation was exchanged between them.

"We care about you, Uncle George," Rowan said. "After Father died, you stayed with us and took care of us. We play together. You help me with my homework. Don't we mean anything to you?"

George worked his jaw as his gaze became suspiciously shiny.

Rowan wasn't finished. "When my mother left, you went after her because you didn't want to see me crying. Tristan told me how at Christmas you always shared dinner with him and Papa, even when they didn't have a penny. We're your family. Can't you find another way to confront Lord Winchester?" Rowan asked. "A way that doesn't hurt Lady Effie or my brother?"

"I'm not hurting Tristan. Quite the opposite." George frowned.

"He cares about Lady Effie, so you're hurting him, and I care about Tristan, so you're hurting me."

He exchanged another stare with his brother, glad they understood each other.

Rowan moved the tip of his crutch in a circle. "It's like a spiderweb. You touch a thread, the whole web ripples."

He tilted his head towards his brother, impressed by his maturity. "Where did you learn that?"

"I've been cooped up in the house for weeks with nothing to do but read." Rowan straightened. "What do you say, Uncle

George? You don't want more boys hobbling around with crutches, do you? You care about us as we care about you."

George shifted his weight, lowering his gaze. Tristan didn't say anything. It was Rowan's moment, and his brother was handling it beautifully.

"Please, Uncle George," Rowan insisted. "For me. I might never walk without a crutch again. If you stop now, I'll be grateful."

"I would do it for you and Tristan," George said in a low voice as if he were ashamed of saying it.

Rowan ran to him as fast as his crutch allowed him and hugged him with one arm. "Thank you, Uncle George."

George hugged him back. They held each other for a long moment. "Well, I must go now, if you want me to set things straight." He exchanged a warm stare with Tristan.

Words weren't needed. Stopping the attack on Winchester required all of George's effort. But his love for his family was bigger than his desire for revenge.

Tristan gave him a nod as a thank you.

"I'll do it for Rowan and for you." George squeezed Tristan's shoulder.

"I won't forget it."

When George left, Tristan was alone with Rowan, and a moment of silence thickened between them.

"You were brilliant," he said. "I didn't know how to convince him to stop."

Rowan didn't say anything.

"You're an excellent negotiator. Thank you." He stretched out his arm towards Rowan who ignored it.

"Will you stop hurting yourself?"

"I will. I promise. It won't happen again."

"You won't leave me as my mother did, will you?" Rowan's voice cracked with the sound of a young heart broken.

"Never. You have my word."

Rowan hugged him in a surprisingly strong embrace. Tristan held him as emotion clogged his throat.

"I love you, brother," Rowan said.

"So do I."

If he needed a new reason to leave his addiction behind, his brother had just given it to him.

<h1 style="text-align:right">forty-three</h1>

Effie observed her father sitting on the armchair, reading the *London Financial Guide*. His shoulders were rigid, and his face was stern. He hadn't talked to her much, aside from a few civil words.

She couldn't read his mood. The new attack had stopped. Mr. Fleet had repaired some of the damage he'd done, and Tristan should be here any minute to talk to them. Papa had many reasons to be happy, but his flat attitude didn't reveal any emotion.

She lowered the latest issue of *The Veterinary Record*. "Aren't you happy about your situation now?"

He lowered the newspaper. "No. Between Montcrest and his henchman, I lost a few important assets, just because they played a game with me."

"Assets that Lord Montcrest promised to restore."

"Montcrest promised a great many things."

"We're lucky he's a man of his word."

He angled towards her. "Lucky isn't the word I have in mind."

"Lord Montcrest," Doyle announced, interrupting yet another pointless argument with her father.

She beamed when Tristan entered the room. His freshly

pressed dark suit and white shirt gave him an air of authority suiting him. But when he smiled back at her, he simply looked like a dashing gentleman in love.

"Effie." He kissed her hand, his eyes like blue flames. "I've missed you."

"As I have you."

"I hope we can spend some time together this afternoon. I would like to take a drive through the park."

"It would be lovely."

Papa cleared his throat. "Montcrest, we're starting this meeting on the wrong foot."

"I beg to differ." She sat on the armchair, and Papa and Tristan sat down as well.

"Mr. Fleet stopped his financial moves," Tristan said, all businesslike. "I didn't participate in his latest attack, nor did I know about it, as I wrote in the letter I sent you yesterday. I trust your finances are recovering, Winchester."

"Slowly." Papa's tone matched Tristan's. "Destroying takes a moment. Rebuilding is a slow process."

He didn't flinch. "It is, but I'll help in any way I can."

"Thank you, but you'll forgive me if I find it difficult to trust you," Papa said.

"Papa." She gave a shake of her head. "Can we go past this quarrel?"

Papa scoffed. "This *quarrel* almost bankrupted me."

"Maybe next time you'll remember not to meddle with the anarchists," Tristan said through his teeth.

"Gentlemen, please." She held up a hand when her father opened his mouth to reply. "We're here not to discuss who did what, but because I want to marry Tristan, and I hope you two will leave behind any animosity for each other for my sake. I love you both. Don't put me in a difficult place."

A murmur that could mean anything rippled through the room.

"I'm not happy to have Montcrest as a member of our family," Papa said. "And quite frankly, I'm not sure I'll ever be."

"Papa, whatever your opinion, it won't change the fact I want to be Tristan's wife." She blew out a nervous puff of air.

Tristan sucked in a deep breath, his chest rising. "And I want to be your husband."

"But." Papa pinned her with a glare. "I admit Montcrest helped stop Mr. Fleet from causing further damage, and that warrants some gratitude. Not much, but some."

Tristan's eyes became two slits. "What is that supposed to mean?"

"Please." She touched his hand. "Let Papa talk."

But Papa didn't go on. He drummed his fingers on the armrest.

"Papa? I'm sure there's a 'but' coming." She pressed her lips hard.

He was pushing her to elope. She would do it if he didn't leave her any choice.

Papa cleared his throat. Once, twice. He started to talk, then stopped, then started again. "If marrying Montcrest makes you happy, then I won't oppose the union, only and exclusively because I love you, Effie. There isn't any other reason."

She shot up and hugged him. "Thank you."

Papa patted her back. "But don't expect me to become his best friend or sit with him in the drawing room at Christmas and smoke cigars."

"As if I would ever want that," Tristan muttered.

"Please," she mouthed, shaking her head. "Would you shake hands now? Like two businessmen," she said loudly.

She'd seen rival cats less belligerent than them. At first, neither of them moved, and she feared they might shout at each other.

"Please," she said again, glancing from Tristan to Papa. "For me."

Tristan's jaw clenched as he shook Papa's hand. Papa stared at him as if he were ready for a duel.

"Make her happy," Papa said.

"I will make her very happy," Tristan said in a steely tone.

They stood in front of each other for a moment too long, and the handshake became a tug-of-war with them squeezing each other's hand too tightly.

She slid between them, separating them. "Excellent. So all is well."

They both muttered under their breaths, and she chose not to bother understanding what they were saying. Besides, she didn't care.

She was more than happy. "Would you mind leaving us alone for a moment?"

Papa's expression said he didn't approve. "Effie."

"Please?"

He shook his head and took her hand before he looked at Tristan.

"Thank you." She kissed his cheek, aware she was pushing her luck.

Tristan said nothing, which was a good thing.

"We don't have anything else to say for now." Papa squared his shoulders. "Montcrest."

"Winchester."

If she paid attention, she could hear the noise of frost growing between them.

The moment Papa left, she jumped into Tristan's arms. "I'm going to be Lady Montcrest."

"And I'm going to be happy." He kissed her almost savagely, causing her toes to curl. But what made her heart soar was knowing that feeling wasn't going to end.

Tristan had no idea a cat could sleep for so many hours without moving.

Kettle had curled up on his lap a while ago and fallen asleep instantly while he had been sitting at his desk to work.

He hadn't moved from his chair for fear of waking the cat up. He and Kettle were still trying to get to know each other better. It'd been easier to form a civil, if not warm, relationship with Winchester. They'd stopped barking at each other on every occasion—also because Effie had grown tired of the arguments—and they were tentatively talking in more calm tones. Winchester had even relented and sold the bloody field in Easthollow to him. A miracle. They were far from being best friends, but their relationship was slowly getting better.

Kettle, on the other hand, was a different matter.

After marrying Effie, he'd quickly learnt Kettle had a volatile mood, was fussy, and enjoyed cuddles only when he decided so, at least with Tristan. The cat could scratch, hiss, purr, or be the gentlest creature on Earth without rhyme or reason. With Effie, Kettle was always the perfect pet, but with him, the result was anyone's guess.

The good thing about his current predicament was that while he'd been confined to his desk, he'd replied to several letters, paid bills, and read the reports from his stewards. The bad thing was that he needed to stretch out his legs.

Hell, he couldn't even reach the bell rope to call Harris. Shouting would scare Kettle and diminish his chances of becoming friends with the feline, so that wasn't an option. Besides, he'd been scratched too many times.

He sagged on the chair, resigned to his fate, wondering if every cat owner shared his situation.

He was Lord Tristan, the 15th Marquess of Montcrest. He owned the London and West Marches Railway company, a dozen estates, and a mansion in Paris, but a cat owned him.

He used that moment to also contemplate all the changes Effie had brought to the house. She'd added coloured curtains, bright carpets, and books on veterinary medicine. At first, he'd feared he would feel constricted in a house full of paintings, books, and mismatched furniture, but it was the opposite. He felt surrounded by care.

"Tristan?" Effie entered the study in a flutter of light green fabric. "Are you still here?" She dropped her medical bag on a chair. Her expertise in veterinary medicine was highly requested. Hardly a day passed without her visiting a patient.

"Thank goodness." He spread his arms. "Please come here."

"What's the matter?" She eyed Kettle, then him.

"I've been trapped here for hours."

Her mouth twitched until she burst out laughing. "You could have gently picked him up and laid him on the sofa." She did just that, hauling up Kettle.

The cat meowed and unsheathed his claws, blinking sleepy eyes, but he didn't dare as much as give her the evil eye.

"I missed a meeting because of him." Tristan brushed off black hairs from his trousers.

"There's no need to be his slave." Effie kissed Kettle's head many times. "He won't hurt you if you want to stand up."

"He will, as he's done several times. And it's rude." He rose and stretched out his legs. "Kettle would have worked better than the rope to stop me from going to The Octagon."

"Are we ready?" Rowan entered the study, fixing his tie.

Pepper followed him, his tail drawing circles in the air. That dog didn't know what being sad meant.

It'd taken two years of exercises and pain after a second surgery, but Rowan had recovered the use of his leg. He still walked with a small limp, and the fact that he was growing by the minute didn't make the recovery easy for him, but he didn't need crutches anymore.

"I am." Effie waved towards Tristan. "Your brother needs to change."

"You haven't changed yet?" Rowan widened his eyes.

"We have plenty of time." Tristan tried to pet Kettle, but one harsh glance from the feline discouraged him. Certain battles couldn't be won.

"I know," Rowan said, "but the last time we had lunch with Lord Winchester, he complained about our tardiness."

Yes, the battle with Winchester was still ongoing, but Tristan believed Effie's father would be more easily conquered than Kettle.

"He's grumpy. Don't worry about him," Effie said.

Tristan laced his fingers through Effie's. She smiled, and he smiled back.

He was Lord Tristan, the 15th Marquess of Montcrest. He owned the London and West Marches Railway company, a dozen estates, and a mansion in Paris, but his beautiful wife owned his whole heart.

about me

Love stories have always captured my imagination. What's better than two people falling in love with each other? I write steamy romance, usually with a paranormal twist in an historical setting. Add a touch of suspense and mystery and a pinch of darkness. I love stories with  strong, sexy heroes and mischievous heroines who pull no punches.

I live in the City of Sails, New Zealand, drinking tea (coffee gives me anxiety) and devouring books.

Join my newsletter for exclusive content and the chance to receive an ARC copy of my books. Just copy and paste this link into your browser:

Barbara's Newsletter: https://bit.ly/39yZ4Lw

also by barbara russell

If you want historical romance:

<u>Victorian Outcasts</u>

If you love steamy paranormal romance set in Victorian London, my Royal Occult Bureau series is for you:

<u>The Royal Occult Bureau Series</u>

Are you into shape-shifter romance? Check out my da Vinci's Beasts series, set in WW2:

<u>da Vinci's Beasts Series</u>

For more Victorian paranormal romance with witches and sexy warriors, see the Knights of the White Blade series:

<u>The White Order Series</u>

OLIVERHEBERBOOKS

A small press bound by the belief that every voice matters.

Sign up for our newsletter to learn about new releases and more.
https://oliver-heberbooks.com/subscribe/

Follow us on social media:

facebook.com/oliverheberbooks

instagram.com/oliverheberbooks

amazon.com/oliverheberbooks

youtube.com/@OliverHeberBooksPublisher